BLEAK HOUSE

Published by Priory Books,
© Peter Haddock Publishing,
United Kingdom, YO16 6BT.

BLEAK HOUSE

CHAPTER 1

In Fashion

My Lady Dedlock has returned to her house in town for a few days previous to her departure for Paris, where her ladyship intends to stay some weeks; after which her movements are uncertain. Sir Leicester Dedlock is only a baronet, but there is no mightier baronet than he. His family is as old as the hills, and infinitely more respectable. He has a general opinion that the world might get on without hills, but would be done up without Dedlocks. Sir Leicester is twenty years, full measure, older than my Lady. His gallantry to my Lady, which has never changed since he courted her, is the one little touch of romantic fancy in him. Indeed, he married her for love. Wealth and station soon floated her upward; and for years now, my Lady Dedlock has been at the centre of the fashionable intelligence, and at the top of the fashionable tree.

At her house in town, upon this muddy, murky afternoon, arrives an old-fashioned old gentleman, attorney-at-law, and solicitor of the High Court of Chancery, who has the honour of acting as legal adviser of the Dedlocks. The old gentleman is rusty to look at, but is reputed to have made good thrift out of aristocratic marriage settlements and aristocratic wills, and to be very rich.

Sir Leicester Dedlock is with my Lady, and is happy to see Mr Tulkinghorn.

"My Lady's cause has been again before the Chancellor, has it, Mr Tulkinghorn?" says Sir Leicester, giving him his hand.

"Yes. It has been on again to-day," Mr Tulkinghorn replies; making one of his quiet bows to my Lady who is on a sofa near the fire, shading her face with a hand-screen.

"It would be useless to ask," says my Lady, with the dreariness of the place in Lincolnshire still upon her, "whether anything has been done."

"Nothing that you would call anything, has been done to-day," replies Mr Tulkinghorn.

"Nor ever will be," says my Lady.

3

"As a few fresh affidavits have been put upon the file," says Mr Tulkinghorn.

Mr Tulkinghorn takes out his papers, asks permission to place them on a golden talisman of a table at my Lady's elbow, puts on his spectacles, and begins to read by the light of a shaded lamp.

"'In Chancery. Between John Jarndyce – '"

My Lady interrupts, requesting him to miss as many of the formal horrors as he can.

Mr Tulkinghorn glances over his spectacles, and begins again lower down. My Lady carelessly and scornfully abstracts her attention, then changing her position, sees the papers on the table – looks at them nearer – looks at them nearer still – asks impulsively:

"Who copied that?"

Mr Tulkinghorn stops short, surprised by my Lady's animation and her unusual tone.

"Is it what you people call law-hand?" she asks, looking full at him in her careless way again.

"Not quite. Probably" – Mr Tulkinghorn examines it as he speaks – "the legal character which it has, was acquired after the original hand was formed. Why do you ask?"

"Anything to vary this detestable monotony. O, go on, do!"

Mr Tulkinghorn reads again. The heat is greater, my Lady screens her face. Sir Leicester dozes, starts up suddenly, and cries, "Eh? What do you say?"

"I say I am afraid," says Mr Tulkinghorn, who had risen hastily, "that Lady Dedlock is ill."

"Faint," my Lady murmurs, with white lips, "only that; but it is like the faintness of death. Don't speak to me. Ring, and take me to my room!"

Mr Tulkinghorn retires into another chamber; bells ring, feet shuffle and patter, silence ensues.

CHAPTER 2

Quite at Home

Richard Carston and Ada Clare are orphans who expect to inherit a vast fortune if ever the endless case of Jarndyce v. Jarndyce is settled. Meantime their cousin, John Jarndyce, has offered them a home at Bleak House together with another young lady, Esther Summerson, to whom he has acted as anonymous guardian for many years. Esther takes up their story:

When we turned out of the town, round a corner we both stood up in the carriage (Richard holding Ada, lest she should be jolted down), and gazed round upon the open country and the starlight night, for our destination.

There was a light sparkling on the top of a hill before us, and the driver, pointing to it with his whip and crying, "That's Bleak House!" put his horses into a canter.

Presently we lost the light, presently saw it, presently lost it, presently saw it, and turned into an avenue of trees, and cantered up towards where it was beaming brightly. It was in a window of what seemed to be an old-fashioned house, with three peaks in the roof in front, and a circular sweep leading to the porch. A bell was rung as we drew up, and amidst the sound of its deep voice in the still air, and the distant barking of some dogs, and a gush of light from the opened door, and the smoking and steaming of the heated horses, and the quickened beating of our own hearts, we alighted in no inconsiderable confusion.

"Ada, my love, Esther, my dear, you are welcome. I rejoice to see you! Rick, if I had a hand to spare at present, I would give it you!"

The gentleman who said these words in a clear, bright, hospitable voice, had one of his arms round Ada's waist, and the other round mine, and kissed us both in a fatherly way, and bore us across the hall into a ruddy little room, all in a glow with a blazing fire. Here he kissed us again, and, opening his arms, made us sit down side by side, on a sofa ready drawn out near the hearth. I felt that if we had been at all demonstrative, he would have run away in a moment.

"Now, Rick!" said he, "I am heartily glad to see you. You are at home. Warm yourself!"

5

Richard shook him by both hands. "You are very kind, sir! We are very much obliged to you!"

"It makes no pretensions; but it is a comfortable little place, I hope, and will be more so with such bright young looks in it. You have barely half an hour before dinner. Come along!"

Our luggage having arrived, and being all at hand, I was dressed in a few minutes, and engaged in putting my worldly goods away, when a maid brought a basket into my room, with two bunches of keys in it, all labelled.

"For you, miss, if you please," said she.

"For me?" said I.

"The housekeeping keys, miss."

I showed my surprise; for she added, "Miss Summerson, if I don't deceive myself?"

"Yes," said I. "That is my name."

"The large bunch is the housekeeping, and the little bunch is the cellars, miss. Any time you was pleased to appoint to-morrow morning, I am to show you the presses and things they belong to."

I said I would be ready at half-past six; and, after she was gone, stood looking at the basket, quite lost in the magnitude of my trust.

When we went downstairs, we were presented to Mr Skimpole, who was standing before the fire, telling Richard how fond he used to be, in his school-time, of football. There was an easy negligence in his manner, and even in his dress (his hair carelessly disposed, and his neckerchief loose and flowing, as I have seen artists paint their own portraits).

"I covet nothing," said Mr Skimpole. "Possession is nothing to me. Here is my friend Jarndyce's excellent house. I feel obliged to him for possessing it. I can sketch it, and alter it. I can set it to music. When I am here, I have sufficient possession of it, and have neither trouble, cost, nor responsibility. My steward's name, in short, is Jarndyce, and he can't cheat me."

The more we listened, the more gaily Mr Skimpole talked. And what with his fine hilarious manner, and his engaging candour, and his genial way of lightly tossing his own weaknesses about, the effect was absolutely dazzling.

In the evening when I was preparing to make tea, and Ada was touching the piano in the adjoining room and softly humming a tune to her cousin Richard, he came and sat down on the sofa near me, and so spoke of Ada that I almost loved him.

"She is like the morning," he said. "With that golden hair, those blue eyes, and that fresh bloom on her cheek, she is like the summer morning. She is the child of the universe."

Mr Jarndyce, I found, was standing near us, with his hands behind him, and an attentive smile upon his face.

"The universe," he observed, "makes rather an indifferent parent, I am afraid."

"O! I don't know!" cried Mr Skimpole, buoyantly.

"I think I do know," said Mr Jarndyce.

"Well!" cried Mr Skimpole. "You know the world (which in your sense is the universe), and I know nothing of it, so you shall have your way."

Mr Jarndyce patted him on the head with a smile, as if he had been really a child; and passing a step or two on, and stopping a moment, glanced at the young cousins. Ada sat at the piano; Richard stood beside her, bending down. Ada touched the notes so softly, and sang so low, that the wind, sighing away to the distant hills, was as audible as the music.

Though Mr Jarndyce's glance, as he withdrew it, rested for but a moment on me, I felt as if, in that moment, he confided to me – and knew that he confided to me, and that I received the confidence – his hope that Ada and Richard might one day enter on a dearer relationship.

CHAPTER 3

Covering a Multitude of Sins

Mr Skimpole was as agreeable at breakfast, as he had been overnight. There was honey on the table, and it led him into a discourse about bees. He pursued this fancy with the lightest foot over a variety of ground, and made us all merry. I left them still listening to him, when I withdrew to attend to my new duties. They had occupied me for some time, and I was passing through the passages on my return with my basket of keys on my arm, when Mr Jarndyce called me into a small room next to his bedchamber, which I found to be in part a little library of books and papers, and in part quite a little museum of his boots and shoes, and hat-boxes.

"Sit down, my dear," said Mr Jarndyce. "This, you must know, is the Growlery. When I am out of humour, I come and growl here."

"You must be here very seldom, sir," said I.

"O, you don't know me!" he returned. "When I am deceived or disappointed I take refuge here. The Growlery is the best-used room in the house. You are not aware of half my humours yet. My dear, how you are trembling!"

I could not help it: I tried very hard: but being alone with that benevolent presence, and meeting his kind eyes, and feeling so happy, and so honoured there, and my heart so full –

I kissed his hand. I don't know what I said, or even that I spoke. He was disconcerted, and walked to the window; I almost believed with an intention of jumping out, until he turned, and I was reassured by seeing in his eyes what he had gone there to hide. He gently patted me on the head, and I sat down.

"There! There!" he said. "That's over. Pooh! Don't be foolish."

"It shall not happen again, sir," I returned, "but at first it is difficult – "

"Nonsense!" he said. "It's easy, easy. Why not? I hear of a good little orphan girl without a protector, and I take it into my head to be that protector. She grows up, and more than justifies my good opinion, and I remain her guardian and her friend. What is there in all this? So, so! Now, we have cleared off old scores, and I have before me thy pleasant, trusting, trusty face again."

I folded my hands upon my basket and quite recovered myself. Mr Jarndyce began to talk to me as confidentially, as if I had been in the habit of conversing with him every morning for I don't know how long. I almost felt as if I had.

"Of course, Esther," he said, "you don't understand this Chancery business?"

And of course I shook my head.

"I don't know who does," he returned. "It's about a Will, and the trusts under a Will – or it was, once. It's about nothing but Costs, now. That's the great question. All the rest, by some extraordinary means, has melted away."

"But it was, sir," said I, to bring him back, for he began to rub his head, "about a Will?"

"Why, yes, it was about a Will when it was about anything," he returned. "A certain Jarndyce, in an evil hour, made a great fortune, and made a great Will. And thus, through years and years, and lives and lives, everything goes on, constantly beginning over and over again, and nothing ever ends. And we can't get out of the suit on any terms, for we are made parties to it, and must be parties to it, whether we like it or not. But it won't do to think of it! When my great uncle, poor Tom Jarndyce, began to think of it, it was the beginning of the end!"

"The Mr Jarndyce, sir, whose story I have heard?"

He nodded gravely. "I was his heir, and this was his house, Esther. When I came here, it was bleak indeed. He had left the signs of his misery upon it."

"How changed it is!" I said.

"Why, so it is," he answered much more cheerfully; "and it is wisdom in you to keep me to the bright side. You are clever enough to be the good little woman of our lives here, my dear," he returned playfully; "the little old woman of the child's rhyme:

'Little old woman, and whither so high?' –
'To sweep the cobwebs out of the sky.'

You will sweep them so neatly out of our sky, in the course of your housekeeping, Esther, that one of these days, we shall have to abandon the Growlery, and nail up the door."

He drew my hand through his arm, and we went away to look for Ada. From that hour I felt quite easy with him, quite unreserved, quite content to know no more, quite happy.

CHAPTER 4

The Law-Writer

On the eastern borders of Chancery Lane, that is to say, more particularly, in Cook's Court, Cursitor Street, Mr Snagsby, Law-Stationer, pursues his lawful calling. The day is closing in and the gas is lighted, but is not yet fully effective, for it is not quite dark. Mr Snagsby standing at his shop-door looking up at the clouds, sees a crow, who is out late, skim westward over the slice of sky belonging to Cook's Court. The crow flies straight across Chancery Lane and Lincoln's Inn Garden, into Lincoln's Inn Fields.

Here, in a large house, formerly a house of state, lives Mr Tulkinghorn. He keeps no staff. Mr Tulkinghorn is not in a common way. He wants no clerks. His clients want him; he is all in all. Fair copies that he requires to be made, are made at the stationers', expense being no consideration.

Mr Tulkinghorn goes, as the crow came – not quite so straight, but nearly – to Cook's Court, Cursitor Street. To Snagsby's, Law Stationer's, Deeds engrossed and copied, Law-Writing executed in all its branches.

Mr Snagsby appears: greasy, warm, herbaceous, and chewing. Bolts a bit of bread and butter. Says, "Bless my soul, sir! Mr Tulkinghorn!"

"I want half a word with you, Snagsby."

"Certainly, sir! Pray walk into the back shop, sir." Snagsby has brightened in a moment.

The confined room, smelling strong of parchment-grease, is warehouse, counting-house, and copying-office. Mr Tulkinghorn sits, facing round, on a stool at the desk.

"Jarndyce and Jarndyce, Snagsby."

"Yes, sir." Mr Snagsby turns up the gas, and coughs behind his hand, modestly anticipating profit.

"You copied some affidavits in that cause for me lately."

"Yes, sir, we did."

"There was one of them," says Mr Tulkinghorn, "the handwriting of which is peculiar, and I rather like. As I happened to be passing, and thought I had it about me, I looked in to ask you who copied this?"

"Who copied this, sir?" says Mr Snagsby, taking it, laying it flat on the desk. "We gave this out, sir. I can tell you in a moment who copied it, sir, by referring to my Book."

Mr Snagsby takes his Book down from the safe, eyes the affidavit aside, and brings his right forefinger travelling down a page of the Book. "Jewby – Packer – Jarndyce."

"Jarndyce! Here we are, sir," says Mr Snagsby. "To be sure! I might have remembered it. This was given out, sir, to a Writer who lodges just over on the opposite side of the lane."

Mr Tulkinghorn has seen the entry, found it before the Law-stationer, read it while the forefinger was coming down the hill.

"What do you call him? Nemo?" says Mr Tulkinghorn.

"Nemo, sir. Here it is. Given out on the Wednesday night, at eight o'clock; brought in on the Thursday morning, at half after nine."

"Nemo!" repeats Mr Tulkinghorn. "Nemo is Latin for no one."

"It must be English for some one, sir, I think," Mr Snagsby submits, with his deferential cough.

"Have you given this man work before?" asks Mr Tulkinghorn.

"O dear, yes, sir! Work of yours."

"Thinking of more important matters, I forget where you said he lived?"

"Across the lane, sir. In fact, he lodges at a Rag and Bottle shop."

"Can you show me the place as I go back?"

"With the greatest pleasure, sir!"

Mr Snagsby pulls off his sleeves and his grey coat, pulls on his black coat, takes his hat from its peg.

"You will find that the place is rough, sir," says Mr Snagsby, walking deferentially in the road, and leaving the narrow pavement to the lawyer.

The lawyer and the stationer come to a Rag and Bottle shop, lying in the shadow of the wall of Lincoln's Inn, and kept, as is announced in paint, to all it may concern, by one Krook.

"This is where he lives, sir," says the law-stationer.

"This is where he lives, is it?" says the lawyer unconcernedly. "Thank you."

"Are you not going in, sir?"

"No, thank you, no; I am going on to the Fields at present. Good evening. Thank you!" Mr Snagsby lifts his hat, and returns to his little woman and his tea.

But, Mr Tulkinghorn does not go on to the Fields at present. He goes a short way, turns back, comes again to the shop of Mr Krook, and enters it straight. It is dim enough, with a blot-headed candle or so in the windows, and an old man and a cat sitting in the back part by a fire. The old man rises and comes forward, with another blot-headed candle in his hand.

"Pray, is your lodger within?"

"Male or female, sir?" says Mr Krook.

"Male. The person who does copying."

Mr Krook has eyed his man narrowly. Knows him by sight. Has an indistinct impression of his aristocratic repute.

"Did you wish to see him, sir?"

"Yes."

"It's what I seldom do myself," says Mr Krook with a grin. "Shall I call him down? But it's a weak chance if he'd come, sir!"

"I'll go up to him, then," says Mr Tulkinghorn.

"Second floor, sir. Take the candle. Up there!" Mr Krook, with his cat beside him, stands at the bottom of the staircase, looking after Mr Tulkinghorn.

Mr Tulkinghorn with a nod goes on his way. He comes to the dark door on the second floor. He knocks, receives no answer, opens it, and accidentally extinguishes his candle in doing so.

The discoloured shutters are drawn together; and through the two gaunt holes pierced in them, famine might be staring in – the Banshee of the man upon the bed.

For, on a low bed opposite the fire, a confusion of dirty patchwork, lean-ribbed ticking, and coarse sacking, the lawyer, hesitating just within the doorway, sees a man. He lies there, dressed in shirt and trousers, with bare feet. He has a yellow look in the spectral darkness of a candle that has guttered down, until the whole length of its wick (still burning) has doubled over. His hair is ragged, mingling with his whiskers and his beard foul and filthy as the room is, foul and filthy as the air, but through the general sickliness and faintness, and the odour of stale tobacco, there comes into the lawyer's mouth the bitter, vapid taste of opium.

"Hallo, my friend!" he cries, and strikes his iron candlestick against the door.

He thinks he has awakened his friend. He lies a little turned away, but his eyes are surely open.

"Hallo, my friend!" he cries again. "Hallo! Hallo!"

As he rattles on the door, the candle which has drooped so long, goes out, and leaves him in the dark; with the gaunt eyes in the shutters staring down upon the bed.

CHAPTER 5

Our Dear Brother

The welcome light soon shines upon the wall, as Krook comes slowly up, with his green-eyed cat following at his heels.

"Does the man generally sleep like this?" inquired the lawyer, in a low voice.

"I don't know," says Krook. "I know next to nothing of his habits, except that he keeps himself very close."

Thus whispering, they both go in together. As the light goes in, the great eyes in the shutters, darkening, seem to close. Not so the eyes upon the bed.

"God save us!" exclaims Mr Tulkinghorn. "He is dead!" Krook drops the heavy hand he has taken up, so suddenly that the arm swings over the bedside.

They look at one another for a moment.

"Send for some doctor! Call out for Flite. Here's poison by the bed!" says Krook, with his lean hands spread out above the body like a vampire's wings.

Mr Tulkinghorn hurries to the landing, and calls "Make haste, here, whoever you are! Flite!" Krook follows him with his eyes, and, while he is calling, finds opportunity to steal to the old portmanteau, and steal back again.

"Run, Flite, run! The nearest doctor! Run!" So Mr Krook addresses a crazy little woman, who is his female lodger: who appears and vanishes in a breath: who soon returns, accompanied by a dark young man.

The dark young surgeon passes the candle across and across the face, and carefully examines the law-writer.

"I knew this person by sight, very well," says Mr Woodcourt. "He has purchased opium of me, for the last year and a half. Was anybody present related to him?" glancing round upon the three bystanders.

"I was his landlord," grimly answers Krook, taking the candle from the surgeon's outstretched hand. "He told me once, I was the nearest relation he had."

"He has died," says Woodcourt, "of an over-dose of opium, there is no

13

doubt. The room is strongly flavoured with it. There is enough here now," taking an old teapot from Mr Krook, "to kill a dozen people."

"Do you think he did it on purpose?" asks Krook.

"Took the over-dose?"

"Yes!" Krook almost smacks his lips with the unction of a horrible interest.

"I can't say. I should think it unlikely, as he has been in the habit of taking so much. But nobody can tell. He was very poor, I suppose?"

"I suppose he was. His room – don't look rich," says Krook as he casts his sharp glance around.

"Did he owe you any rent?"

"Six weeks."

"He will never pay it!" says the young man, resuming his examination. "It is beyond a doubt that he is indeed as dead as Pharaoh; and to judge from his appearance and condition, I should think it a happy release. Yet he must have been a good figure when a youth, and I dare say, good-looking." He says this, not unfeelingly.

During this dialogue, Mr Tulkinghorn has stood aloof by the old portmanteau, with his hands behind him, his imperturbable face as inexpressive as his rusty clothes.

He now interposes; addressing the young surgeon, in his unmoved, professional way.

"I looked in here," he observes, "just before you, with the intention of giving this deceased man, whom I never saw alive, some employment at his trade of copying. I had heard of him from my stationer – Snagsby of Cook's Court. Since no one here knows anything about him, it might be as well to send for Snagsby. Ah!" to the little crazy woman, Flite, "Suppose you do!"

While she is gone, the surgeon abandons his hopeless investigation, and covers its subject with the patchwork counterpane. Mr Krook and he interchange a word or two. Mr Tulkinghorn says nothing; but stands, ever, near the old portmanteau.

Mr Snagsby arrives hastily in his grey coat and his black sleeves. "Dear me, dear me," he says; "and it has come to this, has it! Bless my soul!"

"Can you give the person of the house any information about this unfortunate creature, Snagsby?" inquires Mr Tulkinghorn. "He was in arrears with his rent, it seems. And he must be buried, you know."

14

"Well, sir," says Mr Snagsby, coughing his apologetic cough behind his hand; "I really don't know what advice I could offer, except sending for the beadle."

"I don't speak of advice," returns Mr Tulkinghorn. "I speak of affording some clue to his connexions, or to where he came from, or to anything concerning him."

"I assure you, sir," says Mr Snagsby, "that I no more know where he came from, than I know – "

"Where he has gone to, perhaps," suggests the surgeon, to help him out.

A pause. Mr Tulkinghorn looking at the law-stationer. Mr Krook, with his mouth open, looking for somebody to speak next.

"Hadn't you better see," says Mr Tulkinghorn to Krook, "whether he had any papers that may enlighten you? There will be an inquest, and you will be asked the question. You can read?"

"No, I can't," returns the old man, with a sudden grin.

"Snagsby," says Mr Tulkinghorn, "look over the room for him. He will get into some trouble or difficulty, otherwise. Being here, I'll wait, and then I can testify on his behalf. If you will hold the candle for Mr Snagsby, my friend, he'll soon see whether there is anything to help you."

"In the first place, here's an old portmanteau, sir," says Snagsby.

Ah, to be sure, so there is! Mr Tulkinghorn does not appear to have seen it before, though he is standing so close to it, and though there is very little else.

There are some worthless articles of clothing in the old portmanteau; there is a bundle of pawnbrokers' tickets, there is a crumpled paper, smelling of opium. There are a few dirty scraps of newspapers, all referring to Coroners' Inquests; there is nothing else. They search the cupboard, and the drawer of the ink-splashed table. There is not a morsel of an old letter, or of any other writing in either. The young surgeon examines the dress on the law-writer. A knife and some odd halfpence are all he finds.

And, all that night, the coffin stands ready by the old portmanteau; and the lonely figure on the bed, whose path in life has lain through five-and-forty years, lies there, with no more track behind him, that any one can trace, than a deserted infant.

Next day at the appointed hour arrives the Coroner, for whom the Jurymen are waiting. The Coroner is conducted by the beadle and the landlord to the Harmonic Meeting Room, where he puts his hat on the piano, and takes a Windsor-chair at the head of a long table. As many of the Jury as can crowd together at the table sit there. The rest get among the spittoons and pipes, or lean against the piano.

Mr Tulkinghorn is received with distinction, and seated near the Coroner; between that high judicial officer, a bagatelle board, and the coal-box. The inquiry proceeds. The Jury learn how the subject of their inquiry died, and learn no more about him. "A very eminent solicitor is in attendance, gentlemen," says the Coroner, "who, I am informed, was accidentally present, when discovery of the death was made; but he could only repeat the evidence you have already heard from the surgeon, the landlord, the lodger, and the law-stationer; and it is not necessary to trouble him. Is anybody in attendance who knows anything more?"

"Only the boy that sweeps the crossing down the lane over the way round the corner which if he was here would tell you that he has been seen a-speaking to him frequent."

"Here's the boy, gentlemen!"

"Here he is, very muddy, very hoarse, very ragged. Now, boy! – But stop a minute. Caution. This boy must be put through a few preliminary paces."

Name, Jo. Nothing else that he knows on. Don't know that everybody has two names. Don't know that Jo is short for a longer name. No. he can't spell it. No father, no mother, no friends. Never been to school. What's home? Knows a broom's a broom, and knows it's wicked to tell a lie and so he'll tell the truth.

"This won't do, gentlemen!" says the Coroner, with a melancholy shake of the head.

"Don't you think you can receive his evidence, sir?" asks an attentive Juryman.

"Out of the question," says the Coroner. "You have heard the boy. We can't take that, in a Court of Justice, gentlemen, put the boy aside."

"Now. Is there any other witness?" No other witness.

"Very well, gentlemen! If you think it is a case of accidental death, you will find a verdict accordingly."

"Verdict accordingly. Accidental death. No doubt. Gentlemen, you are discharged. Good afternoon."

While the coroner buttons his great coat, Mr Tulkinghorn and he give private audience to the rejected witness in a corner.

That graceless creature only knows that one cold winter night, when he, the boy, was shivering in a doorway near his crossing, the man turned to look at him, and came back, and, having questioned him and found that he had not a friend in the world, said, "Neither have I. Not one!" and gave him the price of a supper and a night's lodging. That the man had often spoken to him since; and asked him whether he slept sound at night, and how he bore cold and hunger, and whether he ever wished to die; and similar strange questions. That when the man had no money, he would say in passing, "I am as poor as you to-day, Jo", but that when he had any, he had always been glad to give him some.

"He wos wery good to me," says the boy, wiping his eyes with his wretched sleeve. "He wos wery good to me, he wos!"

As he shuffles downstairs, Mr Snagsby, lying in wait for him, puts a half-crown in his hand.

With the night, comes a slouching figure through the tunnel-court, to the outside of the iron gate. It holds the gate with its hands, and looks in between the bars; stands looking in, for a little while.

It then, with an old broom it carries, softly sweeps the step, and makes the archway clean. It does so, very busily and trimly; looks in again, a little while; and so departs.

"He wos wery good to me, he wos!"

CHAPTER 6

On the Watch

It has left off raining down in Lincolnshire, at last, and Chesney Wold has taken heart for Sir Leicester and my Lady are coming home from Paris.

Through the cold sunshine, and sharp wind my Lady and Sir Leicester start for home. They cannot go away too fast; for, even here, my Lady Dedlock has been bored to death. She cannot, therefore, go too fast from Paris.

Sir Leicester is generally in a complacent state, and rarely bored. When he has nothing else to do, he can always contemplate his own greatness. After reading his letters, he leans back in his corner of the carriage, and generally reviews his importance to society.

"You have an unusual amount of correspondence this morning?" says my Lady, after a long time. She is fatigued with reading. Has almost read a page in twenty miles.

"Nothing in it, though. Nothing whatever."

"I saw one of Mr Tulkinghorn's long effusions, I think?"

"You see everything," says Sir Leicester, with admiration.

"He is the most tiresome of men!" sighs my Lady.

"He sends a message to you," says Sir Leicester, selecting the letter, and unfolding it. "He says, 'Will you do me the favour to mention to my Lady, in reference to the person who copied the affidavit, which so powerfully stimulated her curiosity. I have seen him.'"

My Lady, leaning forward, looks out of her window.

"That's the message," observes Sir Leicester.

"I should like to walk a little," says my Lady, still looking out of her window.

"Walk?" repeats Sir Leicester, in a tone of surprise.

"I should like to walk a little," says my Lady, with unmistakable distinctness. "Please to stop the carriage."

The carriage is stopped, the affectionate man alights from the rumble, opens the door, and lets down the steps, obedient to an impatient motion of my Lady's hand. My Lady alights so quickly, and walks away so quickly, that Sir Leicester, for all his scrupulous politeness, is unable to assist her, and is left behind. A space of a minute or two has elapsed before he comes up with her. She smiles, looks very handsome, takes his arm, lounges with him for a quarter of a mile, is very much bored, and resumes her seat in the carriage.

Every night after that, my Lady casually asks her maid:

"Is Mr Tulkinghorn come?"

Every night the answer is, "No, my Lady, not yet."

One night, while having her hair undressed, my Lady loses herself in deep thought after this reply, until she sees her own brooding face in the opposite glass, and a pair of black eyes curiously observing her.

"Be so good as to attend," says my Lady then, addressing the reflection

18

of Hortense, "to your business. You can contemplate your beauty at another time."

"Pardon! It was your Ladyship's beauty."

"That," says my Lady, "you needn't contemplate at all."

At length, one afternoon a little before sunset, when Sir Leicester and my Lady remain upon the terrace, Mr Tulkinghorn appears. He comes towards them at his usual methodical pace, wears his usual expressionless mask and carries family secrets in every limb of his body, and every crease of his dress.

"How do you do, Mr Tulkinghorn?" says Sir Leicester, giving him his hand.

Mr Tulkinghorn is quite well. Sir Leicester is quite well. My Lady is quite well. All highly satisfactory. The lawyer, with his hands behind him, walks, at Sir Leicester's side, along the terrace. My Lady walks upon the other side.

"But night is coming on," says he, "and my Lady will take cold. My dear, let us go in."

As they turn towards the hall-door, Lady Dedlock addresses Mr Tulkinghorn for the first time.

"You sent me a message respecting the person whose writing I happened to inquire about. I had quite forgotten it. I can't imagine what association I had, with a hand like that; but I surely had some."

"You had some?" Mr Tulkinghorn repeats.

"O yes!" returns my Lady, carelessly. "I think I must have had some. And did you really take the trouble to find out the writer of that actual thing – what is it! – Affidavit?"

"Yes."

"How very odd!"

They pass into a sombre breakfast-room on the ground-floor, lighted in the day by two deep windows. It is now twilight.

My Lady lounges in a great chair in the chimney-corner, and Sir Leicester takes another great chair opposite. The lawyer stands before the fire, with his hand out at arm's length, shading his face. He looks across his arm at my Lady.

"Yes," he says, "I inquired about the man, and found him. And, what is very strange, I found him – "

"Not to be any out-of-the-way person, I am afraid!" Lady Dedlock languidly anticipates.

19

"I found him dead."

"O dear me!" remonstrated Sir Leicester. Not so much shocked by the fact, as by the fact of the fact being mentioned.

"I was directed to his lodging – a miserable, poverty-stricken place – and I found him dead."

"You will excuse me, Mr Tulkinghorn," observes Sir Leicester. "I think the less said – "

"Pray, Sir Leicester, let me hear the story out;" (it is my Lady speaking). "It is quite a story for twilight. How very shocking! Dead?"

Mr Tulkinghorn re-asserts it by another inclination of his head. "Whether by his own hand – "

"Upon my honour!" cries Sir Leicester. "Really!"

"Do let me hear the story!" says my Lady.

"Whatever you desire, my dear. But, I must say – "

"No, you mustn't say! Go on, Mr Tulkinghorn."

Sir Leicester's gallantry concedes the point; though he still feels that to bring this sort of squalor among the upper classes is really – really –

"I was about to say," resumes the lawyer, with undisturbed calmness, "that whether he had died by his own hand or not, it was beyond my power to tell you. The Coroner's jury found that he took the poison accidentally."

"And what kind of man," my Lady asks, "was this deplorable creature?"

"Very difficult to say," returns the lawyer, shaking his head. "He had lived so wretchedly, and was so neglected, with his gipsy colour, and his wild black hair and beard, that I should have considered him the commonest of the common. The surgeon had a notion that he had once been something better, both in appearance and condition."

"What did they call the wretched being?"

"They called him what he had called himself, but no one knew his name."

"Not even any one who had attended on him?"

"No one had attended on him. He was found dead. In fact, I found him."

"Without any clue to anything more?"

"Without any; there was," says the lawyer, meditatively, "an old portmanteau; but – No, there were no papers."

During the utterance of every word of this short dialogue, Lady Dedlock and Mr Tulkinghorn, without any other alteration in their customary deportment, have looked very steadily at one another.

CHAPTER 7

Tom-all-Alone's

My Lady Dedlock is restless, very restless. She has flitted away to town, with no intention of remaining there, and will soon flit hither again.

What connexion can there be, between the place in Lincolnshire, the house in town and the whereabouts of Jo the outlaw with the broom. Jo sweeps his crossing all day long, unconscious of the link, if any link there be. He sums up his mental condition, when asked a question, by replying that he "don't know nothink." He knows that it's hard to keep the mud off the crossing in dirty weather, and harder still to live by doing it. Nobody taught him, even that much; he found it out.

Jo lives – that is to say, Jo has not yet died – in a ruinous place, known to the like of him by the name of Tom-all-Alone's. It is a black, dilapidated street, avoided by all decent people. Now, these tumbling tenements contain, by night, a swarm of misery. Twice, lately, there has been a crash and a cloud of dust, like the springing of a mine, in Tom-all-Alone's; and, each time, a house has fallen. As several more houses are nearly ready to go, the next crash in Tom-all-Alone's may be expected to be a good one.

Jo comes out of Tom-all-Alone's, meeting the tardy morning which is always late in getting down there, and munches his dirty bit of bread as he goes to his crossing, and begins to lay it out for the day.

The day changes as it wears itself away, and becomes dark and drizzly. Jo fights it out, at his crossing, among the mud and wheels, the horses, whips, and umbrellas, and gets but a scanty sum to pay for the unsavoury shelter of Tom-all-Alone's. Twilight comes on; gas begins to start up in the shops; the lamp-lighter, with his ladder, runs along the margin of the pavement. A wretched evening is beginning to close in.

Like the woman who now leaves her London house behind. Her face is veiled, and she never turns her head. until she comes to the crossing where Jo plies with his broom. He crosses with her, and begs. Still, she does not turn her head until she has landed on the other side. Then, she slightly beckons to him, and says, "Come here!"

Jo follows her, a pace or two, into a quiet court.

"Are you the boy I've read of in the papers?" she asked behind her veil.

"I don't know," says Jo, staring moodily at the veil, "nothink about no papers. I don't know nothink about nothink at all."

"Were you examined at an inquest?"

"I don't know nothink about no – " says Jo. "Was the boy's name at the inkwest Jo?"

"Yes."

"That's me!" says Jo.

"Come farther up."

"You mean about the man?" says Jo, following. "Him as wos dead?"

"Hush! Speak in a whisper! Yes. Did he look, when he was living, so very ill and poor?"

"O, jist!" says Jo.

"Did he look like – not like you?" says the woman.

"O, not so bad as me," says Jo. "I'm a reg'lar one I am! You didn't know him, did you?"

"How dare you ask me if I knew him?"

"No offence, my lady," says Jo with much humility; for even he has got at the suspicion of her being a lady.

"I am not a lady. I am a servant."

"You are a jolly servant!" says Jo without the least idea of saying anything offensive; merely as a tribute of admiration.

"Listen and be silent. Don't talk to me, and stand farther from me! Can you show me all those places that were spoken of in the account I read? The place he wrote for, the place he died at, the place where you were taken to, and the place where he was buried? Do you know the place where he was buried?"

Jo answers with a nod; having also nodded as each other place was mentioned.

"Go before me and show me all those dreadful places. Stop opposite to each, and don't speak to me unless I speak to you. Don't look back. Do what I want, and I will pay you well."

Jo attends closely while the words are being spoken; tells them off on his broom-handle, finding them rather hard; pauses to consider their meaning; considers it satisfactory; and nods his ragged head.

"Go on before! I will give you more money than you ever had in your life."

Jo screws up his mouth into a whistle, gives his ragged head a rub, takes his broom under his arm, and leads the way; passing deftly, with his bare feet, over the hard stones, and through the mud and mire.

Cook's Court. Jo stops. A pause.

"Who lives here?"

"Him wot give him his writing, and give me half a crown," says Jo in a whisper, without looking over his shoulder.

"Go on to the next."

Krook's house. Jo stops again. A longer pause.

"Who lives here?"

"He lived here," Jo answers as before.

After a silence, he is asked, "In which room?"

"In the back room up there. You can see the winder from this corner. Up there! That's where I see him stritched out. This is the public ouse where I was took to."

"Go on to the next!"

It is a longer walk to the next; but Jo, relieved of his first suspicions, sticks to the forms imposed upon him, and does not look round. By many devious ways, reeking with offence of many kinds, they come to the little tunnel of a court, and to the gas-lamp (lighted now), and to the iron gate.

"He was put there," says Jo, holding to the bars and looking in.

"Where? O, what a scene of horror!"

"There!" says Jo, pointing. "Over yinder. Among them piles of bones, and close to that there kitchin winder! They put him wery nigh the top. They was obliged to stamp upon it to git it in. I could unkiver it for you, with my broom if the gate was open. That's why they locks it, I s'pose," giving it a shake. "It's always locked. Look at the rat!" cries Jo, excited. "Hi! Look! There he goes! Ho! Into the ground!"

The servant shrinks into a corner – into a corner of that hideous archway, with its deadly stains contaminating her dress; and putting out her two hands and passionately telling him to keep away from her, for he is loathsome to her, so remains for some moments. Jo stands staring, and is still staring when she recovers herself.

"Is this place of abomination, consecrated ground?"

"I don't know nothink of consequential ground," says Jo, still staring.

"Is it blessed?"

"I'm blest if I know," says Jo, staring more than ever; "but I shouldn't think it warn't. Blest?" repeats Jo, something troubled in his mind. "It an't done it much good if it is. Blest? I should think it was t'othered myself. But I don't know nothink!"

The servant takes as little heed of what he says, as she seems to take of what she has said herself. She draws off her glove, to get some money from her purse. Jo silently notices how white and small her hand is, and what a jolly servant she must be to wear such sparkling rings.

She drops a piece of money in his hand, without touching it, and shuddering as their hands approach. "Now," she adds, "show me the spot again!"

Jo thrusts the handle of his broom between the bars of the gate, and with his utmost power of elaboration, points it out. At length he finds that he is alone.

His first proceeding, is, to hold the piece of money to the gas-light, and to be overpowered at finding that it is yellow – gold. His next, is, to give it a one-sided bite at the edge, as a test of its quality. His next, to put it in his mouth for safety, and to sweep the step and passage with great care. His job done, he sets off for Tom-all-Alone's; stopping in the light of innumerable gas-lamps to produce the piece of gold, and give it another one-sided bite, as a reassurance of its being genuine.

CHAPTER 8

Esther's Narrative

I was little inclined to sleep that night so I sat up working. I was wakeful and rather low-spirited and if I could have made myself go to sleep, I would have done it directly; but, not being able to do that, I took out of my basket some ornamental work for our house that I was busy with at that time, and I soon found myself very busy. But I had left some silk downstairs in a work-table drawer so I took my candle and went softly down to get it. To my great surprise, I found my guardian still there, and sitting looking at the ashes. Almost frightened by coming upon him so unexpectedly, I stood still for a moment.

"Esther!"

I told him what I had come for.

"At work so late, my dear?"

"I am working late to-night," said I, "because I couldn't sleep, and wished to tire myself. But, dear guardian, you are late too, and look weary. You have no trouble, I hope, to keep you waking?"

"None, little woman, that you would readily understand," said he.

He spoke in a regretful tone.

"Remain a moment, Esther," said he, "You were in my thoughts."

"I hope I was not the trouble, guardian?"

He slightly waved his hand, and fell into his usual manner.

"Little woman," said my guardian, "I was thinking that you ought to know of your own history, all I know. It is very little. Next to nothing."

"If you think so, guardian, it is right."

"I think so," he returned, very gently, and kindly, and very distinctly.

I sat down; and said, after a little effort to be as calm as I ought to be, "One of my earliest remembrances, guardian, is of these words. 'Your mother, Esther, is your disgrace, and you were hers.'"

I had covered my face with my hands, in repeating the words; but I took them away now and told him, that to him I owed the blessing that I had from my childhood to that hour never, never, never felt it. He put up his hand as if to stop me. I well knew that he was never to be thanked, and said no more.

"Nine years, my dear," he said after thinking for a little while, "have passed since I received a letter from a lady living in seclusion. It told me of a child, an orphan girl then twelve years old, in some such cruel words as those which live in your remembrance. It told me that the writer had bred her in secrecy from her birth, had blotted out all trace of her existence, and that if the writer were to die before the child became a woman, she would be left entirely friendless, nameless, and unknown. It asked me, to consider if I would, in that case, finish what the writer had begun?"

25

I listened in silence, and looked attentively at him.

"I felt concerned for the little creature, in her darkened life; and replied to the letter."

I took his hand and kissed it.

"The lady said that she was, if there were any ties of blood in such a case, the child's aunt. That more than this she would never, for any human consideration, disclose her real name. My dear, I have told you all."

I held his hand for a little while in mine.

"I saw my ward oftener than she saw me," he added, cheerily making light of it, "and I always knew she was beloved, useful, and happy. She repays me twenty-thousand fold, and twenty more to that, every hour in every day!"

"And oftener still," said I, "she blesses the guardian who is a Father to her!"

At the word Father, I saw his former trouble come into his face. He subdued it as before, and it was gone in an instant; but, it had been there, and it had come so swiftly upon my words that I felt as if they had given him a shock. I did not understand it. Not for many and many a day.

"Take a fatherly good-night, my dear," said he, kissing me on the forehead, "and so to rest. These are late hours for working and thinking. You do that for all of us, all day long, little housekeeper!"

I neither worked nor thought, any more, that night. I opened my grateful heart to Heaven in thankfulness for its providence to me and its care of me, and fell asleep.

CHAPTER 9

Lady Dedlock

Midsummer arrived before Richard finally entered on an experimental course of Messrs Kenge and Carboy. For all his waywardness, he took great credit to himself as being determined to be in earnest "this time." And he was so good-natured throughout, and in such high spirits, and so fond of Ada, that it was very difficult indeed to be otherwise than pleased with him.

At length, Richard having taken possession of his lodging, there was nothing to prevent our departure to stay with my guardian's great friend, Mr Boythorn.

We made a pleasant journey down into Lincolnshire by the coach, and had an entertaining companion in Mr Skimpole. His furniture had been all cleared off, it appeared, by the person who took possession of it on his blue-eyed daughter's birthday; but, he seemed quite relieved to think that it was gone.

"The oddity of the thing is," said Mr Skimpole, with a quickened sense of the ludicrous, "that my chairs and tables were not paid for, and yet my landlord walks off with them!"

"Well," said my guardian, good-humouredly, "it's pretty clear that whoever became security for those chairs and tables will have to pay for them."

"Exactly!" returned Mr Skimpole. "I said to my landlord, 'My good man, you are not aware that my excellent friend Jarndyce will have to pay for those things that you are sweeping off in that indelicate manner. Have you no consideration for his property?' He hadn't the least."

If these were some of the inconveniences of Mr Skimpole's it assuredly possessed its advantages too. On the journey he had a very good appetite for such refreshment as came in our way but never thought of paying for anything. So, when the coachman came round for his fee, he pleasantly asked him what he considered a very good fee and, on his replying, half-a-crown for a single passenger, said it was little enough too, all things considered; and left Mr Jarndyce to give it him.

At the inn we found Mr Boythorn on horseback, waiting with an open carriage.

"I am sorry, ladies," he said, standing bare-headed at the carriage-door, when all was ready, "that I am obliged to conduct you nearly two miles out of the way. But, our direct road lies through Sir Leicester Dedlock's park; and, in that fellow's property, I have sworn never to set foot of mine, or horse's foot of mine, pending the present relations between us, while I breathe the breath of life!" And here, catching my guardian's eye, he broke into one of his tremendous laughs, which seemed to shake even the motionless little market-town.

"Are the Dedlocks down here, Lawrence?" said my guardian as we drove along, and Mr Boythorn trotted on the green turf by the roadside.

"Sir Arrogant Numskull is here," replied Mr Boythorn. "Ha ha ha! Sir Arrogant is here, and, I am glad to say, has been laid by the heels here. My Lady," in naming whom he always made a courtly gesture as if particularly to exclude her from any part in the quarrel, "is expected, I believe, daily. I am not in the least surprised that she postpones her appearance as long as possible."

"I suppose," said my guardian laughing, "*we* may set foot in the park while we are here?"

"I can lay no prohibition on my guests," he said, bending his head to Ada and me, with the smiling politeness which sat so gracefully upon him.

Our coming to the ridge of a hill we had been ascending, enabled our friend to point out Chesney Wold itself to us, and diverted his attention from its master.

When we came into the little village, and passed a small inn with the sign of the Dedlock Arms swinging over the road in front, Mr Boythorn interchanged greetings with a young gentleman sitting on a bench outside the inn-door, who had some fishing-tackle lying beside him.

"That's the housekeeper's grandson, Mr Rouncewell by name," said he; "and he is in love with a pretty girl up at the House. Lady Dedlock has taken a fancy to the pretty girl, and is going to keep her about her own fair person – an honour which my young friend himself does not at all appreciate!"

"Are he and the pretty girl engaged, Mr Boythorn?" asked Ada.

"Why, my dear Miss Clare," he returned, "I think they may perhaps understand each other; but you will see them soon, I dare say, and I must learn from you on such a point – not you from me."

Ada blushed; and Mr Boythorn, trotting forward on his comely grey horse, dismounted at his own door, and stood ready, with extended arm and uncovered head, to welcome us when we arrived.

He lived in a pretty house, formerly the Parsonage-house, with a lawn in front, a bright flower-garden at the side, and a well-stocked orchard and kitchen-garden in the rear, enclosed with a venerable wall that had of itself a ripened ruddy look. On one side of it was the terrible piece of ground in dispute, where Mr Boythorn maintained a sentry day and night, whose duty was supposed to be, in cases of aggression, immediately to ring a large bell hung up there for the purpose, to unchain

28

a great bull-dog established in a kennel as his ally, and generally to deal destruction on the enemy.

"But, this is taking a good deal of trouble," said Mr Skimpole in his light way, "when you are not in earnest after all."

"Not in earnest!" returned Mr Boythorn with unspeakable warmth. "Not in earnest! Let Sir Leicester Dedlock consent to come out and decide this question by single combat, and I will meet him with any weapon known to mankind in any age or country. I am that much in earnest. Not more!"

We arrived at his house on a Saturday. On the Sunday morning we all set forth to walk to the little church in the park. Entering the park, almost immediately by the disputed ground, we pursued a pleasant footpath winding among the verdant turf and the beautiful trees, until it brought us to the church porch.

As the bell was yet ringing and the great people were not yet come, I had leisure to glance over the church, which smelt as earthy as a grave, and to think what a shady, ancient, solemn little church it was. But a stir, a gathering of reverential awe in the rustic faces, forewarned me that the great people were come, and that the service was going to begin.

"'Enter not into judgment with thy servant, O Lord, for in thy sight – '"

Shall I ever forget the rapid beating at my heart, occasioned by the look I met, as I stood up! Shall I ever forget the manner in which those handsome proud eyes seemed to spring out of their languor, and to hold mine! It was only a moment before I cast mine down on my book but I knew the beautiful face quite well, in that short space of time.

And, very strangely, there was something quickened within me, associated with the lonely days at my godmother's; yes, away even to the days when I had stood on tiptoe to dress myself at my little glass. And this although I had never seen this lady's face before in all my life – I was quite sure of it – absolutely certain.

It was easy to know that the ceremonious, gouty, grey-haired gentleman, the only other occupant of the great pew, was Sir Leicester Dedlock; and that the lady was Lady Dedlock. But why her face should be, in a confused way, like a broken glass to me, in which I saw scraps of old remembrances; and why I should be so fluttered and troubled (for I was still), by having casually met her eyes; I could not think.

It made me tremble so, to be thrown into this unaccountable agitation, that I was conscious of being distressed even by the observation of the French maid, though I knew she had been looking watchfully here, and there, and everywhere, from the moment of her coming into the church. By degrees, though very slowly, I at last overcame my strange emotion. After a long time, I looked towards Lady Dedlock again and the beating at my heart was gone. Neither did it revive for more than a few moments, when she once or twice afterwards glanced at Ada or at me.

Mr Skimpole often betook himself to beginning some sketch in the park which be never finished, or to playing fragments of airs on the piano, or to singing scraps of songs, or to lying down on his back under a tree, and looking at the sky – which he couldn't help thinking, he said, was what he was meant for; it suited him so exactly.

I always wondered on these occasions whether he ever thought of Mrs Skimpole and the children. So far as I could understand, they rarely presented themselves in his mind at all.

The week had gone round to the Saturday following that beating of my heart in the church; and every day had been so bright and blue, that to ramble in the woods had been most delightful. We had one favourite spot, deep in moss and last year's leaves, where there were some felled trees from which the bark was all stripped off. Upon the Saturday we sat here, Mr Jarndyce, Ada, and I, until we heard thunder muttering in the distance, and felt the large rain-drops rattle through the leaves.

The weather had been all the week extremely sultry; but, the storm broke so suddenly – upon us, at least, in that sheltered spot – that before we reached the outskirts of the wood, the thunder and lightning were frequent, and the rain came plunging through the leaves, as if every drop were a great leaden bead. As it was not a time for standing among trees, we ran out of the wood and made for a keeper's lodge which was close at hand.

The lattice-windows were all thrown open, and we sat, just within the doorway, watching the storm. It was grand to see how the wind awoke, and bent the trees, and drove the rain before it like a cloud of smoke; and to hear the solemn thunder, and to see the lightning.

"Is it not dangerous to sit in so exposed a place?"

The beating of my heart came back again. I had never heard the voice, as I had never seen the face, but it affected me in the same strange way.

Lady Dedlock had taken shelter in the lodge, before our arrival there, and had come out of the gloom within. She stood behind my chair, with her hand upon it. I saw her with her hand close to my shoulder, when I turned my head.

"I have frightened you?" she said.

No. It was not fright. Why should I be frightened!

"I believe," said Lady Dedlock to my guardian, "I have the pleasure of speaking to Mr Jarndyce."

"Your remembrance does me more honour than I had supposed it would, Lady Dedlock," he returned.

She had given him her hand, in an indifferent way that seemed habitual to her, and spoke in a correspondingly indifferent manner, though in a very pleasant voice. She was as graceful as she was beautiful; perfectly self-possessed; and had the air, I thought, of being able to attract and interest any one, if she had thought it worth her while. There was something very winning in her haughty manner; and it became more familiar – I was going to say more easy, but that could hardly be – as she spoke to him over her shoulder.

"I presume this is your ward, Miss Clare?"

He presented Ada, in form.

"But present me," and she turned full upon me, "to this young lady too!"

"Miss Summerson really is my ward," said Mr Jarndyce. "I am responsible to no Lord Chancellor in her case."

"Has Miss Summerson lost both her parents?" said my Lady.

"Yes."

"She is very fortunate in her guardian."

Lady Dedlock looked at me, and I looked at her, and said I was indeed. All at once she turned from me with a hasty air, almost expressive of displeasure or dislike, and spoke to him over her shoulder again.

"I think you knew my sister, when we were abroad together, better than you know me?" she said, looking at him again.

"Yes, we happened to meet oftener," he returned.

"We went our several ways," said Lady Dedlock, "and had little in common even before we agreed to differ. It is to be regretted, I suppose, but it could not be helped."

Lady Dedlock again sat looking at the rain. The shower greatly abated, the lightning ceased, the thunder rolled among the distant hills, and the sun began to glisten on the wet leaves and the falling rain. As we sat there, silently, we saw a little pony phaeton coming towards us at a merry pace.

As it drove up, we saw that there were two people inside. There alighted from it, with some cloaks and wrappers, first the Frenchwoman whom I had seen in church, and secondly the pretty girl; the Frenchwoman with a defiant confidence; the pretty girl, confused and hesitating.

"What now?" said Lady Dedlock. "Two!"

"I am your maid, my Lady, at the present," said the Frenchwoman. "The message was for the attendant."

"I was afraid you might mean me, my Lady," said the pretty girl.

"I did mean you, child," replied her mistress, calmly. "Put that shawl on me."

She slightly stooped her shoulders to receive it, and the pretty girl lightly dropped it in its place. The Frenchwoman stood unnoticed, looking on with her lips very tightly set.

Lady Dedlock turned to Mr Jarndyce. "You will allow me to send the carriage back for your two wards. It shall be here directly."

But, as he would on no account accept this offer, she took a graceful leave of Ada – none of me – and put her hand upon his proffered arm, and got into the carriage; which was a little, low, park carriage, with a hood.

"Come in, child," she said to the pretty girl, "I shall want you. Go on!"

The carriage rolled away; and the Frenchwoman, with the wrappers she had brought hanging over her arm, remained standing where she had alighted.

Her retaliation was the most singular I could have imagined. She remained perfectly still until the carriage had turned into the drive, and then, without the least discomposure of countenance, slipped off her shoes, left them on the ground, and walked deliberately in the same direction, through the wettest of the wet grass.

"Is that young woman mad?" said my guardian.

We passed not far from the House, a few minutes afterwards. Peaceful as it had looked when we first saw it, it looked even more so now, with a diamond spray glittering all about it, everything refreshed by the late rain, and the little carriage shining at the doorway like a fairy carriage made of silver. Still, very steadfastly and quietly walking towards it, a peaceful figure too in the landscape, went Mademoiselle Hortense, shoeless, through the wet grass.

CHAPTER 10

Mr Bucket

Mr Tulkinghorn, sitting in the twilight by the open window, enjoys his wine. As if it whispered to him of its fifty years of silence and seclusion, it shuts him up the closer.

But, Mr Tulkinghorn is not alone to-night, to ponder at his usual length. Seated at the same table, though with his chair modestly and uncomfortably drawn a little away from it, sits a bald, mild, shining man, who coughs respectfully behind his hand when the lawyer bids him fill his glass.

"Now, Snagsby," says Mr Tulkinghorn, "to go over this odd story again."

"If you please, sir." Mr Snagsby drinks, and murmurs with an admiring cough behind his hand. "Dear me, very fine wine indeed!"

Mr Tulkinghorn assents. "Fill your glass, Snagsby."

"Thank you, sir, I am sure," returns the stationer, with his cough of deference. "This is wonderfully fine wine, sir!"

"It is a rare wine now," says Mr Tulkinghorn. "It is fifty years old."

"Is it indeed, sir? But I am not surprised to hear it, I am sure. It might be – any age almost."

"Will you run over, once again, what the boy said?" asks Mr Tulkinghorn, putting his hands into the pockets of his rusty smallclothes and leaning quietly back in his chair.

"With pleasure, sir."

Then law-stationer repeats Jo's statement made to explain his sudden fortune. On coming to the end of his narrative, he gives a great start, and breaks off with "Dear me, sir, I wasn't aware there was any other gentleman present!"

Mr Snagsby is dismayed to see a person with a hat and stick in his hand who was not there when he himself came in, and has not since entered by the door or by either of the windows.

"Don't mind this gentleman," says Mr Tulkinghorn, in his quiet way. "This is only Mr Bucket."

"O indeed, sir?" returns the stationer, expressing by a cough that he is quite in the dark as to who Mr Bucket may be.

"I wanted him to hear this story," says the lawyer, "because I have half a mind to know more of it, and he is very intelligent in such things. What do you say to this, Bucket?"

"If Mr Snagsby don't object to go down with me to Tom-all-Alone's and point him out, we can have him here in less than a couple of hours' time. I can do it without Mr Snagsby, of course; but this is the shortest way."

"Mr Bucket is a detective officer, Snagsby," says the lawyer in explanation.

"Is he indeed, sir?" says Mr Snagsby, with a strong tendency in his clump of hair to stand on end.

"And if you have no real objection to accompany Mr Bucket to the place in question," pursues the lawyer, "I shall feel obliged to you if you will do so."

In a moment's hesitation on the part of Mr Snagsby, Bucket dips down to the bottom of his mind.

"Don't you be afraid of hurting the boy," he says. "You won't do that. We shall only bring him here to ask him a question or so I want to put to him, and he'll be paid for his trouble, and sent away again."

"Very well, Mr Tulkinghorn!" cries Mr Snagsby cheerfully, and reassured, "Since that's the case – "

"Then here's your hat," returns his new friend, quite as intimate with it as if he had made it; "and if you're ready, I am."

They leave Mr Tulkinghorn, without a ruffle on the surface of his unfathomable depths, drinking his old wine, and go down into the streets.

There is inquiry made, at various houses, for a boy named Jo. As few people are known in Tom-all-Alone's by any Christian sign, there is much reference to Mr Snagsby whether he means Carrots, or the Colonel, or Gallows, or Young Chisel, or Terrier Tip, or Lanky, or the Brick. At last there is a lair found out where Toughy, or the Tough Subject, lays him down at night; and it is thought that the Tough Subject may be Jo.

"And who have we got here to-night?" says Mr Bucket, opening another door and glaring in with his lantern.

The room is so low that the head of the tallest of the visitors would touch the blackened ceiling if he stood upright. It is offensive to every sense; even the gross candle burns pale and sickly in the polluted air.

As Mr Snagsby blows his nose, and coughs his cough of sympathy, a step is heard. Mr Bucket throws his light into the doorway, and says to Mr Snagsby, "Now, what do you say to Toughy? Will he do?"

"That's Jo!" says Mr Snagsby.

Jo stands amazed in the disk of light, like a ragged figure in a magic lantern, trembling to think that he has offended against the law in not having moved on far enough. Mr Snagsby, however, giving him the consolatory assurance, "It's only a job you will be paid for, Jo," he recovers; and, on being taken outside by Mr Bucket for a little private confabulation, tells his tale satisfactorily, though out of breath.

"I have squared it with the lad," says Mr Bucket, returning, "and it's all right. Now, Mr Snagsby, we're ready for you."

Through the clearer and fresher streets, never so clear and fresh to Mr Snagsby's mind as now, they walk and ride, until they come to Mr Tulkinghorn's gate.

They come at last into the hall, where a lamp is burning, and so into Mr Tulkinghorn's usual room – the room where he drank his old wine to-night. He is not there, but his two old-fashioned candlesticks are; and the room is tolerably light.

Mr Bucket, still having his professional hold of Jo, makes a little way into this room, when Jo starts, and stops.

"What's the matter?" says Bucket in a whisper.

"There she is!" cries Jo.

"Who?"

"The lady!"

A female figure, closely veiled, stands in the middle of the room, where the light falls upon it. It is quite still, and silent. The front of the figure is towards them, but it takes no notice of their entrance, and remains like a statue.

"Now, tell me," says Bucket aloud, "how you know that to be the lady."

"I know the veil," replies Jo, staring, "and the bonnet, and the gownd."

"Be quite sure of what you say, Tough," returns Bucket, narrowly observant of him. "Look again."

"I am a looking as hard as ever I can look," says Jo, with starting eyes, "and that there's the veil, the bonnet, and the gownd."

"What about those rings you told me of?" asks Bucket.

"A sparkling all over here," says Jo, rubbing the fingers of his left hand on the knuckles of his right, without taking his eyes from the figure.

35

The figure removes the right hand glove, and shews the hand.

"Now, what do you say to that?" asks Bucket.

Jo shakes his head. "Not rings a bit like them. Not a hand like that."

"What are you talking of?" says Bucket; evidently pleased though, and well pleased too.

"Hand was a deal whiter, a deal delicater and a deal smaller," returns Jo.

"Why, you'll tell me I'm my own mother, next," says Mr Bucket. "Do you recollect the lady's voice?"

"I think I does," says Jo.

The figure speaks. "Was it at all like this? I will speak as long as you like if you are not sure. Was it this voice, or at all like this voice?"

Jo looks aghast at Mr Bucket. "Not a bit!"

"Then, what," retorts that worthy, pointing to the figure, "did you say it was the lady for?"

"Cos," says Jo, with a perplexed stare, but without being at all shaken in his certainty, "cos that there's the veil, the bonnet, and the gownd. It is her and it an't her. It an't her hand, nor yet her rings, nor yet her woice. But that there's the veil, the bonnet, and the gownd, and they're wore the same way wot she wore 'em, and it's her height wot she wos, and she giv me a sov'ring and hooked it."

"Well!" says Mr Bucket slightly, "we haven't got much good out of you. But, however, here's five shillings for you. Take care how you spend it, and don't get yourself into trouble." Bucket takes the coins from one hand into the other and then puts them, in a little pile, into the boy's hand, and takes him out to the door, leaving Mr Snagsby alone with the veiled figure. But, on Mr Tulkinghorn's coming into the room, the veil is raised, and a good-looking Frenchwoman is revealed, though her expression is intense.

"Thank you, Mademoiselle Hortense," says Mr Tulkinghorn, with his usual equanimity. "I will give you no further trouble about this little wager."

"You will do me the kindness to remember, sir, that I am not at present placed?" says mademoiselle.

"Certainly, certainly!"

"And to confer upon me the favour of your distinguished recommendation?"

"By all means, Mademoiselle Hortense."

36

Mademoiselle goes out with an air of native gentility; and Mr Bucket shows her downstairs, not without gallantry.

"Well, Bucket?" quoth Mr Tulkinghorn on his return.

"There an't a doubt that it was the other one with this one's dress on. The boy was exact respecting colours and everything."

Mr Snagsby coughs his cough. "If I can be of no further use, Mr Tulkinghorn, I think, as my little woman will be getting anxious – "

"Thank you, Snagsby, no further use," says Mr Tulkinghorn. "I am quite indebted to you for the trouble you have taken already."

"Not at all, sir. I wish you good night."

Mr Snagsby goes homeward so confused by the events of the evening, that he is doubtful of his being awake and out – doubtful of the reality of the streets through which he goes – doubtful of the reality of the moon that shines above him.

CHAPTER 11

Esther's Narrative

We came home from Mr Boythorn's after six pleasant weeks. We were often in the park, and in the woods but we saw no more of Lady Dedlock, except at church on Sundays. I had a fancy, on more than one of these Sundays, that what this lady so curiously was to me, I was to her – I mean that I disturbed her thoughts as she influenced mine, though in some different way.

One incident that occurred before we quitted Mr Boythorn's house, I had better mention in this place.

I was walking in the garden with Ada, when I was told that some one wished to see me. Going into the breakfast-room where this person was waiting, I found it to be the French maid who had cast off her shoes and walked through the wet grass, on the day when it thundered and lightened.

"Mademoiselle," she began, looking fixedly at me with her too-eager eyes and speaking neither with boldness nor servility, "I have taken a great liberty in coming here, but you know how to excuse it, being so amiable, mademoiselle."

"No excuse is necessary," I returned, "if you wish to speak to me."

"That is my desire, mademoiselle. A thousand thanks for the permission. I have your leave to speak. Is it not?" she said, in a quick natural way.

"Certainly," said I.

"Listen then, if you please. I have left my Lady. We could not agree. My Lady is so high; so very high. Pardon! Mademoiselle, you are right!" Her quickness anticipated what I might have said presently, but as yet had only thought. "It is not for me to come here to complain of my Lady. But I say she is so high, so very high. I will not say a word more. All the world knows that.'

"Go on, if you please," said I.

"Mademoiselle, you are good, accomplished, and beautiful as an angel. Ah, could I have the honour of being your domestic!"

"I am sorry – " I began.

"Do not dismiss me so soon, mademoiselle!" she said, with a contraction of her fine black eyebrows. "Let me hope, a moment! Mademoiselle, I know this service would be more retired than that which I have quitted. Well! I wish that. I know this service would be less distinguished than that which I have quitted. Well! I wish that. I know that I should win less, as to wages, here. Good. I am content."

"I assure you," said I, quite embarrassed by the mere idea of having such an attendant, "that I keep no maid – "

"Ah, mademoiselle, but why not? Why not, when you can have one so devoted to you? Who would be enchanted to serve you; who would be so true, so zealous, and so faithful, every day! Mademoiselle, I wish with all my heart to serve you. Do not speak of money at present. Take me as I am. For nothing!"

She was so singularly earnest that I drew back, almost afraid of her. She still pressed herself upon me; speaking in a rapid subdued voice.

"Receive me as your domestic, and I will serve you well. I will do more for you, than you figure to yourself now. I will serve you well. You don't know how well!"

There was a lowering energy in her face, as she stood looking at me while I explained the impossibility of my engaging her. She heard me out without interruption; and then said, with her pretty accent, and in her mildest voice:

"Mademoiselle, I have received my answer! I am sorry of it. But I must go elsewhere, and seek what I have not found here. Will you graciously let me kiss your hand?"

She looked at me more intently as she took it, and seemed to take note of every vein in it. "I fear I surprised you, mademoiselle, on the day of the storm?" she said, with a parting curtsy.

I confessed that she had surprised us all.

"I took an oath, mademoiselle," she said, smiling, "and I wanted to stamp it on my mind, so that I might keep it faithfully. And I will! Adieu, mademoiselle!"

So ended our conference, which I was very glad to bring to a close. I supposed she went away from the village, for I saw her no more; and nothing else occurred to disturb our tranquil summer pleasures, until six weeks were out, and we returned home.

At that time, and for a good many weeks after that time, Richard was constant in his visits. Besides coming every Saturday or Sunday, and remaining with us until Monday morning, he sometimes rode out on horseback unexpectedly, and passed the evening with us, and rode back again early next day. He was as vivacious as ever, and told us he was very industrious; but I was not easy in my mind about him. It appeared to me that his industry was all misdirected. I could not find that it led to anything, but the formation of delusive hopes in connexion with the suit already the pernicious cause of so much sorrow and ruin. He had got at the core of that mystery now, he told us; and nothing could be plainer than that the will under which he and Ada were to take, I don't know how many thousands of pounds, must be finally established, if there were any sense or justice in the Court of Chancery. He proved this to himself by all the weary arguments on that side he had read, and every one of them sunk him deeper in the infatuation. He had even begun to haunt the court.

Ada loved him too well, to mistrust him much in anything he said or did, and my guardian, though he frequently complained and read more than usual in the Growlery, preserved a strict silence on the subject. So, I thought, one day when I went to London to meet Caddy Jellyby, I would ask Richard to be in waiting for me at the coach-office, that we might have a little talk together. I found him there when I arrived, and we walked away arm in arm.

"Well, Richard," said I, as soon as I could begin to be grave with him, "are you beginning to feel more settled now?"

"O yes, my dear!" returned Richard. "I'm all right enough."

"But settled?" said I.

"How do you mean, settled?" returned Richard, with his gay laugh.

"Settled in the law," said I.

"O aye," replied Richard, "I'm all right enough."

"You said that before, my dear Richard."

"And you don't think it's an answer, eh? Well! Perhaps it's not. Settled? You mean, do I feel as if I were settling down?"

"Yes."

"Why, no, I can't say I am settling down," said Richard, strongly emphasising "down," as if that expressed the difficulty; "because one can't settle down while this business remains in such an unsettled state. When I say this business, of course I mean the – forbidden subject."

"Do you think it will ever be in a settled state?" said I.

"Not the least doubt of it," answered Richard.

We walked a little way without speaking; and presently Richard addressed me in his frankest and most feeling manner, thus:

"My dear Esther, I understand you, and I wish to heaven I were a more constant sort of fellow. If I were a more constant sort of fellow, I should have begun to be steady and systematic by this time, and shouldn't be in debt, and – "

"Are you in debt, Richard?"

"Yes," said Richard, "I am a little so, my dear. Also, I have taken rather too much to billiards, and that sort of thing. Now the murder's out; you despise me, Esther, don't you?"

"You know I don't," said I.

"You are kinder to me than I often am to myself," he returned. "My dear Esther, I am a very unfortunate dog not to be more settled, but how can I be more settled? I was born into this unfinished contention and it began to unsettle me before I quite knew the difference between a suit at law and a suit of clothes; and it has gone on unsettling me ever since; and here I am now, conscious sometimes that I am but a worthless fellow to love my confiding cousin Ada."

We were in a solitary place, and he put his hands before his eyes and sobbed as he said the words.

"O Richard!" said I, "do not be so moved. You have a noble nature, and Ada's love may make you worthier every day."

"I know, my dear," he replied, pressing my arm, "I know what the thought of Ada ought to do for me, but it doesn't do it. I am too unsettled even for that. I love her most devotedly; and yet I do her wrong, in doing myself wrong, every day and hour. But it can't last for ever. We shall come on for a final hearing, and get judgement in our favour; and then you and Ada shall see what I can really be!"

It had given me a pang to hear him sob, and see the tears start out between his fingers; but that was infinitely less affecting to me, than the hopeful animation with which he said these words.

"I have looked well into the papers, Esther – I have been deep in them for months," he continued, recovering his cheerfulness in a moment, "and you may rely upon it that we shall come out triumphant. As to years of delay, there has been no want of them, Heaven knows! and there is the greater probability of our bringing the matter to a speedy close; in fact, it's on the paper now. It will be all right at last, and then you shall see!"

I asked him when he intended to be articled in Lincoln's Inn.

"There again! I think not at all, Esther," he returned with an effort. "I fancy I have had enough of it. Having worked at Jarndyce and Jarndyce like a galley slave, I have slaked my thirst for the law, and satisfied myself that I shouldn't like it. Besides, I find it unsettles me more and more to be so constantly upon the scene of action. So what," continued Richard, confident again by this time, "do I naturally turn my thoughts to?"

"I can't imagine," said I.

"What," said Richard, in a tone of perfect conviction, "but the army!"

"The army?" said I.

"The army, of course. What I have to do, is, to get a commission; and – there I am, you know!" said Richard.

I spoke to Richard with all the earnestness I felt, and all the hope I could not quite feel then; and implored him, for Ada's sake, not to put any trust in Chancery. To all I said, Richard readily assented; riding over the court and everything else in his easy way, and drawing the brightest pictures of the character he was to settle into when the grievous suit should loose its hold upon him! We had a long talk, but it always came back to that, in substance.

CHAPTER 12

An Appeal Case

As soon as Richard and I had held the conversation, of which I have given an account, Richard communicated the state of his mind to Mr Jarndyce. I doubt if my guardian were altogether taken by surprise, when he received the representation; though it caused him much uneasiness and disappointment. He and Richard were often closeted together, late at night and early in the morning, and passed whole days in London, and had innumerable appointments with Mr Kenge, and laboured through a quantity of disagreeable business.

At last it was settled that his application should be granted. His name was entered at the Horse Guards, as an applicant for an ensign's commission; the purchase-money was deposited at an agent's; and Richard, in his usual characteristic way, plunged into a violent course of military study, and got up at five o'clock every morning to practise the broadsword exercise.

Thus, vacation succeeded term, and term succeeded vacation. We sometimes heard of Jarndyce and Jarndyce, as being in the paper or out of the paper, or as being to be mentioned, or as being to be spoken to; and it came on, and it went off. My guardian still maintained the same reserve; and so time passed until the commission was obtained, and Richard received directions with it to join a regiment in Ireland.

He arrived post-haste with the intelligence one evening, and had a long conference with my guardian. Upwards of an hour elapsed before my guardian put his head into the room where Ada and I were sitting, and said, "Come in, my dears!" We went in, and found Richard, whom we had last seen in high spirits, leaning on the chimney-piece, looking mortified and angry.

"Rick and I, Ada," said Mr Jarndyce, "are not quite of one mind. Come, come, Rick, put a brighter face upon it!"

"You are very hard with me, sir," said Richard. "The harder, because you have been so considerate to me in all other respects, and have done me kindnesses that I can never acknowledge. I never could have been set right without you, sir."

"Well, well!" said Mr Jarndyce. "I want to set you more right yet. I want to set you more right with yourself."

"I hope you will excuse my saying, sir," returned Richard in a fiery way, but yet respectfully, "that I think I am the best judge about myself."

"I hope you will excuse my saying, my dear Rick," observed Mr Jarndyce with the sweetest cheerfulness and good humour, "that's it's quite natural in you to think so, but I don't think so. I must do my duty, Rick, or you could never care for me in cool blood; and I hope you will always care for me, cool and hot."

Ada had turned so pale that he made her sit down in his reading-chair, and sat beside her.

"It's nothing, my dear," he said, "it's nothing. Rick and I have only had a friendly difference, which we must state to you, for you are the theme. Now you are afraid of what's coming."

"I am not indeed, cousin John," replied Ada, with a smile, "if it is to come from you."

"Thank you, my dear. Do you give me a minute's calm attention, without looking at Rick. And, little woman, do you likewise. My dear girl," putting his hand on hers, as it lay on the side of the easy-chair, "you recollect the talk we had, we four, when the little woman told me of a little love-affair?"

"It is not likely that either Richard or I can ever forget your kindness that day, cousin John."

"I can never forget it," said Richard.

"And I can never forget it," said Ada.

"So much the easier what I have to say, and so much the easier for us to agree," returned my guardian, his face irradiated by the gentleness and honour of his heart. "Ada, my bird, you should know that Rick has now chosen his profession for the last time. He has exhausted his resources."

"Quite true that I have exhausted my present resources, and I am quite content to know it. But what I have of certainty, sir," said Richard, "is not all I have."

"Rick, Rick!" cried my guardian, with a sudden terror in his manner, and in an altered voice, and putting up his hands as if he would have stopped his ears, "for the love of God, don't found a hope or expectation on the family curse! Whatever you do on this side the grave, never give one lingering glance towards the horrible phantom that has haunted us so many years. Better to borrow, better to beg, better to die!"

We were all startled by the fervour of this warning. Richard bit his lip and held his breath, and glanced at me, as if he felt, and knew that I felt too, how much he needed it.

"Ada, my dear," said Mr Jarndyce, recovering his cheerfulness, "these are strong words of advice; but I live in Bleak House, and have seen a sight here. All Richard had, to start him in the race of life, is ventured. I recommend to him and you, for his sake and your own, that there is no sort of contract between you. I must go further. I will be plain with you both. I ask you wholly to relinquish, for the present, any tie but your relationship."

"Better to say at once, sir," returned Richard, "that you renounce all confidence in me, and that you advise Ada to do the same."

"Better to say nothing of the sort, Rick, because I don't mean it."

"You think I have begun ill, sir," retorted Richard. "I have, I know."

"You have not made that beginning yet; but there is a time for all things, and yours is not gone by – rather, it is just now fully come. Make a clear beginning altogether. You two are cousins. As yet, you are nothing more. What more may come, must come of being worked out, Rick; and no sooner."

"You are very hard with me, sir," said Richard. "Harder than I could have supposed you would be."

"My dear boy," said Mr Jarndyce, "I am harder with myself when I do anything that gives you pain. You have your remedy in your own hands. Ada, it is better for him that he should be free, and that there should be no youthful engagement between you. Rick, it is better for her, much better; you owe it to her. Come! Each of you will do what is best for the other, if not what is best for yourselves."

"Why is it best, sir?" returned Richard, hastily. "It was not, when we opened our hearts to you. You did not say so, then."

"I have had experience since. I don't blame you, Rick – but I have had experience since."

"You mean of me, sir."

"Well! Yes, of both of you," said Mr Jarndyce, kindly. "The time is not come for your standing pledged to one another. It is not right, and I must not recognize it. Come, come, my young cousins, begin afresh! Bygones shall be bygones, and a new page turned for you to write your lives in."

A long silence succeeded.

"Cousin Richard," said Ada, then, raising her blue eyes tenderly to his face, "after what our cousin John has said, I think no choice is left us. Your mind may be quite at ease about me; for you will leave me here under his care, and will be sure that I can have nothing to wish for; quite sure, if I guide myself by his advice. Even cousins may be sorry to part; and in truth I am very, very sorry, Richard, though I know it's for your welfare. So now," said Ada, going up to him and giving him her trembling hand, "we are only cousins again, Richard – for the time perhaps – and I pray for a blessing on my dear cousin, wherever he goes!"

But I observed, with great regret, that from this hour Richard never was as free and open with Mr Jarndyce as he had been before.

In the business of preparation and equipment he soon lost himself, and even his grief at parting from Ada, who remained in Hertfordshire, while he, Mr Jarndyce, and I, went up to London for a week. He remembered her by fits and starts, even with bursts of tears; and at such times would confide to me the heaviest self-reproaches. But, in a few minutes he would recklessly conjure up some undefinable means by which they were both to be made rich and happy for ever, and would become as gay as possible.

There used, in that week, to come backward and forward to our lodging, to fence with Richard, a person who had formerly been a cavalry soldier; he was a fine bluff-looking man with whom Richard had practised for some months. I heard so much about him, not only from Richard, but from my guardian too, that I was purposely in the room, with my work, one morning after breakfast when he came.

"Good morning, Mr George," said my guardian, who happened to be alone with me. "Mr Carstone will be here directly. Meanwhile, Miss Summerson is very happy to see you, I know. Sit down."

He sat down, a little disconcerted by my presence, I thought; and, without looking at me, drew his heavy sunburnt hand across his upper lip.

"You are as punctual as the sun," said Mr Jarndyce.

"Military time, sir," he replied. "Force of habit. A mere habit in me, sir. I am not at all business-like."

"Yet you have a large establishment, too, I am told?" said Mr Jarndyce.

"Not much of a one, sir. I keep a shooting gallery, but not much of a one."

"And what kind of a shot, and what kind of a swordsman, do you make of Mr Carstone?" said my guardian.

"Pretty good, sir," he replied, folding his arms upon his broad chest, and looking very large. "If Mr Carstone was to give his full mind to it, he would come out very good."

"But he don't, I suppose?" said my guardian.

"He did at first, sir, but not afterwards. Not his full mind. Perhaps he has something else upon it – some young lady, perhaps." His bright dark eyes glanced at me for the first time.

"He has not me upon his mind, I assure you, Mr George," said I, laughing, "though you seem to suspect me."

He reddened a little through his brown, and made me a trooper's bow. "No offence, I hope, miss. I am one of the roughs."

"Not at all," said I. "I take it as a compliment."

If he had not looked at me before, he looked at me now, in three or four quick successive glances. "I beg your pardon, sir," he said to my guardian, with a manly kind of diffidence, "but you did me the honour to mention the young lady's name – "

"Miss Summerson."

"Miss Summerson," he repeated, and looked at me again.

"Do you know the name?" I asked.

"No, miss. To my knowledge, I never heard it. I thought I had seen you somewhere."

"I think not," I returned, raising my head from my work to look at him; and there was something so genuine in his speech and manner, that I was glad of the opportunity. "I remember faces very well."

"So do I, miss!" he returned, meeting my look with the fullness of his dark eyes and broad forehead.

"Have you many pupils, Mr George?" asked my guardian.

"All sorts, sir. From gentlemen to 'prentices. I have had French women come, before now, and show themselves dabs at pistol-shooting."

"People don't come with grudges, and schemes of finishing their practice with live targets, I hope?" said my guardian, smiling.

"Not much of that, sir, though that has happened. Mostly they come for skill – or idleness. Six of one, and half a dozen of the other."

Richard's entrance stopped the conversation. Mr George rose, made me another of his soldierly bows, wished my guardian a good day, and strode heavily out of the room.

This was the morning of the day appointed for Richard's departure. We had no more purchases to make now; I had completed all his packing early in the afternoon; and our time was disengaged until night, when he was to go to Liverpool for Holyhead. Jarndyce and Jarndyce being again expected to come on that day, Richard proposed to me that we should go down to the court and hear what passed. As it was his last day, and he was eager to go, and I had never been there, I gave my consent, and we walked down to Westminster where the court was then sitting. We beguiled the way with arrangements concerning the letters that Richard was to write to me, and the letters that I was to write to him; and with a great many hopeful projects. My guardian knew where we were going, and therefore was not with us.

When we came to the court, there was the Lord Chancellor sitting, in great state and gravity, on the bench; with the mace and seals on a red table below him, and an immense flat nosegay, like a little garden, which scented the whole court. Below the table, again, was a long row of solicitors, with bundles of papers on the matting at their feet; and then there were the gentlemen of the bar in wigs and gowns – some awake and some asleep, and one talking, and nobody paying much attention to what he said. The Lord Chancellor leaned back in his very easy chair, with his elbow on the cushioned arm, and his forehead resting on his hand; some of those who were present, dozed; some read the newspapers; some walked about, or whispered in groups; all seemed perfectly at their ease, by no means in a hurry, very unconcerned, and extremely comfortable.

I sat where Richard put me, and tried to listen, and looked about me; but there seemed to be no reality in the whole scene.

When we had been there half an hour or so, the case in progress – if I may use a phrase so ridiculous in such a connexion – seemed to die out of its own vapidity, without coming, or being by anybody expected to come, to any result. The Lord Chancellor then threw down a bundle of papers from his desk to the gentlemen below him, and somebody said, "*Jarndyce and Jarndyce*." Upon this there was a buzz, and a laugh, and a general withdrawal of the bystanders, and a bringing in of great heaps, and piles, and bags and bags-full of papers.

I think it came on "for further directions," – about some bill of costs, to the best of my understanding, which was confused enough. But I counted twenty-three gentlemen in wigs, who said they were "in it," and none of them appeared to understand it much better than I. They chatted about it with the Lord Chancellor, and contradicted and explained among themselves, and some of them said it was this way, and some of them said it was that way, and some of them jocosely proposed to read huge volumes of affidavits, and there was more buzzing and laughing, and everybody concerned was in a state of idle entertainment, and nothing could be made of it by anybody. After an hour or so of this, and a good many speeches being begun and cut short, it was "referred back for the present," and the papers were bundled up again, before the clerks had finished bringing them in.

I glanced at Richard, on the termination of these hopeless proceedings, and was shocked to see the worn look of his handsome young face. "It can't last for ever, Dame Durden. Better luck next time!" was all he said.

CHAPTER 13

Sharpshooters

The wintry morning wakes Mr George of the Shooting Gallery, and his man, Phil. They arise, roll up and stow away their mattresses. Mr George, having shaved himself before a looking-glass of minute proportions, then marches out, bare-headed and bare-chested, to the Pump, in the little yard, and anon comes back shining with yellow soap, friction, drifting rain, and exceedingly cold water. Mr George's toilet is soon performed. He fills his pipe, lights it, and marches up and down smoking, as his custom is, while Phil, raising a powerful odour of hot rolls and coffee, prepares breakfast.

Master and man are at length disturbed by footsteps in the passage, where they make an unusual sound, denoting the arrival of unusual company.

It consists of a limp and ugly figure carried in a chair by two bearers, and attended by a lean female with a face like a pinched mask.

"Mr George, my dear friend," says Grandfather Smallweed. "I have brought my grand-daughter Judy. She longed so much to see you."

"Hum! She bears it calmly!" mutters Mr George, wheeling his chair to face the old man. "Now then?"

"My friend in the city, Mr George, has done a little business with a pupil of yours."

"Has he?" says Mr George. "I am sorry to hear it."

"Yes, sir." Grandfather Smallweed rubs his legs. "He is a fine young soldier now, Mr George, by the name of Carstone. Friends came forward, and paid it all up, honourable."

"Did they?" returns Mr George. "Do you think your friend in the city would like a piece of advice?"

"I think he would, my dear friend. From you."

"I advise him, then, to do no more business in that quarter. There's no more to be got by it. The young gentleman, to my knowledge, is brought to a dead halt."

"No, no, my dear friend. No, no, Mr George. No, no, no, sir," remonstrates Grandfather Smallweed, cunningly rubbing his spare legs. "Not quite a dead halt, I think. He has good friends, and he is good for his pay, and he is good for the selling price of his commission, and he is good for his chance in a lawsuit, and he is good for his chance in a wife, and – oh, do you know, Mr George, I think my friend would consider the young gentleman good for something yet!" says Grandfather Smallweed, turning up his velvet cap, and scratching his ear like a monkey. "But to pass, Mr George, from the ensign to the captain."

"What are you up to, now?" asks Mr George, pausing with a frown in stroking the recollection of his moustache. "What captain?"

"Our captain. The captain we know of. Captain Hawdon."

"My dear friend," returns the old man, "I was applied to, yesterday, about the captain. Now, what do you think the lawyer making the inquiries wants?"

"A job," says Mr George.

"My dear friend, he is a lawyer, and a famous one. He wants to see some fragment in Captain Hawdon's writing. He don't want to keep it. He only wants to see it, and compare it with a writing in his possession."

"Well, Mr Smallweed?" says Mr George again, after going through the ceremony with some stiffness.

"I had no such thing. I have nothing but his signature. I have half a million of his signatures, I think! But you, my dear Mr George, are likely to have some letter or paper that would suit the purpose. Anything would suit the purpose, written in the hand."

"Some writing in that hand," says the trooper, pondering, "may be, I have."

"My dearest friend!"

"May be, I have not."

"No!" says Grandfather Smallweed, crest-fallen.

"But if I had bushels of it, I would not show as much as would make a cartridge, without knowing why."

"Sir, I have told you why. My dear Mr George, I have told you why."

"Not enough," says the trooper, shaking his head. "I must know more, and approve it."

"Then, will you come to the lawyer? My dear friend, will you come and see the gentleman?" urges Grandfather Smallweed, pulling out a lean old silver watch, with hands like the legs of a skeleton.

"Hum!" says he, gravely. "I don't mind that. Though why this should concern you so much, I don't know."

"Everything concerns me, that has a chance in it of bringing anything to light about him. Didn't he owe us immense sums, all round?" says Grandfather Smallweed, lowering his tone, "Are you ready to come, my dear friend?"

"Aye! I'll come in a moment. I promise nothing, you know."

"No, my dear Mr George; no."

"And you mean to say you're going to give me a lift to this place, wherever it is, without charging for it?" Mr George inquires, getting his hat, and thick wash-leather gloves.

"I am ready," says the trooper. "Phil, you can carry this old gentleman to his coach, and make nothing of him."

"O dear me! O Lord! Stop a moment!" says Mr Smallweed. "Are you sure you can do it carefully, my worthy man?"

Phil makes no reply; but seizing the chair and its load sidles away, tightly hugged by the now speechless Mr Smallweed, and bolts along the passage, terminating at the cab, deposits him there; and the fair Judy takes her place beside him, and the chair embellishes the roof, and Mr George takes the vacant place upon the box.

CHAPTER 14

More Old Soldiers than One

Mr George has not far to ride with folded arms upon the box, for their destination is Lincoln's Inn Fields. When the driver stops his horses, Mr George alights, and looking in at the window, says:

"What, Mr Tulkinghorn's your man, is he?"

"Yes, my dear friend. Do you know him, Mr George?"

"Why, I have heard of him – seen him too, I think. But I don't know him, and he don't know me."

There ensues the carrying of Mr Smallweed upstairs; which is done to perfection with the trooper's help. He is borne into Mr Tulkinghorn's great room, and deposited on the Turkey rug before the fire.

Mr George is mightily curious in respect of the room. He looks up at the painted ceiling, looks round at the old law-books, contemplates the portraits of the great clients, reads aloud the names on the boxes.

"'Sir Leicester Dedlock, Baronet,'" Mr George reads thoughtfully. "Ha! 'Manor of Chesney Wold.' Humph!" Mr George stands looking at these boxes a long while – as if they were pictures – and comes back to the fire, repeating, "Sir Leicester Dedlock, Baronet, and Manor of Chesney Wold, hey?"

"Worth a mint of money, Mr George!" whispers Grandfather Smallweed, rubbing his legs. "Powerfully rich!"

"Who do you mean? This old gentleman, or the Baronet?"

"This gentleman, this gentleman."

"So I have heard; and knows a thing or two, I'll hold a wager. Not bad quarters, either," says Mr George, looking round again. "See the strong box, yonder!"

This reply is cut short by Mr Tulkinghorn's arrival. There is no change in him, of course. In manner, close and dry. In voice, husky and low. In face, watchful behind a blind.

"Good morning, Mr Smallweed, good morning!" he says as he comes in. "You have brought the serjeant, I see. Sit down, serjeant."

As Mr Tulkinghorn takes off his gloves and puts them in his hat, he looks with half-closed eyes across the room to where the trooper stands.

"Sit down, serjeant," he repeats as he comes to his table, which is set on one side of the fire, and takes his easy chair. "Cold and raw this morning, cold and raw!" Mr Tulkinghorn warms before the bars, alternately, the palms and knuckles of his hands, and looks at the trio sitting in a little semicircle before him.

"Mr George," says Grandfather Smallweed, with a tremulous wave of his shrivelled hand, "this is the gentleman, sir."

Mr George salutes the gentleman; but otherwise sits bolt upright and profoundly silent.

Mr Tulkinghorn proceeds: "Well, George? – I believe your name is George?"

"It is so, sir."

"What do you say, George?"

"I ask your pardon, sir," returns the trooper, "but I should wish to know what you say?"

"Do you mean in point of reward?"

"I mean in point of everything, sir."

"I supposed, serjeant," Mr Tulkinghorn resumes, "that Mr Smallweed might have sufficiently explained the matter. You served under Captain Hawdon at one time, and were his attendant in illness, and were rather in his confidence, I am told. That is so, is it not?"

"Yes, sir, that is so," says Mr George, with military brevity.

"Therefore you may happen to have in your possession something – anything, no matter what – accounts, instructions, orders, a letter, anything – in Captain Hawdon's writing. I wish to compare his writing with some that I have. If you can give me the opportunity, you shall be rewarded for your trouble. Three, four, five, guineas, you would consider handsome, I dare say."

"Noble, my dear friend!" cries Grandfather Smallweed, screwing up his eyes.

Mr George sits squared in exactly the same attitude, looks at the ground, looks at the painted ceiling, and says never a word.

"The question is," says Mr Tulkinghorn in his methodical way, "first, whether you have any of Captain Hawdon's writing?"

"First, whether I have any of Captain Hawdon's writing, sir," repeats Mr George.

"Secondly, what will satisfy you for the trouble of producing it?"

"Secondly, what will satisfy me for the trouble of producing it, sir," repeats Mr George.

"Thirdly, you can judge for yourself whether it is at all like that," says

Mr Tulkinghorn, suddenly handing him some sheets of written paper tied together.

"Whether it is at all like that, sir. Just so," repeats Mr George.

All three repetitions Mr George pronounces in a mechanical manner, looking straight at Mr Tulkinghorn; nor does he so much as glance at the affidavit in Jarndyce and Jarndyce, that has been given to him for his inspection (though he still holds it in his hand), but continues to look at the lawyer with an air of troubled meditation.

"Well?" says Mr Tulkinghorn. "What do you say?"

"Well, sir," replies Mr George, rising erect and looking immense, "I would rather, if you'll excuse me, have nothing to do with this."

With that, he takes three strides forward to replace the papers on the lawyer's table, and three strides backward to resume his former station: where he stands perfectly upright, now looking at the ground, and now at the painted ceiling, with his hands behind him as if to prevent himself from accepting any other document whatever.

"You are the best judge of your own interest, serjeant." Mr Tulkinghorn looks over the papers on his table, and prepares to write a letter.

Mr George looks distrustfully from the painted ceiling to the ground, from the ground to Mr Smallweed, from Mr Smallweed to Mr Tulkinghorn, and from Mr Tulkinghorn to the painted ceiling again.

"Will you allow me to ask, why you want to see the captain's hand, in the case that I could find any specimen of it?"

Mr Tulkinghorn quietly shakes his head. "No. There are confidential reasons. But if you are afraid of doing any injury to Captain Hawdon, you may set your mind at rest about that."

"Ay! he is dead, sir."

"Is he?" Mr Tulkinghorn quietly sits down to write.

"Well, sir," says the trooper, looking into his hat, after another disconcerted pause; "I am sorry not to have given you more satisfaction."

"I'll consult my friend, then, by your leave, sir," says the trooper, "and I'll take the liberty of looking in again with the final answer in the course of the day. Mr Smallweed, if you wish to be carried downstairs – "

"I am ready for your kind assistance, my excellent friend!"

Mr Tulkinghorn, with some shadowy sign of amusement manifesting itself through his self-possession, stands on the hearth-rug with his back to the fire, watching the disappearance of Mr Smallweed, and acknowledging the trooper's parting salute with one slight nod.

53

CHAPTER 15

The Young Man

Chesney Wold is shut up, carpets are rolled into great scrolls in corners of comfortless rooms and the Dedlock ancestors retire from the light of day again. But the house in town shines out awakened and Sir Leicester is glad to repose in dignified contentment before the great fire in the library.

Mr Tulkinghorn comes and goes pretty often; there being estate business to do, leases to be renewed, and so on. He sees my Lady pretty often, too; and he and she are as composed, and as indifferent, and take as little heed of one another, as ever. Yet it may be that my Lady fears this Mr Tulkinghorn, and that he knows it. It may be that he pursues her doggedly and steadily, with no touch of remorse, or pity.

Sir Leicester sits in my Lady's room – that room in which Mr Tulkinghorn read the affidavit in Jarndyce and Jarndyce. My Lady sits before the fire with her screen in her hand.

Sir Leicester is reading, with infinite gravity and state, when the door opens, and the Mercury makes this strange announcement:

"The young man, my Lady, of the name of Guppy."

Sir Leicester pauses, stares, repeats in a killing voice:

"The young man of the name of Guppy?"

Looking round, he beholds the young man of the name of Guppy, much discomfited in his manner and appearance.

"I beg your pardon, Sir Leicester, but my Lady said she would see the young man whenever he called," apologised Mercury.

"It's quite right. I gave him those directions," says my Lady. "Let the young man wait."

"By no means, my Lady. Since he has your orders to come, I will not interrupt you." Sir Leicester in his gallantry retires.

Lady Dedlock looks imperiously at her visitor, when the servant has left the room; casting her eyes over him from head to foot. She suffers him to stand by the door, and asks him what he wants.

"That your ladyship would have the kindness to oblige me with a little conversation," returns Mr Guppy, embarrassed.

"You are, of course, the person from Kenge's office who has written me so many letters?"

"Several, your ladyship. Several, before your ladyship condescended to favour me with an answer."

"If it should appear, after all, that what you have to say does not concern me you will allow me to cut you short with but little ceremony. Say what you have to say, if you please."

My Lady, with a careless toss of her screen, turns herself towards the fire again, sitting almost with her back to the young man of the name of Guppy.

"With your ladyship's permission, then," says Mr Guppy, a little emboldened, "I have the pleasure of being acquainted with Mr Tulkinghorn – at least we move when we meet one another – and if it had been any business of another sort, I should have gone to him."

My Lady turns a little round, and says "You had better sit down."

"I am not aware," says Mr Guppy, standing midway between my Lady and his chair, "whether your ladyship ever happened to hear of, or to see, a young lady of the name of Miss Esther Summerson."

My Lady's eyes look at him full. "I saw a young lady of that name not long ago. This past autumn."

"Now, did it strike your ladyship that she was like anybody?" asks Mr Guppy, crossing his arms, holding his head on one side, and scratching the corner of his mouth with his memoranda.

My Lady removes her eyes from him no more.

"No."

"Not like your ladyship's family?"

"No."

"I think your ladyship," says Mr Guppy, "can hardly remember Miss Summerson's face?"

"I remember the young lady very well. What has this to do with me?"

Mr Guppy draws his chair a little forward, and seats himself again. My Lady reclines in her chair composedly, though with a trifle less of graceful ease than usual, perhaps; and never falters in her steady gaze.

"Your ladyship, there is a mystery about Miss Esther Summerson's birth and bringing up. Now, it's a very singular circumstance, your ladyship," says Mr Guppy, "that I have encountered the person, who lived as servant with the lady who brought Miss Summerson up, before Mr Jarndyce took charge of her. That lady was a Miss Barbary, your ladyship."

Is the dead colour on my Lady's face, reflected from the screen which has a green silk ground, and which she holds in her raised hand as if she had forgotten it; or is it a dreadful paleness that has fallen on her?

"Did your ladyship," says Mr Guppy, "ever happen to hear of Miss Barbary?"

"I don't know. I think so. Yes."

"Was Miss Barbary at all connected with your ladyship's family?"

My Lady's lips move, but they utter nothing. She shakes her head.

"Not connected?" says Mr Guppy. "O! Not to your ladyship's knowledge, perhaps? Ah! But might be? Yes." After each of these interrogatories, she has inclined her head. "Very good! Now, this Miss Barbary was extremely close and my witness never had an idea whether she possessed a single relative. On one occasion, and only one, she seems to have been confidential to my witness, on a single point; and she then told her that the little girl's real name was not Esther Summerson, but Esther Hawdon."

"My God!"

Mr Guppy stares. Lady Dedlock sits before him, looking him through, with the same dark shade upon her face, in the same attitude even to the holding of the screen, with her lips a little apart, her brow a little contracted, but for the moment, dead. He sees her consciousness return, sees a tremor pass across her.

"Your ladyship is acquainted with the name of Hawdon?"

"I have heard it before."

"Name of any remote branch of your ladyship's family?"

"No."

"Now, your ladyship," says Mr Guppy, "I come to the last point of the case. Your ladyship must know – if your ladyship don't happen, by any chance, to know already – that there was found dead at the house of a person named Krook, near Chancery Lane, some time ago, a law-writer in great distress. Upon which law-writer, there was an inquest; and which law-writer was an anonymous character, his name being unknown. But, your ladyship, I have discovered, very lately, that that law-writer's name was Hawdon."

"And what is that to me?"

"Aye, your ladyship, that's the question! Now, your ladyship, a queer thing happened after that man's death. A lady started up; a disguised lady, your ladyship, who went to look at the scene of action, and went to look at his grave. She hired a crossing-sweeping boy to show it her. If your ladyship would wish to have the boy produced in corroboration of this statement, I can lay my hand upon him at any time."

The wretched boy is nothing to my Lady, and she does not wish to have him produced.

"Oh, I assure your ladyship it's a very queer start indeed," says Mr Guppy. "If you was to hear him tell about the rings that sparkled on her fingers when she took her glove off, you'd think it quite romantic."

There are diamonds glittering on the hand that holds the screen. My Lady trifles with the screen, and makes them glitter more; again with that expression which in other times might have been so dangerous to the young man of the name of Guppy.

"It was supposed, your ladyship, that he left no rag or scrap behind him by which he could be possibly identified. But he did. He left a bundle of old letters."

The screen still goes, as before. All this time, her eyes never once release him.

"They were taken and hidden away. And to-morrow night, your ladyship, they will come into my possession."

"Still I ask you, what is this to me?"

"Your ladyship, I conclude with that." Mr Guppy rises. "If you think there's enough, in this chain of circumstances put together to give your ladyship a family interest in going further into the case, I will bring these papers here."

Is this the full purpose of the young man of the name of Guppy, or has he any other? He is a match for my Lady there. She may look at him, but he can look at the table, and keep that witness-box face of his from telling anything.

"You may bring the letters," says my Lady, "if you choose."

"Your ladyship is not very encouraging, upon my word and honour," says Mr Guppy, a little injured.

"You may bring the letters," she repeats, in the same tone, "if you – please."

"It shall be done. I wish your ladyship good day."

On a table near her is a rich bauble of a casket, barred and clasped like a strong chest. She, looking at him still, takes it to her and unlocks it.

"Oh! I assure your ladyship I am not actuated by any motives of that sort," says Mr Guppy; "and I couldn't accept of anything of the kind. I wish your ladyship good day, and am much obliged to you all the same."

As Sir Leicester basks in his library, and dozes over his newspaper, is there no influence in the house to startle him; to make the very portraits frown, the very armour stir?

No. Words, sobs, and cries, are but air and yet this cry is in the house, going upward from a wild figure on its knees.

"O my child, my child! Not dead in the first hours of her life, as my cruel sister told me; but kept by her, after she had renounced me and my name! O my child, O my child!"

CHAPTER 16

Nurse and Patient

[Esther's maid, Charley, has reported a wandering, sick young boy who has been taken in by Jenny, a brickmaker's wife in the village.]

My little maid's face was eager, and her quiet hands were folded so closely in one another as she stood looking at me, that I had no great difficulty in reading her thoughts.

"Well, Charley," said I, "it appears to me that you and I can do no better than go round to Jenny's, and see what's the matter."

It was a cold, wild night, and the trees shuddered in the wind. The rain had been thick and heavy all day, and with little intermission for many days. None was falling just then, however. The sky had partly cleared, but was very gloomy – even above us, where a few stars were shining.

We came to the cottage, where there was a feeble candle in the patched window. We tapped at the door, and went in. A wretched boy was cowering on the floor. He held under his arm, like a little bundle, a fragment of a fur cap; and as he tried to warm himself, he shook until the crazy door and window shook. The place was closer than before, and had an unhealthy, and a very peculiar smell.

I had not lifted my veil when I first spoke to the woman and the boy staggered up instantly, and stared at me with a remarkable expression of surprise and terror.

"I won't go no more to the berryin ground," muttered the boy; "I ain't a-going there, so I tell you!"

I lifted my veil and spoke to the woman. She said to me in a low voice, "Don't mind him, ma'am. He'll soon come back to his head;" and said to him, "Jo, Jo, what's the matter?"

"I know wot she's come for!" cried the boy.

"Who?"

"The lady there. She's come to get me to go along with her to the berryin ground. I won't go to the berryin ground. I don't like the name on it. She might go a berryin *me*." His shivering came on again, and as he leaned against the wall, he shook the hovel.

"He has been talking off and on about such like, all day, ma'am," said Jenny softly. "Why, how you stare! This is my lady, Jo."

"Is it?" returned the boy doubtfully, and surveying me with his arm held out above his burning eyes. "She looks to me the t'other one. It ain't the bonnet, nor yet it ain't the gownd, but she looks to me the t'other one."

My little Charley pulled off her bonnet and shawl, and now went quietly up to him with a chair, and sat him down in it, like an old sick nurse.

"I say!" said the boy. "You tell me. Ain't the lady the t'other lady?"

Charley shook her head, as she methodically drew his rags about him and made him as warm as she could.

"O!" the boy muttered. "Then I 'spose she ain't."

"I came to see if I could do you any good," said I, mopping his face with my handkerchief. "What is the matter with you?"

"I'm a being froze," returned the boy hoarsely, with his haggard gaze wandering about me, "and then burnt up, and then froze, and then burnt up, ever so many times in a hour. And my head's all sleepy, and all a going mad-like – and I'm so dry – and my bones isn't half so much bones as pain."

"When did he come here?" I asked the woman.

"This morning, ma'am, I found him at the corner of the town. I had known him up in London yonder. Hadn't I, Jo?"

"Tom-all-Alone's," the boy replied.

Whenever he fixed his attention or his eyes, it was only for a very

59

little while. He soon began to droop his head again, and roll it heavily, and speak as if he were half awake.

"When did he come from London?" I asked.

"I come from London yes'day," said the boy himself, now flushed and hot. "I'm a going somewheres."

"Where is he going?" I asked.

"Somewheres," repeated the boy, in a louder tone. "I have been moved on, and moved on, more nor ever I was afore, since t'other one giv' me the sov'ring. And I'm a-going somewheres. That's where I'm a-going."

"What is to be done with him?" said I, taking the woman aside. "He could not travel in this state, even if he had a purpose, and knew where he was going!"

"I know no more, ma'am, than the dead," she replied, glancing compassionately at him. "Perhaps the dead know better, if they could only tell us. I've kept him here all day for pity's sake, and I've given him broth and physic but I can't keep him long, for if my husband was to come home and find him here, he'd be rough in putting him out, and might do him a hurt."

She put a few halfpence together and hurried them into his hand, and so, in an oblivious, half-thankful, half-insensible way, he shuffled out of the house.

But I said to Charley that we must not leave the boy to die. Charley, who knew what to do much better than I did, glided on before me, and presently we came up with Jo, just short of the brick-kiln.

I think he must have begun his journey with some small bundle under his arm, and must have had it stolen, or lost it. For he still carried his wretched fragment of fur cap like a bundle, though he went bare-headed through the rain, which now fell fast. He stopped when we called to him, and again showed a dread of me when I came up; standing with his lustrous eyes fixed upon me, and even arrested in his shivering fit.

I asked him to come with us, and we would take care that he had some shelter for the night.

"I don't want no shelter," he said; "I can lay amongst the warm bricks."

"But don't you know that people die there?" returned Charley.

"They dies everywheres," said the boy. "They dies in their lodgings – she knows where; I showed her – and they dies down in Tom-all-Alone's in heaps. They dies more than they lives, according to what I see." Then he hoarsely whispered to Charley, "If she ain't the t'other one, she ain't the forrenner. Is there three of 'em then?"

Charley looked at me a little frightened. I felt half frightened at myself when the boy glared on me so.

But he turned and followed, when I beckoned to him; and finding that he acknowledged that influence in me, I led the way straight home.

Leaving him in the hall for a moment, shrunk into the corner of the window-seat, I went into the drawing-room to speak to my guardian. There I found Mr Skimpole, who had come down by the coach, as he frequently did without notice, and never bringing any clothes with him, but always borrowing everything he wanted.

They came out with me directly, to look at the boy. The servants had gathered in the hall, too; and he shivered in the window-seat with Charley standing by him, like some wounded animal that had been found in a ditch.

"This is a sorrowful case," said my guardian, after asking him a question or two, and touching him, and examining his eyes. "What do you say, Harold?"

"You had better turn him out," said Mr Skimpole.

"What do you mean?" inquired my guardian, almost sternly.

"My dear Jarndyce," said Mr Skimpole, "He's not safe, you know. There's a very bad sort of fever about him."

Mr Skimpole had retreated from the hall to the drawing-room again, and said this in his airy way, seated on the music-stool as we stood by.

"You'll say it's childish," observed Mr Skimpole, looking gaily at us. "If you put him out in the road, you only put him where he was before. He will be no worse off than he was, you know. Even make him better off, if you like. Give him sixpence, or five shillings, or five pound ten – you are arithmeticians, and I am not – and get rid of him!"

"And what is he to do then?" asked my guardian.

"Upon my life," said Mr Skimpole, shrugging his shoulders with his engaging smile, "I have not the least idea what he is to do then. But I have no doubt he'll do it."

"In the meantime," I ventured to observe, "he is getting worse."

"In the meantime," said Mr Skimpole cheerfully, "as Miss Summerson, with her practical good sense, observes, he is getting worse. Therefore I recommend your turning him out before he gets still worse."

The amiable face with which he said it, I think I shall never forget.

"Of course, little woman," observed my guardian, turning to me. "There is a bed in the wholesome loft-room by the stable; we had better keep him there till morning, when he can be wrapped up and removed. We'll do that."

"O!" said Mr Skimpole, with his hands upon the keys of the piano, as we moved away. "Are you going back to our young friend?"

"Yes," said my guardian. "You can't recommend anything for the boy, I suppose?"

"My dear Jarndyce, I observed a bottle of cooling medicine in his pocket, and it's impossible for him to do better than take it. You can tell them to sprinkle a little vinegar about the place where he sleeps, and to keep it moderately cool, and him moderately warm."

We went back into the hall, and explained to Jo what we proposed to do, which Charley explained to him again, and which he received with the languid unconcern I had already noticed, wearily looking on at what was done, as if it were for somebody else. We soon got the loft-room ready; and some of the men about the house carried him across the wet yard, well wrapped up. Charley directed the operations, and went to and fro between the loft-room and the house with such little stimulants and comforts as we thought it safe to give him. They had fastened his door on the outside, in case of his being delirious; but had so arranged, that he could not make any noise without being heard.

Charley's last report was, that the boy was quiet. I could see, from my window, the lantern they had left him burning quietly; and I went to bed very happy to think that he was sheltered.

There was more movement and more talking than usual a little before day-break, and it awoke me. As I was dressing, I looked out of my window, and asked one of our men who had been among the active sympathisers last night, whether there was anything wrong about the house. The lantern was still burning in the loft-window.

"It's the boy, miss," said he.

"Is he worse?" I inquired.

"Gone, miss."

"Dead!"

"Dead, miss? No. Gone clean off."

At what time of the night he had gone, or how, or why, it seemed hopeless ever to divine. The door remaining as it had been left, and the lantern standing in the window, it could only be supposed that he had got out by a trap in the floor which communicated with an empty cart-house below. But he had shut it down again, if that were so; and it looked as if it had not been raised. Nothing of any kind was missing. On this fact being clearly ascertained, we all yielded to the painful belief that delirium had come upon him in the night, and that, allured by some imaginary object, or pursued by some imaginary horror, he had strayed away in that worse than helpless state; – all of us, that is to say, but Mr Skimpole, who repeatedly suggested, in his usual easy light style, that it had occurred to our young friend that he was not a safe inmate, having a bad kind of fever upon him; and that he had, with great natural politeness taken himself off.

The search continued for five days. I do not mean that it ceased, even then; but that my attention was then diverted into a current very memorable to me.

I was well enough, however, to be up early in the morning, and to return Ada's cheerful blessing and to talk with her as long as usual. But I was not free from an impression that I had been walking about the room in the night, a little beside myself, though knowing where I was; and I felt confused at times – with a curious sense of fullness, as if I were becoming too large altogether.

In the evening I was so much worse, that I resolved to prepare Charley; with which view, I said, "You're quite strong, Charley, are you not?"

"O quite!" said Charley.

"Strong enough to be told a secret, I think, Charley?"

"Quite strong enough for that, miss!" cried Charley.

"Now, Charley," said I, "I am going to be ill, and my great trust is in you."

"Trust in me, now, if you please, miss," said Charley, quietly. "I am listening to everything you say."

"It's very little at present, Charley. I shall tell the doctor to-night that I don't think I am well, and that you are going to nurse me."

For that, the poor child thanked me with her whole heart.

"And in the morning, when you hear Miss Ada in the garden, if I should not be quite able to go to the window-curtain as usual, do you go, Charley, and say I am asleep – that I have rather tired myself, and am asleep. At all times keep the room as I have kept it, Charley, and let no one come."

"I never will! I never will!" she promised me.

"I believe it, my dear Charley. And now come and sit beside me for a little while, and touch me with your hand. For I cannot see you, Charley; I am blind."

CHAPTER 17

Interlopers

Mr Guppy has a thing to say that must be said to Lady Dedlock.

For which reason, with a sinking heart, and with that hangdog sense of guilt upon him Guppy presents himself at the town mansion at about seven o'clock in the evening, and requests to see her ladyship. Mercury replies that she is going out to dinner; don't he see the carriage at the door? Yes, he does see the carriage at the door; but he wants to see my Lady too.

Mercury sulkily supposes that the young man must come up into the library. There he leaves the young man in a large room, not over-light, while he makes report of him.

Mr Guppy looks into the shade in all directions. Presently he hears a rustling. Is it – ? No, it's no ghost; but fair flesh and blood, most brilliantly dressed.

"I have to beg your ladyship's pardon," Mr Guppy stammers, very downcast. "This is an inconvenient time – "

"I told you, you could come at any time." She takes a chair, looking straight at him as on the last occasion.

"Thank your ladyship. Your ladyship is very affable."

"You can sit down." There is not much affability in her tone.

"I don't know, your ladyship, that it's worth while my sitting down and detaining you, for I – I have not got the letters that I mentioned when I had the honour of waiting on your ladyship."

"Have you come merely to say so?"

"Merely to say so, your ladyship." Mr Guppy, besides being depressed, disappointed, and uneasy, is put at a further disadvantage by the splendour and beauty of her appearance.

She will not speak, it is plain. So he must.

"In short, your ladyship," says Mr Guppy, like a meanly penitent thief, "the person I was to have had the letters of, has come to a sudden end, and – " He stops. Lady Dedlock calmly finishes the sentence.

"And the letters are destroyed with the person?"

Mr Guppy would say no, if he could – as he is unable to hide.

"I believe so, your ladyship."

"Is this all you have to say?" inquires Lady Dedlock.

Mr Guppy thinks that's all.

"You had better be sure that you wish to say nothing more to me; this being the last time you will have the opportunity."

Mr Guppy is quite sure. And indeed he has no such wish at present, by any means.

"That is enough. I will dispense with excuses. Good evening to you!"

And she rings for Mercury to show the young man of the name of Guppy out.

But in that house, in that same moment, there happens to be an old man of the name of Tulkinghorn. And that old man, coming with his quiet footstep to the library, has his hand at that moment on the handle of the door – comes in – and comes face to face with the young man as he is leaving the room.

One glance between the old man and the lady; and for an instant the blind that is always down flies up. Suspicion, eager and sharp, looks out. Another instant; close again.

"I beg your pardon, Lady Dedlock. I beg your pardon a thousand times. I supposed the room was empty. I beg your pardon!"

"Stay!" She negligently calls him back. "Remain here, I beg. I am going out to dinner. I have nothing more to say to this young man!"

The disconcerted young man bows, as he goes out, and cringingly hopes that Mr Tulkinghorn of the Fields is well.

"Aye, aye?" says the lawyer, looking at him from under his bent brows; though he has no need to look again – not he. "From Kenge and Carboy's, surely?"

"Kenge and Carboy's, Mr Tulkinghorn. Name of Guppy, sir."

"To be sure. Why, thank you, Mr Guppy, I am very well!"

"Happy to hear it, sir. You can't be too well, sir, for the credit of the profession."

"Thank you, Mr Guppy!"

Mr Guppy sneaks away. Mr Tulkinghorn, such a foil in his old-fashioned rusty black to Lady Dedlock's brightness, hands her down the staircase to her carriage. He returns rubbing his chin, and rubs it a good deal in the course of the evening.

CHAPTER 18

A Turn of the Screw

"Now, what," says Mr George, "may this be? Is it blank cartridge or ball? A flash in the pan, or a shot?"

An open letter is the subject of the trooper's speculations, and it seems to perplex him mightily.

"Attention, Phil! Listen to this."

"Steady, commander, steady."

"'Sir. Allow me to remind you (though there is no legal necessity for my doing so, as you are aware) that the bill at two months' date, drawn on yourself and by you accepted, for the sum of ninety-seven pounds four shillings and ninepence, will become due to-morrow, when you will please be prepared to take up the same on presentation. Yours, *Joshua Smallweed*.' – What do you make of that, Phil?"

"Mischief, guv'ner."

"Lookye, Phil," says the trooper, sitting on the table. "First and last, I have paid, I may say, half as much again as this principal, in interest and one thing and another. And there has always been an understanding that this bill was to be what they call Renewed. And it has been renewed, no end of times. What do you say now?"

"I say that I think the times is come to an end at last."

"You do? Humph! I am much of the same mind myself."

"Joshua Smallweed is him that was brought here in a chair?"

"The same."

"Guv'ner," says Phil, with exceeding gravity, "he's a leech in his dispositions, he's a screw and a wice in his actions, a snake in his twistings, and a lobster in his claws."

At Grandfather Smallweed's house the door is opened by the perennial Judy, who, having surveyed them from top to toe with a malignant sneer, leaves them standing there, while she consults the oracle as to their admission.

"My dear friend," says Grandfather Smallweed, with those two lean, affectionate arms of his stretched forth. "How de do? How de do?"

"The fact is, Mr Smallweed," proceeds George, "that I find myself in rather an unpleasant state of mind. It appears to me, sir, that your friend in the city has been playing tricks."

"O dear no!" says Grandfather Smallweed. "He never does that!"

"Don't he? Well, I am glad to hear it, because I thought it might be his doing. This, you know, I am speaking of. This letter."

Grandfather Smallweed smiles in a very ugly way, in recognition of the letter.

"What does it mean?" asks Mr George.

"Did you say what does it mean, my good friend?"

"Aye! Now, come, come, you know, Mr Smallweed," urges the trooper, constraining himself to speak as smoothly and confidentially as he can, holding the open letter in one hand, and resting the broad knuckles of the other on his thigh; "a good lot of money has passed between us, and we are face to face at the present moment, and are both well aware of the understanding there has always been. I am prepared to do the usual thing which I have done regularly, and to keep this matter going. I never got a letter like this from you before, and I have been a little put about by it this morning."

"But I think you asked me, Mr George"; old Smallweed, who all this time has had the pipe in his hand, is the speaker now; "I think you asked me, what did the letter mean?"

"Why, yes, I did," returns the trooper, in his off-hand way: "but I don't care to know particularly, if it's all correct and pleasant."

Mr Smallweed, purposely balking himself in an aim at the trooper's head, throws the pipe on the ground and breaks it to pieces.

"That's what it means, my dear friend. I'll smash you. I'll crumble you. I'll powder you. Go to the devil!" cries the old man. "Go to my lawyer and show your independeuce now, will you? Come, my dear friend, there's a chance for you."

When he presents himself in Lincoln's Inn Fields, Mr Tulkinghorn is engaged, and not to be seen. He waits with the perseverance of military tactics; and at last the bell rings again, and Mr Tulkinghorn being heard, "Let 'em come in then!" they pass into the great room with the painted ceiling, and find him standing before the fire.

"Now, what do you want Serjeant? I told you the last time I saw you that I don't desire your company here."

Serjeant replies – dashed within the last few minutes as to his usual manner of speech, and even as to his usual carriage – that he has received this letter, has been to Mr Smallweed about it, and has been referred there.

"I have nothing to say to you," rejoins Mr Tulkinghorn. "If you get into debt, you must pay your debts, or take the consequences. You have no occasion to come here to learn that, I suppose?"

Serjeant is sorry to say that he is not prepared with the money.

"You have had the money and must refund it. You are not to pocket other people's pounds, shillings, and pence, and escape scot free."

The lawyer sits down in his easy chair and stirs the fire.

"I tell you, serjeant, I have nothing to say to you. I don't like your associates, and don't want you here."

"I must make an apology to you, sir," says Mr George, "for pressing myself upon you with so little encouragement but would you let me say a private word to you?"

Mr Tulkinghorn rises with his hands in his pockets, and walks into one of the window recesses. "Now! I have no time to waste."

"Well, sir," says Mr George, "I can find no help for it but to give up what you wanted of me the other day."

"Have you got it here?"

"I have got it here, sir."

"Serjeant," the lawyer proceeds in his dry, passionless manner, "make up your mind while I speak to you, for this is final. After I have finished speaking I have closed the subject, and I won't re-open it. Understand that. Have you decided?"

The trooper puts his hand into his breast, and answers with a long breath, "I must do it, sir."

The trooper then takes from his breast-pocket a folded paper, which he lays with an unwilling hand at the lawyer's elbow. "'Tis ouly a letter of instructions, sir. The last I ever had from him."

Look at a millstone, Mr George, for some change in its expression, and you will find it quite as soon as in the face of Mr Tulkinghorn when he opens and reads the letter! He refolds it, and lays it in his desk, with a countenance as unperturbable as Death.

CHAPTER 19

Esther's Narrative

I lay ill through several weeks, and the usual tenor of my life became like an old remembrance. But, this was not the effect of time, so much as of the change in all my habits, made by the helplessness and inaction of a sick room. In falling ill, I seemed to have crossed a dark lake, and to have left all my experiences, mingled together by the great distance, on the healthy shore.

The repose that succeeded, the long delicious sleep, the blissful rest, when in my weakness I was too calm to have any care for myself, and could have heard (or so I think now) that I was dying; with no other emotion than with a pitying love for those I left behind. I was in this state when I first shrunk from the light as it twinkled on me once more, and knew with a boundless joy, that I should see again.

I had heard my Ada crying at the door, day and night; I had heard her calling to me that I was cruel and did not love her; I had heard her praying and imploring to be let in to nurse and comfort me, and to leave my bedside no more; but I had only said, when I could speak, "Never, my sweet girl, never!" and I had over and over again reminded Charley that she was to keep her from the room whether I lived or died. Charley had been true to me in that time of need, and with her little hand and her great heart had kept the door fast.

But now, my sight strengthening, and the glorious light coming every day more fully and brightly on me. By and by, my strength began to be restored. How well I remember the pleasant afternoon when I was raised in bed with pillows for the first time, to enjoy a great tea-drinking with Charley! When I felt sure I was steady enough to say something to Charley that was not new to my thoughts.

"Are the pictures all as they used to be?" I asked her.

"Every one of them; miss," said Charley.

"And the furniture, Charley?"

"Except where I have moved it about, to make more room, miss."

"And yet," said I, "I miss some familiar object. Ah, I know what it is, Charley! It's the looking-glass."

Charley got up from the table, making as if she had forgotten something, and went into the next room; and I heard her sob there.

I had thought of this very often. I was now certain of it. I could thank God that it was not a shock to me now. I called Charley back; and when she came – at first pretending to smile, but as she drew nearer to me, looking grieved – I took her in my arms, and said, "It matters very little, Charley. I hope I can do without my old face very well."

I was presently so far advanced as to be able to sit up in a great chair, and even giddily to walk into the adjoining room, leaning on Charley. The mirror was gone from its usual place in that room too; but what I had to bear, was none the harder to bear for that.

My guardian came one morning; and when he first came in, could only hold me in his embrace, and say, "My dear, dear girl!"

"O yes!" I thought. "He has seen me and is even fonder of me than he was before; and what have I to mourn for!"

He sat down by me on the sofa, supporting me with his arm. For a little while he sat with his hand over his face, but when he removed it, fell into his usual manner.

"My little woman," said he, "what a sad time this has been. Such an inflexible little woman, too, through all!"

"Only for the best, guardian," said I.

"For the best?" he repeated, tenderly. "Of course, for the best. But here have Ada and I been perfectly forlorn and miserable; here has everyone about the house been utterly lost and dejected; here has even poor Rick been writing – to me too – in his anxiety for you!"

I had read Ada's letters, but never of Richard. I told him so.

"Why, no, my dear," he replied. "I have thought it better not to mention it to her."

"And you speak of his writing to you," said I, repeating his emphasis. "As if it were not natural for him to do so, guardian; as if he could write to a better friend!"

"He thinks he could, my love," returned my guardian, "and to many a better. The truth is, he wrote coldly, haughtily, distantly, resentfully. He is not to blame. Jarndyce and Jarndyce has warped him out of himself. I have known it do as bad deeds, and worse, many a time."

"But it is a terrible misfortune, guardian."

"It is a terrible misfortune, little woman, to be ever drawn within the influences of Jarndyce and Jarndyce. I know none greater."

"But, guardian, may we not hope that a little experience will teach him what a false and wretched thing it is?"

"We will hope so, my Esther," said Mr Jarndyce, "and that it may not teach him so too late. Enough of this, my dear!"

He had supported me, as at first, all this time; and his tenderness was so precious to me, that I leaned my head upon his shoulder and loved him as if he had been my father. I resolved in my own mind in this little pause, by some means, to see Richard when I grew strong, and try to set him right.

"There are better subjects than these," said my guardian, "when shall Ada come to see you, my love?"

I had been thinking of that too. A little in connexion with the absent mirrors, but not much; for I knew my loving girl would be changed by no change in my looks.

"As I have kept Ada out so long," I began after a short while, "I think I should like to have my own way a little longer, guardian. It would be best to be away from here before I see her. If Charley and I were to go to some country lodging as soon as I can move, and if I had a week there, in which to grow stronger and to be revived by the sweet air, and to look forward to the happiness of having Ada with me again, I think it would be better for us."

"Our spoilt little woman," said my guardian, "shall have her own way even in her inflexibility, though at the price of tears downstairs. And see here! Here is Boythorn, heart of chivalry, breathing such ferocious vows that if you don't go and occupy his whole house, by Heaven and by earth he'll pull it down, and not leave one brick standing on another!"

And my guardian put a letter in my hand; without any ordinary beginning such as "My dear Jarndyce," but rushing at once into the words, "I swear if Miss Summerson do not come down and take possession of my house, which I vacate for her this day at one o'clock, p.m.," and then with the utmost seriousness, and in the most emphatic terms, going on to make the extraordinary declaration he had quoted. We did not appreciate the writer the less, for laughing heartily over it; and we settled that I should send him a letter of thanks on the morrow, and accept his offer. It was a most agreeable one to me; for all the places I could have thought of, I should have liked to go to none so well as Chesney Wold.

CHAPTER 20

Chesney Wold

Charley and I did not set off alone upon our expedition into Lincolnshire. My guardian had made up his mind not to lose sight of me until I was safe in Mr Boythorn's house; so he accompanied us, and we were two days upon the road. My guardian intending to go back immediately, we appointed, on our way down, a day when my dear girl should come. I wrote her a letter, of which he took charge; and he left us within half an hour of our arrival at our destination, on a delightful evening in the early summer time.

If a good fairy had built the house for me with a wave of her wand, and I had been a princess and her favoured godchild, I could not have been more considered in it. I made myself very busy in unpacking and arranging; and I sent Charley to bed in good time, and told her I should want her no more that night.

For I had not yet looked in the glass, and had never asked to have my own restored to me. I had wanted to be alone, and therefore I was now alone, in my own room. I sat down for a little while first to reflect upon all my blessings.

My hair had not been cut off, though it had been in danger more than once. It was long and thick. I let it down, and shook it out, and went up to the glass upon the dressing-table. There was a little muslin curtain drawn across it. I drew it back; and stood for a moment looking through such a veil of my own hair, that I could see nothing else. Then I put my hair aside, and looked at the reflection in the mirror: encouraged by seeing how placidly it looked at me. At first, my face was so strange to

72

me, that I almost put my hands before it and started back, but for the encouragement I have mentioned. Very soon it became more familiar, and then I knew the extent of the alteration in it better than I had done at first.

I had never been a beauty, and had never thought myself one; but I had been very different from this. It was all gone now but I could let it go with a few not bitter tears, and could stand there arranging my hair for the night quite thankfully.

I took care to be up early in the morning, and to be before the glass when Charley came in on tiptoe.

"Dear, dear, miss!" cried Charley, starting. "Is that you?"

"Yes, Charley," said I, quietly putting up my hair. "And I am very well indeed, and very happy."

I saw it was a weight off Charley's mind, but it was a greater weight off mine. I knew the worst now, and was composed to it.

The air blew as freshly and revivingly upon me as it had ever blown, and the healthy colour came into my new face as it had come into my old one. Charley was wonderful to see, she was so radiant and so rosy; and we both enjoyed the whole day, and slept soundly the whole night.

There was a favourite spot of mine in the park-woods of Chesney Wold, where a seat had been erected commanding a lovely view. There was a bank here, too, which was a famous one for violets; and as it was a daily delight of Charley's to gather wild flowers, she took as much to the spot as I did.

I was resting at my favourite point, after a long ramble, and Charley was gathering violets at a little distance from me, when I became aware of a figure approaching through the wood. By little and little, it revealed itself to be a woman's – a lady's – Lady Dedlock's. She was alone, and coming to where I sat with a much quicker step than was usual with her. I was fluttered by her being unexpectedly so near and would have risen to continue my walk. But I could not. I was rendered motionless. Not so much by her hurried gesture of entreaty, not so much by her quick advance and outstretched hands, as by a something in her face that I had pined for and dreamed of when I was a little child; something I had never seen in any face; something I had never seen in hers before.

A dread and faintness fell upon me, and I called to Charley. Lady Dedlock stopped, upon the instant, and changed back almost to what I had known her.

"Miss Summerson, I am afraid I have startled you," she said, now advancing slowly. "You can scarcely be strong yet. You have been very ill, I know. I have been much concerned to hear it."

I could no more have removed my eyes from her pale face, than I could have stirred from the bench on which I sat. She gave me her hand; and its deadly coldness, so at variance with the enforced composure of her features, deepened the fascination that overpowered me. I cannot say what was in my whirling thoughts.

"You are recovering again?" she asked, kindly.

"I was quite well but a moment ago, Lady Dedlock."

"Is this your young attendant?"

"Yes."

"Will you send her on before, and walk towards your house with me?"

"Charley," said I, "take your flowers home, and I will follow you directly."

Charley, with her best curtsey, blushingly tied on her bonnet, and went her way. When she was gone, Lady Dedlock sat down on the seat beside me.

I looked at her; but I could not see her, I could not hear her, I could not draw my breath. The beating of my heart was so violent and wild, that I felt as if my life were breaking from me. But when she caught me to her breast, kissed me, wept over me and called me back to myself; when she fell down on her knees and cried to me, "O my child, my child, I am your wicked and unhappy mother! O try to forgive me!"

I raised my mother up, praying and beseeching her not to stoop before me in such affliction and humiliation. I did so, in broken, incoherent words; for, besides the trouble I was in, it frightened me to see her at my feet. I held my mother in my embrace, and she held me in hers; and among the still woods in the silence of the summer day, there seemed to be nothing but our two troubled minds that was not at peace.

"To bless and receive me," groaned my mother, "it is far too late. I must travel my dark road alone, and it will lead me where it will. From day to day, sometimes from hour to hour, I do not see the way before my guilty feet. This is the earthly punishment I have brought upon myself. I bear it, and I hide it."

Even in the thinking of her endurance, she drew her habitual air of proud indifference about her like a veil, though she soon cast it off again.

74

"I must keep this secret, if by any means it can be kept, not wholly for myself. I have a husband, wretched and dishonouring creature that I am!"

My unhappy mother told me that in my illness she had been nearly frantic. She had but then known that her child was living. She could not have suspected me to be that child before. She had followed me down here, to speak to me but once in all her life. We never could associate, never could communicate, never probably from that time forth could interchange another word, on earth. She put into my hands a letter she had written for my reading only; and said, when I had read it, and destroyed it I must evermore consider her as dead.

"But is the secret safe so far?" I asked. "Is it safe now, dearest mother?"

"No," replied my mother. "It has been very near discovery. It was saved by an accident. It may be lost by another accident – tomorrow, any day."

"Do you dread a particular person?"

"I dread one person very much."

"An enemy?"

"Not a friend. One who is too passionless to be either. He is Sir Leicester Dedlock's lawyer; mechanically faithful without attachment, and very jealous of the profit, privilege, and reputation of being master of the mysteries of great houses."

"Has he any suspicions?"

"Many."

"Not of you?" I said alarmed.

"Yes! He is always vigilant, and always near me. I may keep him at a stand still, but I can never shake him off."

"Has he so little pity?"

"He has none, and no anger. He is indifferent to everything but his calling. His calling is the acquisition of secrets, and the holding of such power as they give him."

"Could you trust in him?"

"I shall never try. The dark road I have trodden for so many years will end where it will."

"Dear mother, are you so resolved?"

"I am resolved. I will outlive this danger, and outdie it, if I can."

"Mr Jarndyce – " I was beginning, when my mother hurriedly inquired:
"Does he suspect?"

"No," said I. "No, indeed! Be assured that he does not!" And I told her

75

what he had related to me as his knowledge of my story. "But he is so good and sensible," said I.

"Confide fully in him," she said. "You have my free consent – a small gift from such a mother to her injured child! – but do not tell me of it. Some pride is left in me, even yet."

I explained, or tried to do it, how I had only hoped that Mr Jarndyce, who had been the best of fathers to me, might be able to afford some counsel and support to her. But my mother answered no, it was impossible; no one could help her.

"My child, my child!" she said. "For the last time! These kisses for the last time! If you hear of Lady Dedlock, brilliant, prosperous, and flattered; think of your wretched mother, conscience-stricken, underneath that mask! And then forgive her, if you can; and cry to Heaven to forgive her, which it never can!"

We held one another for a little space yet, but she was so firm, that she took my hands away, and, with a last kiss as she released them, went from me into the wood.

I went home very slowly, and told Charley, whom I found at the gate looking for me, that I had been tempted to extend my walk after Lady Dedlock had left me, and that I was over-tired and would lie down. Safe in my own room, I read the letter. I clearly derived from it – and that was much then – that I had not been abandoned by my mother. Her elder and only sister, the godmother of my childhood, discovering signs of life in me when I had been laid aside as dead, had, in her stern sense of duty, reared me in rigid secrecy, and had never again beheld my mother's face from within a few hours of my birth. So strangely did I hold my place in this world that, until within a short time back, I had never, to my own mother's knowledge, breathed, had never borne a name.

My first care was to burn what my mother had written, and to consume even its ashes. I hope it may not appear very unnatural or bad in me, that I then became heavily sorrowful to think I had ever been reared.

I fell asleep, worn out and when I awoke, I cried afresh to think that I was back in the world, with my load of trouble for others and I felt as if the blame and the shame were all in me, and the visitation had come down.

My dear girl was to arrive at five o'clock in the afternoon. There were more than two full hours yet to elapse, before she could come; and in that interval, which seemed a long one, I must confess I was nervously anxious about my altered looks.When she first saw me, might she not be a little shocked and disappointed? Might it not prove a little worse than she had expected?

At last, when I believed there was at least a quarter of an hour more yet, Charley all at once cried out to me as I was trembling in the garden, "Here she comes, miss! Here she is!"

I did not mean to do it, but I ran upstairs into my room, and hid myself behind the door. There I stood, trembling, even when I heard my darling calling as she came upstairs, "Esther, my dear, my love, where are you?"

She ran in, and was running out again when she saw me. Ah, my angel girl! The old dear look, all love, all fondness, all affection. Nothing else in it – no, nothing, nothing!

O how happy I was with my sweet beautiful girl holding my scarred face to her lovely cheek, bathing it with tears and kisses, rocking me to and fro like a child, calling me by every tender name that she could think of, and pressing me to her faithful heart.

CHAPTER 21

Jarndyce and Jarndyce

We were to stay a month at Mr Boythorn's. My pet had scarcely been there a bright week, as I recollect the time, when one evening after we had finished helping the gardener in watering his flowers, and just as the candles were lighted, Charley, appearing with a very important air behind Ada's chair, beckoned me mysteriously out of the room.

"Oh! If you please, miss," said Charley, in a whisper, with her eyes at their roundest and largest. "You're wanted at the Dedlock Arms."

"Why, Charley," said I, "who can possibly want me at the public-house?"

"I don't know, miss," returned Charley, putting her head forward, and folding her hands tight upon the band of her little apron, "but it's a gentleman, miss, and his compliments, and will you please to come without saying anything about it."

77

I thought it best to go to this place by myself. I bade Charley be quick with my bonnet and veil, and my shawl; and having put them on, went away down the little hilly street.

The door of the tavern parlour being open, I heard some voices, familiar in my ears I thought, which stopped. A quick light step approached and who should stand before me but Richard!

"My dear Esther!" he said. "My best friend!" and he really was so warm-hearted and earnest, that in the first surprise and pleasure of his brotherly greeting, I could scarcely find breath to tell him that Ada was well.

"Answering my very thoughts – always the same dear girl!" said Richard, leading me to a chair, and seating himself beside me.

I put my veil up, but not quite.

"Always the same dear girl!" said Richard, just as heartily as before.

I put my veil up altogether, and laying my hand on Richard's sleeve, and looking in his face, told him how much I thanked him for his kind welcome, and how greatly I rejoiced to see him.

"My love," said Richard, "there is no one with whom I have a greater wish to talk, than you, for I want you to understand me."

"And I want you, Richard," said I, shaking my head, "to understand some one else."

"Since you refer so immediately to John Jarndyce," said Richard – "I suppose you mean him?"

"Of course I do."

"I am not accountable to Mr Jarndyce, or Mr Anybody."

"My dear Richard," I returned, "you know you would be heartily welcome at his house and you are as heartily welcome here!"

"Spoken like the best of little women!" cried Richard, gaily.

I asked him how he liked his profession.

"Oh, I like it well enough!" said Richard. "It does as well as anything else, for a time. I am in town on leave, just now."

"Indeed?"

"Yes. I have run over to look after my – my Chancery interests," said Richard, forcing a careless laugh. "We are beginning to spin along with that old suit at last, I promise you."

No wonder that I shook my head!

"As you say, it's not a pleasant subject." Richard spoke with the same shade crossing his face as before. "Who do you suppose is with me?"

"Was it Mr Skimpole's voice I heard?"

"That's the man! He does me more good than anybody."

He came in, and was charmed to see me; said he had been shedding tears of joy and sympathy, at intervals for six weeks, on my account.

"My dear Miss Summerson, here is our friend Richard," said Mr Skimpole, "full of the brightest visions of the future, which he evokes out of the darkness of Chancery."

I began seriously to think that Richard could scarcely have found a worse friend than this.

They both walked back with me; and Mr Skimpole leaving us at the gate, I walked softly in with Richard, and said, "Ada, my love, I have brought a gentleman to visit you." It was not difficult to read the blushing, startled face. She loved him dearly, and he knew it, and I knew it.

But I was not so sure that Richard loved her dearly. He admired her very much – but I had a tormenting idea that he was postponing all things until Jarndyce and Jarndyce should be off his mind.

But there was other trouble.

Richard was a little late in the morning, but I had not to wait for him long, and we turned into the park.

"I tell you what, my dear girl," said Richard, "when I get affairs in general settled, I shall come down here, I think, and rest."

"Would it not be better to rest now?" I asked.

"Oh, as to resting now," said Richard, "or as to doing anything very definite now, that's not easy."

"Why not?" said I.

"There you come back to John Jarndyce!" said Richard, impatiently. "My dear Esther, how can you be so blind? Don't you see that he is an interested party, and that it may be very well for him to wish me to know nothing of the suit?"

"O Richard," I remonstrated, "is it possible that you can breathe such unworthy suspicions?"

He was silent for a little while, before he replied in a subdued voice:

"Esther, I am sure you know that I am not a mean fellow, and that I have some sense of suspicion and distrust being poor qualities in one of my years."

"I know it very well," said I. "I am not more sure of anything."

"That's a dear girl," retorted Richard, "and like you, because it gives me comfort. I had need to get some scrap of comfort out of all this business."

"But I may ask you a question, Richard?"

"I think so," said he, laughing. "I don't know who may not, if you may not."

"You say, yourself, you are not leading a very settled life."

"How can I, my dear Esther, with nothing settled!"

"Are you in debt again?"

"Why of course I am," said Richard, astonished at my simplicity.

"Is it of course?"

"Bless your heart, my excellent girl," said Richard, quite amused with me, "I shall be all right! I shall pull through, my dear!"

When our walk brought us round to the village again, and I went home to breakfast, I prepared Ada for the account I was going to give her, and told her exactly what reason we had to dread that Richard was losing himself, and scattering his whole life to the winds. It made her very unhappy, of course; though she had a far, far greater reliance on his correcting his errors than I could have.

My dear girl told me, that night, how Richard's being prosperous or ruined, befriended or deserted, she would think of him at all times: never of herself, if she could devote herself to him.

And she kept her word!

CHAPTER 22

In Mr Tulkinghorn's Room

At Chesney Wold Mr Tulkinghorn arrives in his turret-room.

The eyes that meet his own, are looking in through the glass from the corridor outside. He knows them well. The blood has not flushed into his face so suddenly and redly for many a long year, as when he recognises Lady Dedlock.

She steps into the room, closing both the doors behind her. There is a wild disturbance – is it fear or anger? – in her eyes. He cannot be sure. Both might be as pale, both as intent.

"Lady Dedlock?"

She does not speak at first, nor even when she has slowly dropped into the easy chair by the table. They look at each other, like two pictures.

"How long have you known?"

"I have suspected it a long while – fully known it, a little while."

"Months?"

"Days."

He stands before her, with one hand on a chair-back and the other in his old-fashioned waistcoat and shirt-frill, exactly as he has stood before her at any time since her marriage.

"Is it the town-talk yet? Is it chalked upon the walls and cried in the streets?"

Mr Tulkinghorn looks at her, with his ragged grey eyebrows.

"No, Lady Dedlock."

"Then they do not know it yet?"

"No."

"You have prepared me for my exposure, and I thank you for that too. Is there anything that you require of me? I will write anything, here and now, that you will dictate. I am ready to do it."

And she would do it, thinks the lawyer, watchful of the firm hand with which she takes the pen!

"I will not trouble you, Lady Dedlock. Pray spare yourself."

"I have long expected this, as you know. I neither wish to spare myself, nor to be spared. You can do nothing worse to me than you have done. Do what remains, now."

"Lady Dedlock, there is nothing to be done. I will take leave to say a few words, when you have finished."

"My jewels are all in their proper places of keeping. They will be found there. So, my dresses. So, all the valuables I have. Some ready money I had with me, please to say, but no large amount. I did not wear my own dress, in order that I might avoid observation. I went, to be henceforward lost. Make this known. I leave no other charge with you."

"Excuse me, Lady Dedlock," says Mr Tulkinghorn, quite unmoved. "I am not sure that I understand you. You want? – "

"To be lost to all here. I leave Chesney Wold to-night. I go this hour."

81

Mr Tulkinghorn shakes his head. She rises; but he, without removing hand from chair-back or from old-fashioned waistcoat and shirt-frill, shakes his head.

"What? Not go as I have said?"

"No, Lady Dedlock," he very calmly replies.

"Sir," she returns, without looking up from the ground, on which her eyes are now fixed, "I had better have gone. It would have been far better not to have detained me. I have no more to say."

"Lady Dedlock, I am not clear what to do, or how to act next. I must request you, in the mean time, to keep your secret as you have kept it so long."

He pauses, but she makes no reply.

"The sole consideration in this unhappy case is Sir Leicester."

"Then why," she asks in a low voice, "do you detain me in his house?"

"When I speak of Sir Leicester being the sole consideration, he and the family credit are one. Sir Leicester and the baronetcy, Sir Leicester and Chesney Wold, Sir Leicester and his ancestors;" Mr Tulkinghorn very dry here; "are, I need not say to you, Lady Dedlock, inseparable."

"Go on!"

"Therefore," says Mr Tulkinghorn, pursuing his case in his jog-trot style, "This is to be hushed up, if it can be."

She stands looking out at the stars, without a word. They are beginning to pale, and she looks as if their coldness froze her.

"My experience teaches me," says Mr Tulkinghorn, "that most of the people I know would do far better to leave marriage alone. So I thought when Sir Leicester married, and so I always have thought since. In the meanwhile I beg you to keep your own counsel, and I will keep mine."

"I am to drag my present life on, holding its pains at your pleasure, day by day?" she asks, still looking at the distant sky.

"Yes, I am afraid so, Lady Dedlock."

"It is necessary, you think, that I should be so tied to the stake?"

"I am sure that what I recommend is necessary."

"We are to meet as usual?"

"Precisely as usual, if you please."

"And I am to hide my guilt, as I have done so many years?"

"As you have done so many years. I know it certainly, but I believe we have never wholly trusted each other."

She stands absorbed in the same frozen way for some little time, before asking: "Is there anything more to be said to-night?"

"Why," Mr Tulkinghorn returns methodically, as he softly rubs his hands, "I should like to be assured of your acquiescence in my arrangements, Lady Dedlock."

"You may be assured of it."

She remains absorbed; but at length moves, and turns, unshaken in her natural and acquired presence, towards the door. Mr Tulkinghorn opens both the doors exactly as he would have done yesterday, or as he would have done ten years ago, and makes his old-fashioned bow as she passes out.

CHAPTER 23

In Mr Tulkinghorn's Chambers

Mr Tulkinghorn transfers himself to the stale heat and dust of London. He melted out of his turret-room this morning, just as now, in the late twilight, he melts into his own square.

He unlocks his door, gropes his way into his murky rooms, lights his candles, and looks about him. He is going towards the door with a candle in his hand, when a knock comes.

"Who's this? Aye, aye, mistress, it's you, is it? Now! What do you want?"

He addresses these words of welcome to Mademoiselle Hortense. That feline personage, with her lips tightly shut, and her eyes looking out at him sideways, softly closes the door before replying.

"I have had great deal of trouble to find you, sir."

"Have you!"

"I have been here very often, sir. It has always been said to me, he is not at home, he is engage, he is this and that, he is not for you."

"Quite right, and quite true."

"Not true. Lies!"

"Now, mistress," says the lawyer, "If you have anything to say, say it, say it."

"Sir, you have not use me well. You have been mean and shabby."

"Mean and shabby, eh?" returns the lawyer, rubbing his nose.

"You know you have. You have catched me to give you information; to show you the dress of mine my Lady must have wore that night, you have prayed me to come in it here to meet that boy – Say! Is it not?" Mademoiselle Hortense makes another spring.

"You are a vixen, a vixen!" Mr Tulkinghorn seems to meditate, as he looks distrustfully at her; then he replies, "Well, wench, well. I paid you."

"You paid me!" she repeats, with fierce disdain. "Two sovereign! I ref-use them, I des-pise them, I throw them from me!" Which she literally does, flinging them with such violence on the floor, that they jerk up again into the light before they roll away into corners.

"Now!" says Mademoiselle Hortense, darkening her large eyes again. "You have paid me?"

Mr Tulkinghorn rubs his head. "You must be rich, my fair friend," he composedly observes, "to throw money about in that way!"

"I am rich," she returns, "I am very rich in hate. I hate my Lady, of all my heart. You know that."

"Know it? How should I know it?"

"I am not blind. You have made sure of me because you knew that. You had reason. I det-est her." Mademoiselle folds her arms, and throws this last remark at him over one of her shoulders.

"Having said this, have you anything else to say, mademoiselle?"

"I am not yet placed. Place me well. Find me a good condition! If you cannot do that, employ me to pursue her, to chase her, to disgrace and to dishonour her. It is what you do. Do I not know that?"

"Now, let us see," says Mr Tulkinghorn, tapping his chin, and looking imperturbably at her, "how this matter stands."

"Ah! Let us see," Mademoiselle assents, with many angry and tight nods of her head.

"You come here to make a modest demand and, it not being met, you will come again."

"And again," says Mademoiselle, with more tight and angry nods. "And yet again. And yet again. And many times again. In effect, for ever!"

"Very well. Now Mademoiselle Hortense, let me recommend you to take the candle and pick up that money of yours."

She merely throws a laugh over her shoulder, and stands her ground with folded arms.

"You will not, eh?"

"No, I will not!" replies Mademoiselle, "I think that you are a miserable wretch."

"Probably," returns Mr Tulkinghorn, quietly. "But I don't ask what you think of myself; I ask what you think of prison."

"Nothing. What does it matter to me?"

"My fair friend," says Mr Tulkinghorn, "make another visit here, and you shall learn."

"In that case you will send me to the prison perhaps?"

"In a word, mistress," says Mr Tulkinghorn, "if you ever present yourself uninvited here again, I will give you over to the police."

"I will prove you," whispers Mademoiselle, stretching out her hand, "I will try if you dare to do it!"

"And now," proceeds the lawyer, still without minding her, "you had better go. Think twice, before you come here again."

"Think you," she answers, "twice two hundred times!"

"You were dismissed by your lady, you know," Mr Tulkinghorn observes, following her out upon the staircase, "as the most implacable and unmanageable of women. Now turn over a new leaf, and take warning by what I say to you. For what I say, I mean; and what I threaten, I will do, mistress."

She goes down without answering or looking behind her. When she is gone, he goes down too; and returning with a cobweb-covered bottle, devotes himself to a leisurely enjoyment of its contents.

CHAPTER 24

Esther's Narrative

It matters little now, how much I thought of my living mother who had told me evermore to consider her dead. I could not venture to approach her, or to communicate with her in writing, at no time did I dare to utter her name. I felt as if I did not even dare to hear it. If the conversation anywhere, when I was present, took that direction, as it sometimes naturally did, I tried not to hear – I mentally counted, repeated something that I knew, or went out of the room, in the dread I had of hearing anything that might lead to her betrayal through me.

When we were settled at home again, I made up my mind that I must tell my guardian what I knew. I went out at my door and sought my guardian among his books. I knew he always read at that hour; and as I drew near, I saw the light shining out into the passage from his reading-lamp.

"May I come in, guardian?"

"Surely, little woman. What's the matter?"

"Nothing is the matter. I thought I would like to take this quiet time of saying a word to you about myself."

He put a chair for me, shut his book, and put it by, and turned his kind attentive face towards me.

"You cannot be more ready to speak than I am to hear."

"I know that, guardian. But I have such need of your advice and support. O! You don't know how much need I have to-night."

He crossed to the door to see that it was shut (but I had seen to that), and resumed his seat before me.

"Guardian," said I, "do you remember, when we were overtaken by the thunderstorm, Lady Dedlock's speaking to you of her sister?"

"Of course. Of course I do."

"And reminding you that she and her sister had differed; had 'gone their several ways?'"

"Of course."

"Why did they separate, guardian?"

His face quite altered as he looked at me. "My child, what questions are these! I never knew. No one but themselves ever did know, I believe. Who could tell what the secrets of those two handsome and proud women were! You have seen Lady Dedlock. If you had ever seen her sister, you would know her to have been as resolute and haughty as she."

"That secluded sister is my first remembrance."

"No, no!" he cried, starting.

"Yes, guardian, yes! And her sister is my mother!"

I would have told him all my mother's letter, but he would not hear it then. He spoke so tenderly and wisely to me I believed I had never loved

86

him so dearly, never thanked him in my heart so fully, as I did that night. And when he had taken me to my room and kissed me at the door, and when at last I lay down to sleep, my thought was how could I ever be good enough, devoted enough to him, to show him how I blessed and honoured him.

CHAPTER 25

The Letter and the Answer

My guardian called me into his room next morning, and then I told him what had been left untold on the previous night. There was nothing to be done, he said, but to keep the secret, and to avoid any encounter with that family. If her mistrust of the lawyer whom she had mentioned were well-founded, which he scarcely doubted, he dreaded discovery. He knew something of him, both by sight and by reputation, and it was certain that he was a dangerous man.

"But I think we may dismiss him for the present. Is there any other might prove dangerous to my Lady?"

I called to his recollection the French maid, and the eager offer of herself she had made to me.

"But after all, she merely proposed herself for your maid, you know. She did nothing more."

"Her manner was strange," said I.

"Yes, and her manner was strange when she took her shoes off, and showed that cool relish for a walk that might have ended in her death-bed," said my guardian. "It would be useless self-distress and torment to reckon up such chances and possibilities. Be hopeful, little woman. It is the best you can do, for everybody's sake. I, sharing the secret with you will be attentive to what passes in that family, so far as I can observe it from my distance. And if the time should come when I can stretch out a hand to render the least service to one whom it is better not to name even here, I will not fail to do it for her dear daughter's sake."

I thanked him with my whole heart. What could I ever do but thank him! I was going out at the door, when he asked me to stay a moment.

Quickly turning round, I saw that odd expression on his face again; and all at once, I don't know how, it flashed upon me as a new and far off possibility that I understood it.

"My dear Esther," said my guardian, "I have long had something in my thoughts that I have wished to say to you."

"Indeed?"

"I have had some difficulty in approaching it, and I still have. Would you object to my writing it?"

"Dear guardian, how could I object to your writing anything for me to read?"

"Can you fully trust me, and thoroughly rely on what I profess, Esther?"

"Most thoroughly," said I with my whole heart.

"That's much," he answered. "That's everything. If you are sure of that, on good consideration, send Charley to me this night week – 'for the letter.' But if you are not quite certain on that one point, never send!"

"Guardian," said I, "I am already certain. I shall send Charley for the letter."

He shook my hand and said no more. Nor was any more said in reference to this conversation, either by him or me, through the whole week. When the appointed night came, I said to Charley as soon as I was alone, "Go and knock at Mr Jarndyce's door, Charley, and say you have come from me – 'for the letter.'" Charley went up the stairs, and down the stairs, and along the passages – the zig-zag way about the old-fashioned house seemed very long in my listening ears that night – and so came back, along the passages, and down the stairs, and up the stairs, and brought the letter. "Lay it on the table, Charley," said I. So Charley laid it on the table and went to bed, and I sat looking at it without taking it up, thinking of many things. I thought of myself so altered and of those around me so unchanged; and all this happiness shone like a light, from one central figure, represented before me by the letter on the table.

I opened it and read it. It was so impressive in its love for me, and in the unselfish caution it gave me, and the consideration it showed for me in every word, that my eyes were too often blinded to read much at a time. But I read it through three times, before I laid it down. I had thought beforehand that I knew its purpose and I did. It asked me would I be the mistress of Bleak House.

But he did not hint to me, that when I had been better-looking, he had

88

had this same thought, and had refrained from it. That when my old face was gone from me, and I had no attractions, he could love me just as well as in my fairer days. That the discovery of my birth gave him no shock. That his generosity rose above my disfigurement, and my inheritance of shame.

But I knew it well now. It came upon me that I had but one thing to do. I was very happy, very thankful, very hopeful; but I cried very much.

On entering the breakfast-room next morning, I found my guardian just as usual; quite as frank, as open, and free. I was with him several times in the course of the morning, in and out, when there was no one there; and I thought it not unlikely that he might speak to me about the letter; but he did not say a word.

So, on the next morning, and the next, and for at least a week; over which time Mr Skimpole prolonged his stay. I expected, every day, that my guardian might speak to me about the letter; but he never did.

I thought then, growing uneasy, that I ought to write an answer. I tried over and over again in my own room at night, but I could not write an answer that at all began like a good answer; so I thought each night I would wait one more day. And I waited seven more days, and he never said a word.

At last Mr Skimpole having departed, we three were one afternoon going out for a ride; and I being dressed before Ada, and going down, came upon my guardian, with his back towards me, standing at the drawing-room window looking out.

He turned on my coming in, and said, smiling, "Aye, it's you, little woman, is it?" and looked out again.

I had made up my mind to speak to him now. In short, I had come down on purpose. "Guardian," I said, rather hesitating and trembling, "when would you like to have the answer to the letter Charley came for?"

"When it's ready, my dear," he replied.

"I think it is ready," said I.

"Is Charley to bring it?" he asked, pleasantly.

"No. I have brought it myself, guardian," I returned.

I put my two arms round his neck and kissed him; and he said was this the mistress of Bleak House; and I said yes; and it made no difference presently, and we all went out together, and I said nothing to my precious pet about it.

CHAPTER 26

Stop Him!

It is a moot point whether Tom-all-Alone's be uglier by day or by night. The day begins to break now; and in truth it might be better for the national glory even that the sun should sometimes set than that it should ever rise upon so vile a wonder as Tom-all-Alone's.

A brown sunburnt gentleman, strolls hitherward at this quiet time. Attracted by curiosity, he often pauses and looks about him, up and down the miserable by-ways. Nor is he merely curious, for in his bright dark eye there is compassionate interest; and as he looks here and there, he seems to understand such wretchedness, and to have studied it before.

As he retraces his way he sees a ragged figure coming very cautiously along, crouching close to the soiled walls and furtively thrusting a hand before it. It is the figure of a youth, whose face is hollow, and whose eyes have an emaciated glare. He shades his face with his ragged elbow as he passes on the other side of the way, and goes shrinking and creeping on, with his anxious hand before him, and his shapeless clothes hanging in shreds.

Allan Woodcourt pauses to look after him and note all this, with a shadowy belief that he has seen the boy before. He cannot recall how, or where; but there is some association in his mind with such a form.

He is gradually emerging from Tom-all-Alone's in the morning light, thinking about it, when he hears running feet behind him; and looking round, sees the boy scouring towards him at great speed, followed by a woman.

"Stop him, stop him!" cries the woman, almost breathless. "Stop him, sir!"

Allan, not knowing but that he has just robbed her of her money, follows in chase, and runs so hard that at last the fugitive is brought to bay, and tumbles down, lying gasping at his pursuer, who stands and gasps at him until the woman comes up.

"O you, Jo!" cries the woman. "What? I have found you at last!"

"Jo," repeats Allan, looking at him with attention, "Jo! To be sure! I recollect this lad some time ago being brought before the coroner."

"I've been a chivied and a chivied, fust by one on you and nixt by another on you, till I'm worried to skins and bones. I don't know why I don't go and make a hole in the water, I'm sure I don't."

Jo says it with such a pitiable air, and his grimy tears appear so real that Allan Woodcourt is softened towards him.

He says to the woman, "Has he robbed you?"

"No, sir, no. Robbed me? He did nothing but what was kind-hearted by me."

Allan looks from Jo to the woman, and from the woman to Jo, waiting for one of them to unravel the riddle.

"But he was along with me, sir," says the woman, "he was along with me, sir, down at Saint Albans, ill, and a young lady Lord bless her for a good friend to me took pity on him and took him home."

Allan shrinks back from him with a sudden horror.

"Yes, sir, yes. Took him home, and made him comfortable, and like a thankless monster he ran away in the night. And that young lady caught his illness, lost her beautiful looks. Do you know it? You ungrateful wretch, do you know that this is all along of you and of her goodness to you?" demands the woman, beginning to rage at him as she recalls it, and breaking into passionate tears.

Allan restrains the woman by a quiet gesture.

"Richard told me – " he falters, " – I mean, I have heard of this – don't mind me for a moment."

He turns away, and stands for a while looking out. When he comes back, he has recovered his composure.

"You hear what she says. But get up, get up!"

Jo, shaking and chattering, slowly rises.

"Have you been here ever since?"

"Wishermaydie if I seen Tom-all-Alone's till this blessed morning," replies Jo, hoarsely.

"Why have you come here now?"

Jo looks all round the confined court, looks at his questioner no higher than the knees, and finally answers:

"I don't know how to do nothink, and I can't get nothink to do. I'm wery poor and ill, and I thought I'd come back here when there warn't nobody about, and lay down and hide somewheres till arter dark, and then go and beg a trifle of Mr Snagsby."

"Where have you come from?"

Jo looks all round the court again, looks at his questioner's knees again, and concludes by laying his profile against the hoarding in a sort of resignation.

"Did you hear me ask you where you have come from?"

"Tramp then," says Jo.

"Now, tell me," proceeds Allan, making a strong effort to overcome his repugnance, going very near to him, "tell me how it came about that you left that house, when the good young lady had been so unfortunate as to pity you, and take you home."

Jo suddenly comes out of his resignation, and excitedly declares, that he never known about the young lady, that he would sooner have hurt his own self, and that she wos wery good to him, she wos, winding up with some very miserable sobs.

Allan Woodcourt sees that this is not a sham. He constrains himself to touch him. "Come, Jo. Tell me."

"No. I dustn't," says Jo, relapsing into the profile state. "I dustn't, or I would."

"But I must know," returns the other, "all the same. Come, Jo."

After two or three such adjurations, Jo lifts up his head again, looks round the court again, and says in a low voice, "Well, I'll tell you somethink. I was took away. There!"

"Took away? In the night?"

"Ah!" Very apprehensive of being overheard, Jo looks about him.

"Who took you away?"

"I dustn't name him," says Jo. "I dustn't do it, sir."

"But I want, in the young lady's name, to know. You may trust me. No one else shall hear."

"Ah, but I don't know," replies Jo, shaking his head fearfully, "as he don't hear."

"Why, he is not in this place."

"Oh, ain't he though?" says Jo. "He's in all manner of places, all at wunst."

Allan patiently awaits an explicit answer; and Jo, more baffled by his patience than by anything else, at last desperately whispers a name in his ear.

"Why," says Allan, "what had you been doing?"

"Nothink, sir. Never done nothink to get myself into no trouble, 'cept in not moving on. But I'm a moving on now. I'm a moving on to the berryin ground -- that's the move as I'm up to."

"No, no, we will try to prevent that. But what did he do with you?"

"Put me in a horsepittle," replied Jo, whispering, "till I was discharged, then giv me a little money and ses 'Don't let me ever see you nowheres within forty mile of London, or you'll repent it.' So I shall, if ever he does see me, and he'll see me if I'm above ground," concludes Jo.

"Now, Jo," says Allan, keeping his eye upon him, "come with me, and I will find you a better place than this to lie down and hide in. Come along. Good day again, my good woman."

"Good day again, sir, and I thank you kindly many times again."

She has been sitting on her bag, deeply attentive, and now rises and takes it up. Jo, repeating, "Ony you tell the young lady as I never went fur to hurt her and wot the gen'l'm'n ses!" nods and shambles and shivers, and smears and blinks, and half laughs and half cries, and takes his creeping way along after Allan Woodcourt, close to the houses on the opposite side of the street. In this order, the two come up out of Tom-all-Alone's into the broad rays of the sunlight and the purer air.

CHAPTER 27

Jo's Will

Allan looks about for an apothecary's shop. There is none at hand, but a tavern does as well or better. He obtains a little measure of wine, and gives the lad a portion of it very carefully. He begins to revive, almost as soon as it passes his lips. "We may repeat that dose, Jo," observes Allan, after watching him with his attentive face. "So! Now we will take five minutes rest, and then go on again."

Observant of these signs of improvement, Allan engages him in conversation; and elicits to his no small wonder the adventure of the lady in the veil, with all its consequences. So he tells Jo, for his encouragement, that this walking about will soon be over now, it is not far.

Soon, Allan Woodcourt sees the figure of Mr George himself, striding towards them in his morning exercise with his pipe in his mouth, and his muscular arms, developed by broadsword and dumb-bell, weightily asserting themselves through his light shirt-sleeves.

"Your servant, sir," says Mr George, with a military salute. "Excuse me, sir. A sailor, I believe?" says Mr George.

"I am proud to find I have the air of one," returns Allan; "but I am only a sea-going doctor."

"Indeed, sir! I should have thought you was a regular blue-jacket, myself."

Allan proceeds to tell him all he knows about Jo; unto which the trooper listens with a grave face.

"And that's the lad, sir, is it?" he inquires, looking along the entry to where Jo stands staring up at the great letters on the whitewashed front, which have no meaning in his eyes.

"That's he," says Allan. "And, Mr George, I am in this difficulty about him. I am unwilling to place him in a hospital, even if I could procure him immediate admission, because I foresee that he would not stay there many hours, if he could be so much as got there. The same objection applies to a workhouse; supposing I had the patience to be evaded and shirked, and handed about from post to pillar in trying to get him into one – which is a system that I don't take kindly to."

"No man does, sir," returns Mr George.

"I am convinced that he would not remain in either place, because he is possessed by an extraordinary terror of this person who ordered him to keep out of the way; in his ignorance, he believes this person to be everywhere, and knowing everything."

"I ask your pardon, sir," says Mr George. "But you have not mentioned that party's name. Is it a secret, sir?"

"The boy makes it one. But his name is Bucket."

"Bucket the detective, sir?"

"The same man."

"The man is known to me, sir," returns the trooper, after blowing out a cloud of smoke, and squaring his chest; "and the boy is so far correct that he undoubtedly is a – rum customer." Mr George smokes with a profound meaning after this.

"Now, I wish Mr Jarndyce and Miss Summerson at least to know that this Jo has reappeared; and to have it in their power to speak with him, if they should desire to do so. Therefore I want to get him, for the present moment, into any poor lodging kept by decent people, where he would be admitted," says Allan. "Do you happen to know any one in this neighbourhood, who would receive him for a while, on my paying for him beforehand?"

"Well, sir," says Mr George, "We are naturally in the vagabond way here, sir, both myself and Phil. You see what the place is. You are welcome to a quiet corner of it for the boy. No charge made, except for rations. We are not in a flourishing state of circumstances here, sir. We are liable to be tumbled out neck and crop, at a moment's notice. However, sir, such as the place is, and so long as it lasts, here it is at your service."

With a comprehensive wave of his pipe, Mr George places the whole building at his visitor's disposal.

"I take it for granted, sir," he adds, "you being one of the medical staff, that there is no present infection about this unfortunate subject?"

Allan is quite sure of it.

"But the boy is deplorably low and reduced; and that he may be – I do not say that he is – too far gone to recover."

"Do you consider him in present danger, sir?" inquires the trooper.

"Yes, I fear so."

"Then, sir," returns the trooper, in a decisive manner, "it appears to me – being naturally in the vagabond way myself – that the sooner he comes out of the street, the better. You, Phil! Bring him in!"

As the trooper speaks, he conducts them to the other end of the gallery, and opens one of the little cabins. "There you are, you see! Here is a mattress, and here you may rest, on good behaviour, as long as Mr Woodcourt pleases. Don't you be alarmed if you hear shots; they'll be aimed at the target, and not you. Now, there's another thing I would recommend, sir," says the trooper, turning to his visitor. "Phil, come here!"

Phil bears down upon them, according to his usual tactics.

"Here is a man, sir, who was found, when a baby, in the gutter. Consequently, it is to be expected that he takes a natural interest in this poor creature. You do, don't you, Phil?"

"Certainly and surely I do, guv'ner," is Phil's reply.

"Now I was thinking, sir," says Mr George, in a martial sort of confidence, as if he were giving his opinion in a council of war at a drumhead, "that if this man was to take him to a bath, and was to lay out a few shillings in getting him one or two coarse articles – "

"Mr George, my considerate friend," returns Allan, taking out his purse, "it is the very favour I would have asked."

Phil Squod and Jo are sent out immediately on this work of improvement. Allan takes the opportunity of going out to procure some restorative medicines; and obtaining them near at hand, soon returns, to find the trooper walking up and down the gallery, and to fall into step and walk with him.

The trooper looks sideways at Allan's sunburnt cheek and bright dark eye, rapidly measures his height and build, and seems to approve of him.

"Since you have been out, sir, I have been thinking that I know the rooms in Lincoln's Inn Fields, where Bucket took the lad. Though he is not acquainted with the name, I can help you to it. It's Tulkinghorn. That's what it is."

Allan looks at him inquiringly, repeating the name.

"Tulkinghorn. That's the name, sir. I know the man, sir. To my sorrow."

Allan naturally asks what kind of man he is?

"What kind of man! Do you mean to look at?"

"I think I know that much of him. I mean to deal with. Generally, what kind of man?"

"Why, then I'll tell you, sir," returns the trooper, stopping short, and folding his arms on his square chest, so angrily, that his face fires and flushes all over; "he is a confoundedly bad kind of man. He is a slow-torturing kind of man. He is a kind of man that has caused me more uneasiness, and more dissatisfaction with myself, than all other men put together. That's the kind of man Mr Tulkinghorn is!"

"I am sorry," says Allan, "to have touched so sore a place."

"It's no fault of yours, sir; but you shall judge. He has got a power over me. He is the man I spoke of just now, as being able to tumble me out of this place neck and crop. He keeps me on a constant see-saw. He won't hold off, and he won't come on. Why, I spend half my life now, pretty well, loitering and dodging about his door. What does he care? Nothing. If I had a chance, in one of the humours he drives me into – he'd go down, sir!"

Mr George has been so excited, that he finds it necessary to wipe his forehead on his shirt-sleeve. Allan Woodcourt has not much doubt about the going down of Mr Tulkinghorn on the field referred to.

Jo and his conductor presently return, and Jo is assisted to his mattress by the careful Phil; to whom, after due administration of medicine by his own hands, Allan confides all needful means and instructions. The morning is by this time getting on apace. He repairs to his lodgings to dress and breakfast; and then, without seeking rest, goes away to Mr Jarndyce to communicate his discovery.

"Let me lay here quiet, and not be chivied no more," falters Jo; "and be so kind as to say to Mr Snagsby that Jo, wot he known once, is a-moving on right forards with his duty."

He makes so many of these references to the law-stationer in the course of a day or two that Allan resolves to call in Cook's Court; the rather, as Jo's health seems to be breaking down.

And being tender-hearted, and affected by the account he hears of Jo's condition, Mr Snagsby readily engages to "look round," as early in the evening as he can manage it.

Jo is very glad to see his old friend; and says, when they are left alone, that he takes it uncommon kind as Mr Snagsby should come so far out of his way on accounts of sich as him. Mr Snagsby, touched by the spectacle before him, immediately lays upon the table half-a-crown: that magic balsam of his for all kinds of wounds.

"And how do you find yourself, my poor lad?" inquires the stationer, with his cough of sympathy.

"Mr Snagsby," says Jo. "I went and giv a illness to the lady but I didn't go fur to do it."

Mr Snagsby deposits another half-crown on the table. Nothing less than a repetition of that infallible remedy will relieve his feelings.

"Wot I was a thinkin on, Mr Sangsby," proceeds Jo, "wos, as you wos able to write wery large, p'raps?"

"Yes, my poor boy."

"Wot I wos a thinking on then, Mr Sangsby, wos, that when I wos moved on as fur as ever I could go whether you might be so good p'raps as to write out, wery large so that any one could see it anywheres, as that I wos wery truly hearty sorry that I done it and that I never went fur to do it; and that though I didn't know nothink at all, I knowd as Mr Woodcot once cried over it and wos allus grieved over it, and that I hoped as he'd be able to forgiv me in his mind. If the writin could be made to say it wery large, he might."

"It shall say it, Jo. Very large."

Jo laughs again. "Thankee, Mr Sangsby. Its wery kind of you, sir, and it makes me more cumfier than I was afore."

The meek little stationer, with a broken and unfinished cough, slips down his next half-crown – he has never been so close to a case requiring so many – and departs. And Jo and he shall meet no more.

Jo is in a sleep or in a stupor to-day, and Allan Woodcourt, newly arrived, stands by him, looking down upon his wasted form. After a while, he softly seats himself upon the bedside with his face towards him and touches his chest and heart.

"Well, Jo! What is the matter? Don't be frightened."

"I thought," says Jo, who has started, and is looking round, "I thought I was in Tom-all-Alone's agin. Ain't there nobody here but you, Mr Woodcot?"

"Nobody."

"And I ain't took back to Tom-all-Alone's. Am I, sir?"

"No."

Jo closes his eyes, muttering, "I'm wery thankful."

After watching him closely a little while, Allan puts his mouth very near his ear, and says to him in a low, distinct voice:

"Jo! Did you ever know a prayer?"

"Never know'd nothink, sir."

"Not so much as one short prayer?"

"No, sir. Nothink at all."

After a short relapse into sleep or stupor, he makes, of a sudden, a strong effort to get out of bed.

"Stay, Jo! What now?"

"It's time for me to go to that there berryin ground, sir," he returns with a wild look.

"Lie down, and tell me. What burying ground, Jo?"

"Where they laid him as wos wery good to me, wery good to me indeed, he wos. I wants to go there and be berried. He used fur to say to me, 'I am as poor as you today, Jo,' he ses. I wants to tell him that I am as poor as him now, and have come there to be laid along with him."

"Bye and bye, Jo. Bye and bye."

"But will you promise to have me took there, sir, and laid along with him?"

"I will, indeed."

"Thankee, sir. Thankee, sir. They'll have to get the key of the gate afore they can take me in, for it's allus locked. And there's a step there, as I used for to clean with my broom. – It's turned wery dark, sir. Is there any light a-comin?"

"It is coming fast, Jo, my poor fellow!"

"I hear you, sir, in the dark, but I'm a-gropin – a-gropin – let me catch hold of your hand."

"Jo, can you say what I say?"

"I'll say anythink as you say, sir, for I knows it's good."

"*Our Father*."

"Our Father! – Yes, that's wery good, sir."

"*Which art in Heaven*."

"Art in Heaven – is the light a-comin, sir?"

"It is close at hand. *Hallowed be thy name!*"

"Hallowed be – thy – "

The light is come upon the dark benighted way. Dead!

Dead, your Majesty. Dead, my lords and gentlemen. Dead, Right Reverends and Wrong Reverends of every order. Dead, men and women, born with Heavenly compassion in your hearts. And dying thus around us, every day.

CHAPTER 28

Closing In

The fashionable world is in full swing and where the throng is thickest, where the lights are brightest, where all the senses are ministered to with the greatest delicacy and refinement, Lady Dedlock is.

Mr Tulkinghorn says nothing, looks nothing. Now, as heretofore, he is to be found in doorways of rooms, with his limp white cravat loosely twisted into its old-fashioned tie. Of all men he is still the last who might be supposed to have any influence upon my Lady. Of all women she is still the last who might be supposed to have any dread of him.

One thing has been much on her mind since their late interview in his turret-room at Chesney Wold. She is now decided, and prepared to throw it off.

Her favoured maid, Rosa, is still with her, and has been writing for her and reading to her. Rosa is now at work upon embroidery, or some such pretty thing; and as she bends her head over it, my Lady watches her in silence. Not for the first time to-day.

"Rosa."

The pretty village face looks brightly up. Then, seeing how serious my Lady is, looks puzzled and surprised.

"See to the door. Is it shut?"

Yes. She goes to it and returns, and looks yet more surprised.

"Do you know," Lady Dedlock asks her, signing to her to bring her chair nearer; "do you know, Rosa, that I am different to you from what I am to any one?"

"Yes, my Lady. Much kinder. But then I often think I know you as you really are."

"You often think you know me as I really am? Poor child, poor child!"

She says it with a kind of scorn – though not of Rosa – and sits brooding, looking dreamily at her.

"And if I were to say to-day, Go! Leave me! I should say what would give me great pain and disquiet, child, and what would leave me very solitary."

"My Lady! Have I offended you?"

"In nothing. Come here."

Rosa bends down on the footstool at my Lady's feet. My Lady lays her hand upon her dark hair, and gently keeps it there.

"There are reasons now known to me, reasons in which you have no part, rendering it far better for you that you should not remain here. You must not remain here. I have determined that you shall not. I have written to Mr Rouncewell, the father of your lover, and he will be here to-day. All this I have done for your sake."

The weeping girl covers her hand with kisses, and says what shall she do, what shall she do, when they are separated! Her mistress kisses her on the cheek, and makes no other answer.

"Now, be happy, child, under better circumstances. Be beloved, and happy!"

"Ah, my Lady, I have sometimes thought – forgive my being so free – that you are not happy."

"I!"

"Will you be more so, when you have sent me away? Pray, pray, think again. Let me stay a little while!"

"I have said, my child, that what I do, I do for your sake, not my own. It is done. What I am towards you, Rosa, is what I am now – not what I shall be a little while hence. Remember this, and keep my confidence. Do so much for my sake, and thus all ends between us!"

She detaches herself from her simple-hearted companion, and leaves the room.

Lady Dedlock dines alone in her own room to-day. Lady Dedlock asks, on sitting down to dinner, still deadly pale, whether Mr Tulkinghorn is gone yet? No. Presently she asks again, is he gone yet? No. What is he doing? He is writing letters in the library. Would my Lady wish to see him? Anything but that.

But he wishes to see my Lady. Within a few more minutes, he is reported as sending his respects, and could my Lady please to receive him for a word or two after her dinner? My Lady will receive him now. He comes now, apologising for intruding, even by her permission, while she is at table. When they are alone, my Lady waves her hand to dispense with such mockeries.

"What do you want, sir?"

"Why, Lady Dedlock," says the lawyer, taking a chair at a little distance from her, "I am rather surprised by the course you have taken."

"Indeed?"

"Yes, decidedly. I was not prepared for it. I consider it a departure from our agreement and your promise."

"I do not quite understand you."

"O yes you do, I think. I think you do. Come, come, Lady Dedlock, we must not fence and parry now. You know you like this girl."

"Well, sir?"

"And you know – and I know – that you have sent her away for the purpose of separating her as much as possible from any reproach and exposure that impend over yourself."

"Well, sir?"

"Well, Lady Dedlock," returns the lawyer, "I object to that. I consider that, a dangerous proceeding. I know it to be unnecessary, and calculated to awaken speculation, doubt, rumour, in the house. Besides, it is a violation of our agreement. You were to be exactly what you were before. Whereas, you have been very different from what you were before."

"If, sir," she begins, "in my knowledge of my secret – " but he interrupts her.

"Now, Lady Dedlock, it is no longer your secret. Excuse me. That is just the mistake. It is my secret, in trust for Sir Leicester and the family. If it were your secret, Lady Dedlock, we should not be here, holding this conversation."

"That is very true. If, in my knowledge of the secret, I do what I can to spare an innocent girl from the taint of my impending shame, I act upon a resolution I have taken. Nothing in the world, and no one in the world, could shake it, or could move me." This she says with great deliberation and distinctness, and with no more outward passion than himself.

"Really? Then you see, Lady Dedlock," he returns, "you are not to be trusted."

For a little while they are silent. Lady Dedlock has eaten no dinner, but has twice or thrice poured out water with a steady hand and drunk it. She rises from table, takes a lounging-chair, and reclines in it, shading her face. She is not the first to speak; appearing so unlikely to be so, though he stood there until midnight, that even he is driven upon breaking silence.

"Lady Dedlock, the most disagreeable part of this business remains. Our agreement is broken. A lady of your sense and strength of character will be prepared for my now declaring it void, and taking my own course."

"I am quite prepared."

Mr Tulkinghorn inclines his head. "That is all I have to trouble you with, Lady Dedlock."

She stops him as he is moving out of the room, by asking, "This is the notice I was to receive? You intend to give me no other notice?"

"You are right. No."

"Do you contemplate undeceiving Sir Leicester to-night?"

Mr Tulkinghorn, with a slight smile, and cautiously shaking his head says, "No, not to-night."

"To-morrow?"

"It may be to-morrow. I would rather say no more. I wish you good evening."

She removes her hand, turns her pale face towards him as he walks silently to the door, and stops him once again as he is about to open it.

"I heard you were writing in the library. Are you going to return there?"

"Only for my hat. I am going home."

She bows her eyes rather than her head, the movement is so slight and curious; and he withdraws.

He passes out into the streets, and walks on, with his hands behind him, under the shadow of the lofty houses, many of whose mysteries, difficulties, mortgages, delicate affairs of all kinds, are treasured up within his old black satin waistcoat, arrives at last in his dull room.

It is a moonlight night; but the moon, being past the full, is only now rising over the great wilderness of London. The stars are shining as they shone above the turret-leads at Chesney Wold. This woman looks out upon them. Her soul is turbulent within her; she is sick at heart, and restless. The large rooms are too cramped and close. She cannot endure their restraint, and will walk alone in a neighbouring garden and, loosely muffled, goes out into the moonlight. Mercury attends with the key. Having opened the garden gate, he delivers the key into his Lady's hands at her request, and is bidden to go back. She will walk there some time, to ease her aching head. She may be an hour; she may be more. She needs no further escort. The gate shuts upon its spring with a clash, and he leaves her, passing on into the dark shade of some trees.

A fine night, and a bright large moon, and multitudes of stars. Mr Tulkinghorn, in repairing to his cellar, and in opening and shutting those resounding doors, has to cross a little prison-like yard. He looks up casually, thinking what a fine night, what a bright large moon, what multitudes of stars! A quiet night, too.

A very quiet night.

But what's that? Who fired a gun or pistol? Where was it?

The few foot-passengers start, stop, and stare about them. Some windows and doors are opened, and people come out to look. It was a loud report, and echoed and rattled heavily. It shook one house, or so a man says who was passing. It has aroused all the dogs in the neighbourhood, who bark vehemently. Terrified cats scamper across the road. While the dogs are yet barking and howling – there is one dog howling like a demon – the church-clocks, as if they were startled too, begin to strike. The hum from the streets, likewise, seems to swell into a shout. But it is soon over. Before the last clock begins to strike ten, there is a lull. When it has ceased, the fine night, the bright large moon, and multitudes of stars, are left at peace again.

Has Mr Tulkinghorn been disturbed? His windows are dark and quiet, and his door is shut. It must be something unusual indeed, to bring him out of his shell. Nothing is heard of him, nothing is seen of him.

But, a little after the coming of the day, come people to clean the rooms. And the foremost of them goes wild; for, looking up at his outstretched hand, and looking down at what is below it, that person shrieks and flies. The others, looking in as the first one looked, shriek and fly too, and there is an alarm in the street.

What does it mean? No light is admitted into the darkened chamber, and people unaccustomed to it, enter, and treading softly, but heavily. There is whispering and wondering all day, strict search of every corner, careful tracing of steps, and careful noting of the disposition of every article of furniture.

So, it shall happen surely, through many years to come, that ghostly stories shall be told of the stain upon the floor, so easy to be covered, so hard to be got out. For Mr Tulkinghorn's time is over for evermore, lying face downward on the floor, shot through the heart.

CHAPTER 29

Enlightened

I proposed to Ada, that morning that we should go and see Richard. It a little surprised me to find that she hesitated, and was not so radiantly willing as I had expected.

"My dear," said I, "you have not had any difference with Richard since I have been so much away?"

"No, Esther."

"Not heard of him, perhaps?" said I.

"Yes, I have heard of him," said Ada.

Such tears in her eyes, and such love in her face. I could not make my darling out.

We were soon equipped, and went out. It was a sombre day, and drops of chill rain fell at intervals.We had first to find out Symond's Inn. We were going to inquire in a shop, when Ada said she thought it was near Chancery Lane.

"We are not likely to be far out, my love, if we go in that direction," said I. So to Chancery Lane we went; and there, sure enough, we saw it written up. Symond's Inn.

We had next to find out the number upon which Ada said, perhaps that was in the corner there. And it really was.

Then came the question, which of the two next doors? I was going for the one, and Ada was going for the other; and she was right again. So up we went to the second storey, when we came to Richard's name in great white letters on a hearse-like panel.

I should have knocked, but Ada said perhaps we had better turn the handle and go in.

Thus we came to Richard, poring over a table covered with dusty bundles of papers which seemed to me like dusty mirrors reflecting his own mind. Wherever I looked, I saw the ominous words that ran in it, repeated. Jarndyce and Jarndyce.

He received us very affectionately, and we sat down. "If you had come a little earlier," he said, "you would have found Woodcourt here. There never was such a good fellow as Woodcourt is, he is so cheery, so fresh, so sensible, so earnest, so everything that I am not, that the place brightens whenever he comes, and darkens whenever he goes again."

As his look wandered over the papers again, and he passed his two hands over his head, I noticed how sunken and how large his eyes appeared, how dry his lips were, and how his finger-nails were all bitten away.

"Is this a healthy place to live in, Richard, do you think?" said I.

"Why, my dear," answered Richard, with his old gay laugh, "it's well enough for the time. It's near the offices and near the court."

"Perhaps," I hinted, "a change from both – "

" – Might do me good?" said Richard, forcing a laugh as he finished the sentence. "I shouldn't wonder! But either the suit must be ended, Esther, or the suitor. But it shall be the suit, the suit, my dear girl!"

These latter words were addressed to Ada, who was sitting nearest to him. Her face being turned away from me and towards him, I could not see it.

"We are doing very well," pursued Richard. "We are really spinning along. We are giving them no rest. We shall rouse up that nest of sleepers, mark my words!"

He took a few turns up and down, and sunk upon the sofa. "I get," he muttered gloomily, "so tired. It is such weary, weary work!"

Then Ada rose, put off her bonnet, kneeled down beside him with her golden hair falling like sunlight on his head, clasped her two arms round his neck, and turned her face to me.

"Esther, dear," she said very quietly, "I am not going home again."

A light shone in upon me all at once.

"Never any more. I am going to stay with my dear husband. We have been married above two months. Go home without me, my own Esther; I shall never go home any more!" With those words my darling drew his head down on her breast, and held it there.

"Speak to Esther, my dearest," said Richard, breaking the silence presently. "Tell her how it was."

I met her before she could come to me, and folded her in my arms. We neither of us spoke; but with her cheek against my own, I wanted to hear nothing. "My pet," said I. "My love. My poor, poor girl!" I pitied her so much. I was very fond of Richard, but the impulse that I had upon me was to pity her so much.

"All I had was Richard's," Ada said; "and Richard would not take it, Esther, and what could I do but be his wife when I loved him dearly!"

"So we went out one morning, and were married," said Richard.

And Ada took her wedding-ring from her bosom, and kissed it, and put it on.

Thus the time went on, until it became necessary for me to think of returning. When that time arrived it was the worst of all, for then my darling completely broke down.

So I said (in a merry, bustling manner) that unless they gave me some encouragement to come back, I was not sure that I could take that liberty; upon which my dear girl looked up, faintly smiling through her tears, and I folded her lovely face between my hands, and gave it one last kiss, and laughed, and ran away.

And when I got downstairs, O, how I cried! It almost seemed to me that I had lost my Ada for ever. I was so lonely, and so blank without her, and it was so desolate to be going home with no hope of seeing her there, that I could get no comfort for a little while, as I walked up and down in a dim corner sobbing and crying.

I came to myself by-and-by, after a little scolding, and took a coach home.

My guardian was standing thoughtfully by the dark window. When I went in, his face cleared and he came to his seat; but he caught the light upon my face, as I took mine.

"Little woman," said he, "You have been crying."

"Why, yes, guardian," said I, "I am afraid I have been, a little. Ada has been in such distress, and is so very sorry, guardian."

I put my arm on the back of his chair; and I saw in his glance that my words, and my look at her empty place, had prepared him.

"Is she married, my dear?"

I told him all about it, and how her first entreaties had referred to his forgiveness.

"She has no need of it," said he. "Heaven bless her, and her husband!" But just as my first impulse had been to pity her, so was his. "Poor girl, poor girl! Poor Rick! Poor Ada!"

Neither of us spoke after that; until he said, with a sigh, "Well, well, my dear! Bleak House is thinning fast."

"But its mistress remains, guardian." Though I was timid about saying it, I ventured because of the sorrowful tone in which he had spoken. "She will do all she can to make it happy," said I.

"She will succeed, my love!"

The letter had made no difference between us, except that the seat by his side had come to be mine; it made none now. He turned his old bright fatherly look upon me, laid his hand on my hand in his old way, and said again, "She will succeed, my dear. Nevertheless, Bleak House is thinning fast, little woman!"

I was sorry presently that this was all we said about that. I was rather disappointed. I feared I might not quite have been all I had meant to be, since the letter and the answer.

CHAPTER 30

Obstinacy

But one other day had intervened, when, early in the morning as we were going to breakfast, Mr Woodcourt came in haste with the astounding news that a terrible murder had been committed, for which Mr George had been apprehended and was in custody. When he told us that a large reward was offered by Sir Leicester Dedlock for the murderer's apprehension, I did not in my first consternation understand why; but a few more words explained to me that the murdered person was Sir Leicester's lawyer, and immediately my mother's dread of him rushed into my remembrance.

"Guardian, you don't think it possible that he is justly accused?"

"My dear, I can't think so; this man justly accused of such a crime? I can't believe it. It's not that I don't or I won't. I can't!"

"And I can't," said Mr Woodcourt. "Still, he bore an animosity towards the deceased gentleman. He has openly mentioned it in many places. He is said to have expressed himself violently towards him, and he certainly did about him, to my knowledge. He admits that he was alone, on the scene of the murder, within a few minutes of its commission. I sincerely believe him to be as innocent of any participation in it, as I am; but these are all reasons for suspicion falling upon him."

"True," said my guardian; and he added, turning to me, "it would be doing him a very bad service, my dear, to shut our eyes to the truth. Nevertheless we will stand by him, as he himself stood by the poor creature who is gone." He meant the boy, to whom Mr George had given shelter.

Mr Woodcourt added that he was now upon his way to see the prisoner himself and my guardian said, directly, he would go too. Now, I had that secret interest in what had happened, which was only known to my guardian, I felt as if it were my duty and obligation to go with them.

In an arched room by himself, like a cellar upstairs: with walls so glaringly white, that they made the massive iron window-bars and iron-bound door even more profoundly black than they were: we found the trooper standing in a corner. He had been sitting on a bench there, and had risen when he heard the locks and bolts turn.

When he saw us, he came forward a step with his usual heavy tread, and there stopped and made a slight bow. But as I still advanced, putting out my hand to him, he understood us in a moment.

"This is a load off my mind, I do assure you, miss and gentlemen," said he. "And now I don't so much care how it ends."

"First," said my guardian, "can we do anything for your personal comfort, George?"

"For which, sir?" he inquired, clearing his throat.

"For your personal comfort. Is there anything you want, that would lessen the hardship of this confinement?"

"Well, sir," replied George, after a little cogitation, "I am equally obliged to you; but tobacco being against the rules, I can't say that there is."

"Next, as to your case," observed my guardian.

"Exactly so, sir," returned Mr George, folding his arms upon his breast with perfect self-possession and a little curiosity.

"How does it stand now?"

"Why, sir, it is under remand at present. Bucket gives me to understand that he will probably apply for a series of remands from time to time, until the case is more complete. How it is to be made more complete, I don't myself see, but I dare say Bucket will manage it somehow."

"That is true enough, to a certain extent," returned my guardian. "But my good fellow, even an innocent man must take ordinary precautions to defend himself."

"Certainly, sir. And I have done so. I have stated to the magistrates, 'Gentlemen, I am as innocent of this charge as yourselves; what has been stated against me in the way of facts, is perfectly true; I know no more about it.' I intend to continue stating that, sir. What more can I do? It's the truth."

"But the mere truth won't do," rejoined my guardian. "You must have a lawyer. We must engage a good one for you."

"I ask your pardon, sir," said Mr George, with a step backward. "I am equally obliged. But I must decidedly beg to be excused from anything of that sort."

"You won't have a lawyer?"

"No, sir." Mr George shook his head in the most emphatic manner. "I thank you all the same, sir, but – no lawyer!"

"Why not?"

"I don't take kindly to the breed," said Mr George.

Unfolding his arms, and changing his position, he stood with one massive hand upon the table, and the other on his hip, as complete a picture of a man who was not to be moved from a fixed purpose as ever I saw. It was in vain that we all three talked to him, and endeavoured to persuade him; he listened with that gentleness which went so well with his bluff bearing, but was evidently no more shaken by our representations than his place of confinement was.

"Pray think, once more, Mr George," said I. "Have you no wish, in reference to your case?"

"More grateful, Miss Summerson, you can't find me," he returned.

"But more persuadable we can, I hope," said I.

He heard me respectfully, but without much heeding these words, which I spoke, a little turned from him, already on my way to the door; he was observing my height and figure, which seemed to catch his attention all at once.

"'Tis curious," said he. "And yet I thought so at the time!"

My guardian asked him what he meant.

"Why, sir," he answered, "when my ill-fortune took me to the dead man's staircase on the night of his murder, I saw a shape so like Miss Summerson's go by me in the dark, that I had half a mind to speak to it."

For an instant, I felt such a shudder as I never felt before or since, and hope I shall never feel again.

"It came downstairs as I went up," said the trooper, "and crossed the moonlighted window with a loose black mantle on; I noticed a deep fringe to it. However, it has nothing to do with the present subject, excepting that Miss Summerson looked so like it at the moment, that it came into my head."

I cannot define the feelings that arose in me after this, without daring to ask myself any question and feeling indignantly sure of there being no possible reason for my being afraid.

CHAPTER 31

The Track

Quiet among the undertakers and the equipages, and the calves of so many legs all steeped in grief, Mr Bucket sits concealed in one of the carriages, and at his ease surveys the crowd through the lattice blinds. He has a keen eye for a crowd – as for what not? – and looking here and there, now from this side of the carriage, now from the other, now up at the house windows, now along the people's heads, nothing escapes him. Mr Bucket sits out the procession, in his own easy manner, and glides from the carriage when the opportunity he has settled with himself arrives. He makes for Sir Leicester Dedlock's, which is at present a sort of home to him, where he comes and goes as he likes at all hours.

No knocking or ringing for Mr Bucket. He has caused himself to be provided with a key, and can pass in at his pleasure. As he is crossing the hall, Mercury informs him, "Here's another letter for you, Mr Bucket, come by post," and gives it him.

"Another one, eh?" says Mr Bucket.

Mr Bucket, with much deliberation walks upstairs to the little library. He often sees damaging letters produced in evidence, and for this reason he has very little to do with letters, either as sender or receiver. And yet he has received a round half-dozen, within the last twenty-four hours.

"And this," says Mr Bucket, spreading it out on the table, "is in the same hand, and consists of the same two words."

What two words?

He turns the key in the door, ungirdles his black pocket-book, lays another letter by it, and reads, boldly written in each, *Lady Dedlock*."

"Yes, yes," says Mr Bucket. "But I could have made the money without this anonymous information."

Mr Bucket softly opens the door of communication between that room and the next, and looks in. The library is deserted, and the fire is sinking low. Mr Bucket's eye alights upon a table where letters are usually put as they arrive. Several letters for Sir Leicester are upon it. Mr Bucket draws near, and examines the directions. "No," he says, "there's none in that hand. It's only me as is written to. I can break it to Sir Leicester Dedlock, Baronet, to-morrow."

In his fondness for society, and his adaptability to all grades, Mr Bucket is presently standing before the hall-fire – bright and warm on the early winter night alongside Mercury.

"My Lady's out, ain't she?"

"Out to dinner."

"Goes out pretty well every day, don't she?"

"Yes."

"My Lady a good temper?"

Mercury replies, "As good as you can expect."

"Ah!" says Mr Bucket. "A little spoilt? A little capricious? Lord! What can you anticipate when they're so handsome as that? And we like 'em all the better for it, don't we?"

Come the roll of wheels and a violent ringing at the bell. "Talk of the angels," says Mr Bucket. "Here she is!"

The doors are thrown open, and she passes through the hall. Still very pale, she is dressed in slight mourning, and wears two beautiful bracelets. Noticing him at his distance, she turns an inquiring look.

"Mr Bucket, my Lady."

Mr Bucket makes a leg, and comes forward, passing his familiar demon over the region of his mouth.

"Are you waiting to see Sir Leicester?"

"No, my Lady, I've seen him!"

"Have you anything to say to me?"

"Not just at present, my Lady."

"Have you made any new discoveries?"

"A few, my Lady."

This is merely in passing. She scarcely makes a stop, and sweeps upstairs alone.

"She's a lovely woman, too, she really is," says Mr Bucket. "Don't look quite healthy though."

Is not quite healthy, he is informed. Suffers much from headaches.

Really? That's a pity! Walking, Mr Bucket would recommend for that. Well, she tries walking, Mercury rejoins. Walks sometimes for two hours, when she has them bad. By night, too.

"Walks by night, does she? When it's moonlight, though?"

O yes. When it's moonlight! Of course. O, of course!

"She went out walking, the very night of this business?"

"To be sure she did! I let her into the garden over the way."

"And left her there. Certainly you did. I saw you doing it."

"I didn't see you," says Mercury.

"I was rather in a hurry," returns Mr Bucket, "chanced to be passing at the time. Let's see. What time might it be? It wasn't ten."

"Half-past nine."

"You're right. So it was. And if I don't deceive myself, my Lady was muffled in a loose black mantle, with a deep fringe to it?"

"Of course she was."

Of course she was. Mr Bucket must return to a little work he has to get on with upstairs.

CHAPTER 32

Springing a Mine

Refreshed by sleep, Mr Bucket rises betimes in the morning, and prepares for a field-day. Smartened up by the aid of a clean shirt and a wet hair-brush he lubricates such thin locks as remain to him after his life of severe study, Mr Bucket lays in a breakfast of two mutton chops as a foundation to work upon, together with tea, eggs, toast, and marmalade on a corresponding scale. Having much enjoyed these strengthening matters, he confidently instructs Mercury "just to mention quietly to Sir Leicester Dedlock, Baronet, that whenever he's ready for me, I'm ready for him."

A gracious message being returned, that Sir Leicester will join Mr Bucket in the library within ten minutes, Mr Bucket repairs to that apartment; and stands before the fire, with his finger on his chin, looking at the blazing coals.

Not in the least anxious or disturbed is Mr Bucket, when Sir Leicester appears; but he eyes the baronet aside as he comes slowly to his easy chair, with that observant gravity of yesterday.

"I am sorry to have kept you waiting, officer, but I am rather later than my usual hour this morning. I am not well. The agitation and the indignation from which I have recently suffered, have been too much for me. I am subject to – gout;" Sir Leicester was going to say indisposition, and would have said it to anybody else, but Mr Bucket palpably knows all about it; "and recent circumstances have brought it on."

As he takes his seat with some difficulty, and with an air of pain, Mr Bucket draws a little nearer, standing with one of his large hands on the library-table.

"I am not aware, officer," Sir Leicester observes, raising his eyes to his face, "whether you wish us to be alone; but that is entirely as you please."

"Why, Sir Leicester Dedlock, Baronet," returns Mr Bucket, "we can't be too private, just at present."

"That is enough."

"So much so, Sir Leicester Dedlock, Baronet," Mr Bucket resumes, "that I was on the point of asking your permission to turn the key in the door."

"By all means."

Mr Bucket skilfully and softly takes that precaution; stooping on his knee for a moment, from mere force of habit, so to adjust the key in the lock as that no one shall peep in from the outer-side.

"Sir Leicester Dedlock, Baronet, I mentioned yesterday evening, that I wanted but a very little to complete this case. I have now completed it, and collected proof against the person who did this crime."

"Against the soldier?"

"No, Sir Leicester Dedlock; not the soldier."

Sir Leicester looks astounded, and inquires, "Is the man in custody?"

Mr Bucket tells him, after a pause, "It was a woman."

Sir Leicester leans back in his chair, and breathlessly ejaculates, "Good Heaven!"

"Now, Sir Leicester Dedlock, Baronet," Mr Bucket begins, standing over him with one hand spread out on the library-table, and the forefinger of the other in impressive use, "it's my duty to prepare you for a train of circumstances that may, and I go so far as to say that will, give you a shock. But Sir Leicester Dedlock, Baronet, you are a gentleman; and a gentleman can bear a shock, when it must come, boldly and steadily. A gentleman can make up his mind to stand up against almost any blow."

Sir Leicester, leaning back in his chair, and grasping the elbows, sits looking at him with a stony face.

"Now, Sir Leicester Dedlock," proceeds Mr Bucket, "thus preparing you, let me beg of you not to trouble your mind, for a moment, as to anything having come to my knowledge. I know so much about so many characters, high and low, that a piece of information more or less, don't signify a straw. I don't suppose there's a move on the board that would surprise me. Therefore what I say to you, Sir Leicester Dedlock, Baronet, is, don't you go and let yourself be put out of the way, because of my knowing anything of your family affairs."

"I thank you for your preparation," returns Sir Leicester, after a silence, without moving hand, foot, or feature; "which I hope is not necessary, though I give it credit for being well intended. Be so good as to go on also, to take a seat, if you have no objection."

None at all. Mr Bucket brings a chair.

"Now, Sir Leicester Dedlock, Baronet, with this short preface, I come to the point. Lady Dedlock – "

Sir Leicester raises himself in his seat, and stares at him fiercely. Mr Bucket brings the finger into play as an emollient.

"Lady Dedlock, you see, she's universally admired. That's what her Ladyship is; she's universally admired," says Mr Bucket.

"I would greatly prefer, officer," Sir Leicester returns, stiffly, "my Lady's name being entirely omitted from this discussion."

"So would I, Sir Leicester Dedlock, Baronet, but – it's impossible."

"Impossible?"

Mr Bucket shakes his relentless head.

"Sir Leicester Dedlock, Baronet, it's altogether impossible. What I have got to say, is about her Ladyship. She is the pivot it all turns on."

"Officer," retorts Sir Leicester, with a fiery eye, and a quivering lip, "you know your duty. Do your duty; but be careful not to overstep it. I would not suffer it. I would not endure it. My Lady's name is not a name for common persons to trifle with!"

"Sir Leicester Dedlock, Baronet, I say what I must say; and no more."

"I hope it may prove so. Very well. Go on. Go on, sir!"

Glancing at the angry eyes which now avoid him, and at the angry figure trembling from head to foot, yet striving to be still, Mr Bucket feels his way with his forefinger, and in a low voice proceeds.

"Sir Leicester Dedlock, Baronet, it becomes my duty to tell you that the deceased Mr Tulkinghorn long entertained mistrusts and suspicions of Lady Dedlock."

"If he had dared to breathe them to me, sir – which he never did – I would have killed him myself!" exclaims Sir Leicester, striking his hand upon the table. But, in the very heat and fury of the act, he stops, fixed by the knowing eyes of Mr Bucket, whose forefinger is slowly going, and who, with mingled confidence and patience, shakes his head.

"Sir Leicester Dedlock, the deceased Mr Tulkinghorn was deep and close; and what he fully had in his mind in the very beginning, I can't quite take upon myself to say. But I know from his lips, that he long ago suspected Lady Dedlock of having discovered, through the sight of some handwriting – in this very house, and when you yourself, Sir Leicester Dedlock, were present – the existence, in great poverty, of a certain person, who had been her lover before you courted her, and who ought to have been her husband;" Mr Bucket stops, and deliberately repeats, "ought to have been her husband; not a doubt about it. I know from his

115

lips, that when that person soon afterwards died, he suspected Lady Dedlock of visiting his wretched lodging, and his wretched grave, alone and in secret. I know from my own inquiries, and through my eyes and ears, that Lady Dedlock did make such visit, in the dress of her own maid; for the deceased Mr Tulkinghorn employed me to reckon up her Ladyship – if you'll excuse my making use of the term we commonly employ – and I reckoned her up, so far, completely. I confronted the maid, in the chambers in Lincoln's Inn Fields, with a witness who had been Lady Dedlock's guide; and there couldn't be the shadow of a doubt that she had worn the young woman's dress, unknown to her. It's my belief that the deceased Mr Tulkinghorn followed up these inquiries to the hour of his death; and that he and Lady Dedlock even had bad blood between them upon the matter, that very night. Now, only you put that to Lady Dedlock, Sir Leicester Dedlock, Baronet; and ask her Ladyship whether, even after he had left here, she didn't go down to his chambers with the intention of saying something further to him, dressed in a loose black mantle with a deep fringe to it."

Sir Leicester sits like a statue, gazing at the cruel finger that is probing the life-blood of his heart.

"You put that to her Ladyship, Sir Leicester Dedlock, Baronet, from me, Inspector Bucket of the Detective. And if her Ladyship makes any difficulty about admitting of it, you tell her that it's no use; that Inspector Bucket knows it, and knows that she passed the soldier, as you called him, and knows that she knows she passed him, on the staircase. Now, Sir Leicester Dedlock, Baronet, why do I relate all this?"

Sir Leicester, who has covered his face with his hands, uttering a single groan, requests him to pause for a moment. By and by, he takes his hands away; and so preserves his dignity and outward calmness, though there is no more colour in his face than in his white hair. Something frozen and fixed is upon his manner, over and above its usual shell of haughtiness; and Mr Bucket soon detects an unusual slowness in his speech, with now and then a curious trouble in beginning, which occasions him to utter inarticulate sounds. With such sounds, he now breaks silence; soon, however, controlling himself to say, that he does not comprehend why a gentleman so faithful and zealous as the late Mr Tulkinghorn should have communicated to him nothing of this painful, this distressing, this overwhelming intelligence.

116

"Again, Sir Leicester Dedlock, Baronet," returns Mr Bucket, "put it to her Ladyship to clear that up. Put it to her Ladyship, if you think it right, from Inspector Bucket of the Detective. You'll find, or I'm much mistaken, that the deceased Mr Tulkinghorn had the intention of communicating the whole to you, as soon as he considered it ripe; and further, that he had given her Ladyship so to understand. Why, he might have been going to reveal it the very morning when I examined the body!"

"True," Sir Leicester, avoiding, with some trouble, those obtrusive sounds, says, "True."

At this juncture, a considerable noise of voices is heard in the hall. Mr Bucket, after listening, goes to the library-door, softly unlocks and opens it, and listens again.

Then he draws in his head, and whispers, hurriedly, but composedly, "Sir Leicester Dedlock, Baronet, this unfortunate family affair has taken air, as I expected it might; the deceased Mr Tulkinghorn being cut down so sudden. The chance to hush it, is to let in these people now in a wrangle with your footmen. Would you mind sitting quiet – on the family account – while I reckon 'em up? And would you just throw in a nod, when I seem to ask you for it?"

Sir Leicester indistinctly answers, "Officer. The best you can, the best you can!" and Mr Bucket, with a nod and a sagacious crook of the forefinger, slips down into the hall, where the voices quickly die away. He is not long in returning, a few paces ahead of Mercury, and a brother deity, who bear between them a chair in which is an incapable old man. Directing the pitching of the chair, in an affable and easy manner, Mr Bucket dismisses the Mercuries, and locks the door again. Sir Leicester looks on at this invasion of the sacred precincts with an icy stare.

"Now, you wanted to see Sir Leicester Dedlock, Baronet. Well! You do see him; and, mind you, it ain't every one as is admitted to that honour. Your name, old gentleman, is Smallweed; that's what your name is; I know it well."

"Well, and you never heard any harm of it!" cries Mr Smallweed in a shrill loud voice.

"You ain't in the habit of conversing with a deaf person, are you?"

"Yes," snarls Mr Smallweed, "my wife's deaf."

"That accounts for your pitching your voice so high. But as she ain't

117

here, just pitch it an octave or two lower, will you, and I'll not only be obliged to you, but it'll do you more credit," says Mr Bucket. "Now, what's up?"

"Do you mean what business have I come upon?" Mr Smallweed asks, a little dashed by the suddenness of this turn.

"Ah! You know what I mean. Let us hear what it's all about in presence of Sir Leicester Dedlock, Baronet. Come."

"I was the client and friend of Mr Tulkinghorn," pipes Grandfather Smallweed then; "I did business with him. I was useful to him, and he was useful to me. Krook, dead and gone, was my brother-in-law. I come into Krook's property. I examined all his papers and all his effects. They was all dug out under my eyes. He hid all manner of things away, everywheres. Mr Tulkinghorn wanted 'em and got 'em, but I looked 'em over first. I'm a man of business, and I took a squint at 'em. They was letters from the lodger's sweetheart, and she signed Honoria. Dear me, that's not a common name, Honoria, is it? There's no lady in this house that signs Honoria, is there? O no, I don't think so! O no, I don't think so! And not in the same hand, perhaps? O no, I don't think so!"

Here Mr Smallweed, seized with a fit of coughing in the midst of his triumph, breaks off to ejaculate, "O dear me! O Lord! I'm shaken all to pieces!"

"Now, when you're ready," says Mr Bucket, after awaiting his recovery, "to come to anything that concerns Sir Leicester Dedlock, Baronet, here the gentleman sits, you know."

"Haven't I come to it, Mr Bucket?" cries Grandfather Smallweed. "Isn't the gentleman concerned yet? Not with Captain Hawdon and his ever affectionate Honoria, and their child into the bargain? Come, then, I want to know where those letters are. That concerns me, if it don't concern Sir Leicester Dedlock. I will know where they are. I won't have 'em disappear so quietly. I handed 'em over to my friend and solicitor, Mr Tulkinghorn; not to anybody else."

"Why, he paid you for them, you know, and handsome too," says Mr Bucket.

"I don't care for that. I want to know who's got 'em. And I tell you what we want – what we all want, Mr Bucket. We want more painstaking and search-making into this murder. We know where the interest and the motive was, and you have not done enough. If George the vagabond dragoon had any hand in it, he was only an accomplice, and was set on. You know what I mean as well as any man."

"Now I tell you what," says Mr Bucket, instantaneously altering his manner, coming close to him, "I am damned if I am a going to have my case spoilt, or interfered with, or anticipated by so much as half a second of time, by any human being in creation. *You* want more painstaking and search-making? *You* do? Do you see this hand, and do you think that I don't know the right time to stretch it out, and put it on the arm that fired that shot?"

Such is the dread power of the man, and so terribly evident it is that he makes no idle boast, that Mr Smallweed begins to apologise.

Mr Bucket, dismissing his sudden anger, checks him.

"The advice I give you is, don't you trouble your head about the murder. That's my affair. You keep half an eye on the newspapers; and I shouldn't wonder if you was to read something about it before long, if you look sharp. I know my business, and that's all I've got to say to you on that subject. Now about those letters. You want to know who's got 'em. I don't mind telling you. I have got 'em. Is that the packet?"

Mr Smallweed looks, with greedy eyes, at the little bundle Mr Bucket produces from a mysterious part of his coat, and identifies it as the same.

"What have you got to say next?" asks Mr Bucket. "Now, don't open your mouth too wide, because you don't look handsome when you do it."

"I want five hundred pound."

"No, you don't; you mean fifty," says Mr Bucket, humorously.

It appears, however, that Mr Smallweed means five hundred.

"That is, I am deputed by Sir Leicester Dedlock, Baronet, to consider (without admitting or promising anything) this bit of business," says Mr Bucket; Sir Leicester mechanically bows his head; "and you ask me to consider a proposal of five hundred pounds. Why, it's an unreasonable proposal! Two fifty would be bad enough, but better than that. Hadn't you better say two fifty?"

Mr Smallweed is quite clear that he had better not.

"Very good," says Mr Bucket. "Now I understand you, you know; and, being deputed by Sir Leicester Dedlock, Baronet, to look into this little matter," again Sir Leicester mechanically bows in confirmation of the statement, "can give it my fair and full attention. Now I won't allude to conspiring to extort money or anything of that sort, because we are men

119

of the world here, and our object is to make things pleasant. But I tell you what I do wonder at; I am surprised that you should think of making a noise below in the hall. It was so opposed to your interests. That's what I look at."

"I wanted to get in," pleads Mr Smallweed.

"Why, of course you wanted to get in," Mr Bucket asserts with cheerfulness; "but for a old gentleman at your time of life – what I call truly venerable, mind you – with his wits sharpened, as I have no doubt they are, by the loss of the use of his limbs, your temper got the better of you; that's where you lost ground," says Mr Bucket, in an argumentative and friendly way.

"I only said I wouldn't go, without one of the servants came up to Sir Leicester Dedlock," returns Mr Smallweed.

"That's it! That's where your temper got the better of you. Now, you keep it under another time, and you'll make money by it. Shall I ring for them to carry you down?"

"When am I to hear more of this?" Mr Smallweed sternly demands.

"I shall have the pleasure of giving you a call to-morrow or next day – not forgetting your proposal of two fifty."

"Five hundred!" exclaims Mr Smallweed.

"All right! Nominally five hundred;" Mr Bucket has his hand on the bell-rope; "shall I wish you good day for the present, on the part of myself and the gentleman of the house?" he asks in an insinuating tone.

Not having the hardihood to object to his doing so, he does it, and the party retire as they came up. Mr Bucket follows them to the door; and returning, says with an air of serious business:

"Sir Leicester Dedlock, Baronet, it's for you to consider whether or not to buy this up. I should recommend, on the whole, it's being bought up myself; and I think it may be bought pretty cheap. Now, with regard to the party to be apprehended."

Sir Leicester seems to wake, though his eyes have been wide open; and he looks intently at Mr Bucket, as Mr Bucket refers to his watch.

"The party to be apprehended is now in this house," proceeds Mr Bucket, putting up his watch with a steady hand, and with rising spirits, "and I'm about to take her into custody in your presence. Sir Leicester Dedlock, Baronet, don't you say a word, nor yet stir. There'll be no noise, and no disturbance at all. I'll come back in the course of the evening, if agreeable to you, and endeavour to meet your wishes respecting this unfortunate family matter, and the nobbiest way of keeping it quiet. Now, Sir Leicester Dedlock, Baronet, don't you be nervous on account of the apprehension at present coming off. You shall see the whole case clear, from first to last."

Mr Bucket rings, goes to the door, briefly whispers to Mercury, shuts the door, and stands behind it with his arms folded. After a suspense of a minute or two, the door slowly opens, and a French woman enters. Mademoiselle Hortense.

The moment she is in the room, Mr Bucket claps the door to, and puts his back against it. The suddenness of the noise occasions her to turn; and then, for the first time, she sees Sir Leicester Dedlock in his chair.

"I ask your pardon," she mutters hurriedly. "They tell me there was no one here."

Her step towards the door brings her front to front with Mr Bucket. Suddenly a spasm shoots across her face, and she turns deadly pale.

"This is my lodger, Sir Leicester Dedlock," says Mr Bucket, nodding at her. "This foreign young woman has been my lodger for some weeks back."

"What do Sir Leicester care for that, you think, my angel?" returns Mademoiselle, in a jocular strain.

"Why, my angel," returns Mr Bucket, "we shall see."

Mademoiselle Hortense eyes him with a scowl upon her tight face, which gradually changes into a smile of scorn. "You are very mysterieuse. Are you drunk?"

"Tolerable sober, my angel," returns Mr Bucket.

"They tell me downstairs that your wife is here. I come here, and your wife is not here. What is the intention of this fool's play, say then?" Mademoiselle demands, with her arms composedly crossed, but with something in her dark cheek beating like a clock.

Mr Bucket merely shakes the finger at her.

"Now, Mademoiselle," says Mr Bucket, in a cool determined way, "you go and sit down upon that sofy."

"I will not sit down upon nothing," she replies, with a shower of nods.

"Now, Mademoiselle," repeats Mr Bucket, making no demonstration, except with the finger; "you sit down upon that sofy."

"Why?"

"Because I take you into custody on a charge of murder, and you don't need to be told it. Now, I want to be polite to one of your sex and a foreigner, if I can. If I can't, I must be rough; and there's rougher ones outside. What I am to be, depends on you. So I recommend you, as a friend, afore another half a blessed moment has passed over your head, to go and sit down upon that sofy."

Mademoiselle complies, saying in a concentrated voice, while that something in her cheek beats fast and hard, "You are a Devil."

"Now, you see," Mr Bucket proceeds approvingly, "you're comfortable, and conducting yourself as I should expect a foreign young woman of your sense to do. So I'll give you a piece of advice, and it's this, Don't you talk too much. You're not expected to say anything here, and you can't keep too quiet a tongue in your head. In short, the less you Parlay, the better, you know." Mr Bucket is very complacent over this French explanation.

Mademoiselle, with that tigerish expansion of the mouth, and her black eyes darting fire upon him, sits upright on the sofa in a rigid state, with her hands clenched – and her feet too, one might suppose – muttering, "O, you Bucket, you are a Devil!"

"Now, Sir Leicester Dedlock, Baronet," says Mr Bucket, and from this time forth the finger never rests, "this young woman, my lodger, was her Ladyship's maid at the time I have mentioned to you; and this young woman, besides being extraordinary vehement and passionate against her Ladyship after being discharged – "

"Lie!" cries Mademoiselle. "I discharge myself."

"Now, why don't you take my advice?" returns Mr Bucket, in an impressive, almost imploring tone. "I'm surprised at the indiscreetness you commit. You'll say something that'll be used against you, you know. You're sure to come to it. Never you mind what I say, till it's given in evidence. It is not addressed to you."

"Discharge, too," cries Mademoiselle, furiously, "by her Ladyship! Eh, my faith, a pretty Ladyship! Why, I r-r-r-ruin my character by remaining with a Ladyship so infame!"

"Upon my soul I wonder at you!" Mr Bucket remonstrates. "I thought the French were a polite nation, I did, really. Yet to hear a female going on like that, before Sir Leicester Dedlock, Baronet!"

"He is a poor abused!" cries Mademoiselle. "I spit upon his house, upon his name, upon his imbecility," all of which she makes the carpet represent. "Oh, that he is a great man! O yes, superb! O Heaven! Bah!"

"Well, Sir Leicester Dedlock," proceeds Mr Bucket, "this intemperate foreigner also angrily took it into her head that she had established a claim upon Mr Tulkinghorn, deceased, by attending on the occasion I told you of, at his chambers; though she was liberally paid for her time and trouble."

"Lie!" cries Mademoiselle. "I ref-use his money all togezzer."

"If you will Parlay, you know," says Mr Bucket, "you must take the consequences. Now, whether she became my lodger, Sir Leicester Dedlock, with any deliberate intention then of doing this deed and blinding me, I give no opinion on; but she lived in my house at the time that she was hovering about the chambers of the deceased Mr Tulkinghorn with a view to a wrangle."

"Lie!" cries Mademoiselle. "All lie!"

"The murder was committed, Sir Leicester Dedlock, Baronet, and you know under what circumstances. Now, I beg of you to follow me close with your attention for a minute or two. I was sent for, and the case was entrusted to me. I examined the place, and the body, and the papers, and everything. From information I received (from a clerk in the same house) I took George into custody, as having been seen hanging about there, on the night, and at very nigh the time, of the murder; also, as having been overheard in high words with the deceased on former occasions – even threatening him, as the witness made out. If you ask me, Sir Leicester Dedlock, whether from the first I believed George to be the murderer, I tell you candidly No; but he might be, notwithstanding; and there was enough against him to make it my duty to take him, and get him kept under remand. Now, observe!"

As Mr Bucket bends forward in some excitement – for him – and inaugurates what he is going to say with one ghostly beat of his forefinger in the air, Mademoiselle Hortense fixes her black eyes upon him with a dark frown, and sets her dry lips closely and firmly together.

"I went home, Sir Leicester Dedlock, Baronet, at night, and found this young woman having supper with my wife, Mrs Bucket. She had made a mighty show of being fond of Mrs Bucket from her first offering herself as our lodger, but that night she made more than ever – in fact, overdid it. Likewise she overdid her respect, and all that, for the lamented memory

123

of the deceased Mr Tulkinghorn. By the living Lord it flashed upon me, as I sat opposite to her at the table and saw her with a knife in her hand, that she had done it!"

Mademoiselle is hardly audible, in straining through her teeth and lips the words, "You are a Devil."

"Now where," pursues Mr Bucket, "had she been on the night of the murder? She had been to the theayter. (She really was there, I have since found, both before the deed and after it.) I knew I had an artful customer to deal with, and that proof would be very difficult; and I laid a trap for her – such a trap as I never laid yet, and such a venture as I never made yet. I worked it out in my mind while I was talking to her at supper. When I went upstairs to bed, our house being small and this young woman's ears sharp, I stuffed the sheet into Mrs Bucket's mouth that she shouldn't say a word of surprise, and told her all about it. – My dear, don't you give your mind to that again, or I shall link your feet together at the ankles." Mr Bucket, breaking off, has made a noiseless descent upon Mademoiselle, and laid his heavy hand upon her shoulder.

"What is the matter with you now?" she asks him.

"Don't you think any more," returns Mr Bucket, with admonitory finger, "of throwing yourself out of window. Come! Just take my arm. You needn't get up; I'll sit down by you. Now take my arm, will you? I'm a married man, you know; you're acquainted with my wife. Just take my arm."

Vainly endeavouring to moisten those dry lips, with a painful sound, she struggles with herself, and complies.

"Now we're all right again. Sir Leicester Dedlock, Baronet, this case could never have been the case it is, but for Mrs Bucket, who is a woman in fifty thousand – in a hundred and fifty thousand! My whispered words to Mrs Bucket, when she had the sheet in her mouth, were, 'My dear, can you throw her off continually with natural accounts of my suspicions against George, and this, and that, and t'other? Can you do without rest, and keep watch upon her, night and day? Can you undertake to say, she shall do nothing without my knowledge, she shall be my prisoner without suspecting it, she shall no more escape from me than from death, and her life shall be my life, and her soul my soul, till I have got her, if she did this murder?' Mrs Bucket says to me, as well as she could speak, on account of the sheet, 'Bucket, I can!' And she has acted up to it glorious!"

"Lies!" Mademoiselle interposes. "All lies, my friend!"

"Sir Leicester Dedlock, Baronet, how did my calculations come out under these circumstances? When I calculated that this impetuous young woman would overdo it in new directions, was I wrong or right? I was right. What does she try to do? Don't let it give you a turn? To throw the murder on her Ladyship."

Sir Leicester rises from his chair, and staggers down again.

"And she got encouragement in it from hearing that I was always here, which was done a' purpose. Now, open that pocket-book of mine, Sir Leicester Dedlock, if I may take the liberty of throwing it towards you, and look at the letters sent to me, each with the two words, *Lady Dedlock*, in it. Open the one directed to yourself, which I stopped this very morning, and read the three words, *Lady Dedlock Murderess*, in it. These letters have been falling about like a shower of lady-birds. What do you say now to Mrs Bucket, from her spy-place, having seen them all written by this young woman? What do you say to Mrs Bucket having, within this half-hour, secured the corresponding ink and paper, fellow half-sheets and what not? What do you say to Mrs Bucket having watched the posting of 'em every one by this young woman, Sir Leicester Dedlock, Baronet?" Mr Bucket asks, triumphant in his admiration of his lady's genius.

"There is no doubt that her Ladyship was on the spot at the eventful period," says Mr Bucket; "and my foreign friend here saw her, I believe, from the upper part of the staircase. Her Ladyship and George and my foreign friend were all pretty close on one another's heels. But that don't signify any more, so I'll not go into it. I found the wadding of the pistol with which the deceased Mr Tulkinghorn was shot. It was a bit of the printed description of your house at Chesney Wold. Not much in that, you'll say, Sir Leicester Dedlock, Baronet. No. But when my foreign friend here is so thoroughly off her guard as to think it a safe time to tear up the rest of that leaf, and when Mrs Bucket puts the pieces together and finds the wadding wanting, it begins to look like Queer Street."

"These are very long lies," Mademoiselle interposes. "You prose great deal. Is it that you have almost all finished, or are you speaking always?"

"Sir Leicester Dedlock, Baronet," proceeds Mr Bucket, "the last point in the case which I am now going to mention, shews the necessity of patience in our business, and never doing a thing in a hurry. Last night, when her Ladyship, as is so universally admired I am sure, come home, looking – why, Lord! a man might almost say like Venus rising from the ocean, it was so unpleasant and inconsistent to think of her being charged with a murder of which she was innocent, that I felt quite to want to put an end to the job. What should I have lost? Sir Leicester Dedlock, Baronet, I should have lost the weapon. My prisoner here proposed to Mrs Bucket, after the departure of the funeral, that they should go and take tea at a very decent house of entertainment. Now, near that house of entertainment there's a piece of water. At tea, my prisoner got up to fetch her pocket-handkerchief from the room where the bonnets was; she was rather a long time gone, and came back a little out of wind. I had the piece of water dragged by moonlight, in presence of a couple of our men, and the pocket-pistol was brought up before it had been there half-a-dozen hours. Now, my dear, put your arm a little further through mine, and hold it steady, and I sha'n't hurt you!"

In a trice Mr Bucket snaps a handcuff on her wrist. "That's one," says Mr Bucket. "Now the other, darling. Two, and all told!"

He rises; she rises too. "Where," she asks him, darkening her large eyes until their drooping lids almost conceal them – and yet they stare, "where is your false, your treacherous, and cursed wife?"

"She's gone forrard to the Police Office," returns Mr Bucket. "You'll see her there, my dear."

"I would like to kiss her!" exclaims Mademoiselle Hortense, panting tigress-like.

"You'd bite her, I suspect," says Mr Bucket.

"I would!" making her eyes very large. "I would love to tear her, limb from limb."

"Bless you, darling," says Mr Bucket, with the greatest composure; "I'm fully prepared to hear that. Your sex have such a surprising animosity against one another, when you do differ. You don't mind me half so much, do you?"

"No. Though you are a Devil still."

"Angel and devil by turns, eh?" cries Mr Bucket. "But I am in my regular employment, you must consider. Let me put your shawl tidy. I've been lady's maid to a good many before now. Anything wanting to the bonnet? There's a cab at the door."

Mademoiselle Hortense, casting an indignant eye at the glass, shakes

126

herself perfectly neat in one shake, and looks, to do her justice, uncommonly genteel.

"Listen then, my angel," says she, after several sarcastic nods. "You are very spiritual. But can you res-tore him back to life?"

Mr Bucket answers, "Not exactly."

"That is droll. Listen yet one time. You are very spiritual. Can you make a honourable lady of Her?"

"Don't be so malicious," says Mr Bucket.

"Or a haughty gentleman of Him?" cries Mademoiselle, referring to Sir Leicester with ineffable disdain. "Eh! O then regard him! The poor infant! Ha! Ha! Ha!"

"Come, come, why this is worse Parlaying than the other," says Mr Bucket. "Come along!"

"You cannot do these things? Then you can do as you please with me. It is but the death, it is all the same. Let us go, my angel. Adieu you old man, grey. I pity you, and I des-pise you!"

With these last words, she snaps her teeth together, as if her mouth closed with a spring. It is impossible to describe how Mr Bucket gets her out, but he accomplishes that feat in a manner so peculiar to himself; enfolding and pervading her like a cloud, and hovering away with her as if she were the object of his affections.

Sir Leicester, left alone, remains in the same attitude as though he were still listening, and his attention were still occupied. At length he gazes round the empty room, and finding it deserted, rises unsteadily to his feet, pushes back his chair, and walks a few steps, supporting himself by the table. Then he stops; and, with more of those inarticulate sounds, lifts up his eyes and seems to stare at something.

Heaven knows what he sees. The green, green woods of Chesney Wold, the noble house, the pictures of his forefathers, strangers defacing them, officers of police coarsely handling his most precious heir-looms, thousands of fingers pointing at him, thousands of faces sneering at him. But if such shadows flit before him to his bewilderment, there is one other shadow which he can name with something like distinctness even yet, and to which alone he addresses his tearing of his white, hair and his extended arms.

It is she, for years a main fibre of the root of his dignity and pride. It is she whom he has loved, admired, honoured, and set up for the world to respect. It is she, who, at the core of all the constrained formalities and conventionalities of his life, has been a stock of living tenderness and love. He sees her, almost to the exclusion of himself; and cannot bear to look upon her cast down from the high place she has graced so well.

And, even to the point of his sinking on the ground, oblivious of his suffering, he can yet pronounce her name with something like distinctness in the midst of those intrusive sounds, and in a tone of mourning and compassion rather than reproach.

CHAPTER 33

Flight

Inspector Bucket of the Detective has not yet struck his great blow, as just now chronicled, but is yet refreshing himself with sleep preparatory to his field-day, when through the night and along the freezing wintry roads, a chaise and pair comes out of Lincolnshire, making its way towards London.

Mrs Rouncewell, so many years housekeeper at Chesney Wold, sits within the chaise! The old lady's hands stray about her as of yore, while she recalls, all in a tremble, what a likely lad, what a fine lad, what a gay good-humoured clever lad he was; how they all took to him, down at Chesney Wold; how Sir Leicester took to him when he was a young gentleman; how the dogs took to him; how even the people who had been angry with him, forgave him the moment he was gone, poor boy. And now to see him after all, and in a prison too! And the broad stomacher heaves, and the quaint upright old-fashioned figure bends under its load of affectionate distress.

He shall have, vows Mrs Rouncewell, "all the help that can be got for him in the world. I will spend all I have, and thankfully, to procure it. Sir Leicester will do his best, the whole family will do their best. I – I know something and will make my own appeal, as his mother parted from him all these years, and finding him in a jail at last."

And Mrs Rouncewell murmurs distractedly, "My Lady, my Lady, my Lady!" over and over again.

The frosty night wears away, and the dawn breaks, and the post-chaise comes rolling on through the early mist, like the ghost of a chaise departed. And when she sets out for the prison where the trooper is confined, the old lady has managed to draw about her, with her lavender-coloured dress, much of the staid calmness which is its usual accompaniment. A wonderfully grave, precise, and handsome piece of old china she looks; though her heart beats fast, and her stomacher is ruffled, more than even the remembrance of this way-ward son has ruffled it these many years.

Approaching the cell, she finds the door opening and a warder in the act of coming out. The old girl promptly makes a sign of entreaty to him to say nothing; assenting with a nod, he suffers her to enter as he shuts the door.

So George, who is writing at his table, supposing himself to be alone, does not raise his eyes, but remains absorbed.

Not a rustle of the housekeeper's dress, not a gesture, not a word, betrays her. She stands looking at him as he writes on, all unconscious, and only her fluttering hands give utterance to her emotions.

"George Rouncewell! O, my dear child, turn and look at me!"

The trooper starts up, clasps his mother round the neck, and falls down on his knees before her. Whether in a late repentance, whether in the first association that comes back upon him, he puts his hands together as a child does when it says its prayers, and raising them towards her breast, bows down his head, and cries.

"My George, my dearest son! Always my favourite, and my favourite still, where have you been these cruel years and years? Grown such a man too, grown such a fine strong man. Grown so like what I knew he must be, if it pleased God he was alive!"

She can ask, and he can answer, nothing connected for a time.

"Mother," says the trooper, when they are more composed; "forgive me first of all, for I know my need of it."

Forgive him! She does it with all her heart and soul. She always has done it. She tells him how she has had it written in her will, these many years, that he was her beloved son George. She has never believed any ill of him, never. If she had died without this happiness – and she is an old woman now, and can't look to live very long – she would have blessed him with her last breath, as her beloved son George.

"Mother, I have been an undutiful trouble to you, and I have my reward; but of late years I have had a kind of glimmering of a purpose in me, too. When I left home I didn't care much, mother – I am afraid not a great deal – for leaving; and went away and 'listed, harum-scarum, making believe to think that I cared for nobody, no not I, and that nobody cared for me."

"I don't find any fault, child – but not to ease my mind, George? Not a word to your loving mother, who was growing older too?"

This almost overturns the trooper afresh, but he sets himself up with a great, rough sounding clearance of his throat.

"Heaven forgive me, mother, but I thought there would be small consolation then in hearing anything about me. There were you, respected and esteemed. There was my brother, as I read in chance north-country papers now and then, rising to be prosperous and famous. There was I, a dragoon, roving, unsettled, not self-made like him, but self-unmade – all my earlier advantages thrown away, all my little learning unlearnt, nothing picked up but what unfitted me for most things that I could think of. What business had I to make myself known? After letting all that time go by me, what good could come of it?"

The old lady sorrowfully shakes her head; and taking one of his powerful hands, lays it lovingly upon her shoulder. And the old lady impresses upon her son George, her own dear recovered boy, her joy and pride, the light of her eyes, the happy close of her life, and every fond name she can think of, that he must be governed by the best advice obtainable by money and influence, that he must yield up his case to the greatest lawyers that can be got; that he must act, in this serious plight, as he shall be advised to act; and must not be self-willed, however right, but must promise to think only of his poor old mother's anxiety and suffering until he is released, or he will break her heart.

"Mother, 'tis little enough to consent to," returns the trooper, stopping her with a kiss; "tell me what I shall do, and I'll make a late beginning, and do it."

"If you'll be acquainted with Mr Jarndyce and Miss Summerson, you will find them of your way of thinking, and they will give you the best advice and assistance."

"And, George," says the old lady, "we must send with all haste for your brother. He is a sensible sound man as they tell me – out in the world beyond Chesney Wold, my dear, though I don't know much of it myself – and will be of great service."

"Mother," returns the trooper, "is it too soon to ask a favour?"

"Surely not, my dear."

"Then grant me this one great favour. Don't let my brother know."

"Not know what, my dear?"

"Not know of me. In fact, mother, I can't bear it; I can't make up my mind to it. How could a man like him be expected to have any pleasure in such a discovery? It's impossible. No, keep my secret from him, mother; do me a greater kindness than I deserve, and keep my secret from my brother, of all men."

"But not always, dear George?"

"Why, mother, perhaps not for good and all – though I may come to ask that too – but keep it now, I do entreat you. If it's ever broke to him that his Rip of a brother has turned up, I could wish," says the trooper, shaking his head very doubtfully, "to break it myself."

As he evidently has a rooted feeling on this point his mother yields her implicit assent to what he asks. For this he thanks her kindly.

"In all other respects, my dear mother, I'll be as tractable and obedient as you can wish; on this one alone, I stand out. So now I am ready even for the lawyers. I have been drawing up," he glances at his writing on the table, "an exact account of what I knew of the deceased, and how I came to be involved in this unfortunate affair. It's entered, plain and regular, like an orderly-book; not a word in it but what's wanted for the facts. I did intend to read it, straight on end, whensoever I was called upon to say anything in my defence. I hope I may be let to do it still; but I have no longer a will of my own in this case, and whatever is said or done, I give my promise not to have any."

Matters being brought to this so far satisfactory pass, and time being on the wane, Mrs Rouncewell proposes a departure. Again the old lady hangs upon her son's neck and again the trooper holds her to his chest.

"But where are you going, mother?"

"I am going to the town house, my dear, the family house," Mrs Rouncewell answers. " I have some business there, that must be looked to directly."

My Lady is in that room in which she held her last conference with the murdered man, and is sitting where she sat that night, and is looking at the spot where he stood upon the hearth, studying her so leisurely, when a tap comes at the door. Who is it? Mrs Rouncewell. What has brought Mrs Rouncewell to town so unexpectedly?

"Trouble, my Lady. Sad trouble. O, my Lady, may I beg a word with you?"

What new occurrence is it that makes this tranquil old woman tremble so? Far happier than her Lady, as her Lady has often thought, why does she falter in this manner, and look at her with such strange mistrust?

"What is the matter? Sit down and take your breath."

"O, my Lady, my Lady. I have found my son – my youngest, who went away for a soldier so long ago. And he is in prison."

"For debt?"

"O, no, my Lady; I would have paid any debt, and joyful."

"For what is he in prison, then?"

"Charged with a murder, my Lady, of which he is as innocent as – as I am. Accused of the murder of Mr Tulkinghorn."

What does she mean by this look and this imploring gesture? Why does she come so close? What is the letter that she holds?

"Lady Dedlock, my dear Lady, my good Lady, my kind Lady! You must have a heart to feel for me, you must have a heart to forgive me. I was in this family before you were born. I am devoted to it. But think of my dear son wrongfully accused."

"I do not accuse him."

"No, my Lady, no. But others do, and he is in prison and in danger. O, Lady Dedlock, if you can say but a word to help to clear him, say it!"

What delusion can this be? What power does she suppose is in the person she petitions, to avert this unjust suspicion, if it be unjust? Her Lady's handsome eyes regard her with astonishment, almost with fear.

"My Lady, as it fell dark last night I got this letter."

"What letter is it?"

"Hush! Hush!" The housekeeper looks round, and answers in a frightened whisper: "My Lady, I have not breathed a word of it, I don't believe what's written in it, I know it can't be true, I am sure and certain that it is not true. But my son is in danger, and you must have a heart to pity me. If you know of anything that is not known to others, if you have any suspicion, if you have any clue at all, and any reason for keeping it in your own breast, O, my dear Lady, think of me, and conquer that reason, and let it be known! This is the most I consider possible. My Lady, you may have some proud or angry reasons for disdaining to utter something that you know; if so, pray, O, pray, think of a faithful servant whose whole life has been passed in this family which she dearly loves, and relent, and help to clear my son! My Lady, my good Lady," the old housekeeper pleads with genuine simplicity, "I am so humble in my place, and you are by nature so high and distant, that you may not think what I feel for my child; but I feel so much, that I have come here to make so bold as to beg and pray you not to be scornful of us, if you can do us any right or justice at this fearful time!"

Lady Dedlock raises her arm without one word, until she takes the letter from her hand.

"Am I to read this?"

"When I am gone, my Lady, if you please; and then remembering the most that I consider possible."

"I know of nothing I can do. I know of nothing I reserve, that can affect your son. I have never accused him."

"My Lady, you may pity him the more, under a false accusation, after reading the letter."

The old housekeeper leaves her with the letter in her hand. In truth she is not a hard lady naturally; and the time has been when the sight of the venerable figure suing to her with such strong earnestness would have moved her to great compassion. But, so long accustomed to suppress emotion, and keep down reality; so long schooled for her own purposes, in that destructive school which shuts up the natural feelings of the heart, like flies in amber, she had subdued even her wonder until now.

She opens the letter. Spread out upon the paper is a printed account of the discovery of the body, as it lay face downward on the floor, shot through the heart; and underneath is written her own name, with the word "murderess" attached.

It falls out of her hand. How long it may have lain upon the ground, she knows not; but it lies where it fell, when a servant stands before her announcing the young man of the name of Guppy. The words have probably been repeated several times, for they are ringing in her head before she begins to understand them.

"Let him come in!"

He comes in. Holding the letter in her hand, which she has taken from the floor, she tries to collect her thoughts. In the eyes of Mr Guppy she is the same Lady Dedlock, holding the same prepared, proud, chilling state.

"Your ladyship may not be at first disposed to excuse this visit from one who has never been welcome to your Ladyship but I hope when I mention my motives to your Ladyship, you will not find fault with me," says Mr Guppy.

"Do so."

"Thank your Ladyship. I ought first to explain to your Ladyship," Mr Guppy sits on the edge of a chair, and puts his hat on the carpet at his feet. "My object being to communicate to your Ladyship, under the seal of confidence, why I am here."

He cannot do so, she tells him, too plainly or too briefly.

"Nor can I," Mr Guppy returns, with a sense of injury upon him, "too particularly request your Ladyship to take particular notice that it's no personal affair of mine that brings me here. I have no interested views of my own to serve in coming here. If it was not for my promise to Miss Summerson, and my keeping of it sacred, – I, in point of fact, shouldn't have darkened these doors again, but should have seen 'em further first."

Mr Guppy considers this a favourable moment for sticking up his hair with both hands.

"Your ladyship will remember when I mention it, that the last time I was here, I run against a party very eminent in our profession, and whose loss we all deplore. That party certainly did from that time apply himself to cutting in against me in a way that I will call sharp practice, and did make it, at every turn and point, extremely difficult for me to be sure that I hadn't inadvertently led up to something contrary to Miss Summerson's wishes."

Lady Dedlock looks at him in stern inquiry. Mr Guppy immediately withdraws his eyes from her face, and looks anywhere else.

"I have now reasons for an apprehension, as to which I come to put your Ladyship upon your guard. First, will your Ladyship allow me to ask you whether you have had any strange visitors this morning? I don't mean fashionable visitors, but such visitors, for instance, as a person without the use of his lower extremities, carried upstairs similarly to a Guy?"

"No!"

"Then I assure your ladyship that such a visitor has been here, and has been received here. Because I saw him at the door, and waited at the corner of the square till he came out, and took half-an-hour's turn afterwards to avoid him."

"What have I to do with that, or what have you? I do not understand you. What do you mean?"

"Your Ladyship, I come to put you on your guard. There may be no occasion for it. Very well. Then I have only done my best to keep my promise to Miss Summerson. I strongly suspect that those letters I was to have brought to your Ladyship were not destroyed when I supposed they were. That the visitor I have alluded to has been here this morning to make money of it. And that the money is made, or making."

Mr Guppy picks up his hat and rises.

"Your Ladyship, you know best, whether there's anything in what I say or whether there's nothing. Something or nothing, I have acted up to Miss Summerson's wishes in letting things alone, and in undoing what I had begun to do, as far as possible; that's sufficient for me. In case I should be taking a liberty in putting your Ladyship on your guard when there's no necessity for it, you will endeavour, I should hope, to outlive my presumption, and I shall endeavour to outlive your disapprobation. I now take my farewell of your Ladyship, and assure you that there's no danger of your ever being waited on by me again."

She scarcely acknowledges these parting words by any look; but when he has been gone a little while, she rings her bell.

"Where is Sir Leicester?"

Mercury reports that he is at present shut up in the library, alone.

"Has Sir Leicester had any visitors this morning?"

Several, on business. Mercury proceeds to a description of one, which has been anticipated by Mr Guppy. Enough; he may go.

So! All is broken down. Her name is in these many mouths, her husband knows his wrongs, her shame will be published – may be spreading while she thinks about it – and in addition to the thunderbolt so long foreseen by her, so unforeseen by him, she is denounced by an invisible accuser as the murderess of her enemy.

Her enemy he was, and she has often, often, often wished him dead. Her enemy he is, even in his grave. This dreadful accusation comes upon her, like a new torment at his lifeless hand. And when she recalls how she was secretly at his door that night, and how she may be represented to have sent her favourite girl away, so soon before, merely to release herself from observation, she shudders as if the hangman's hands were at her neck.

She has thrown herself upon the floor, and lies with her hair all wildly scattered, and her face buried in the cushions of a couch. She rises up, hurries to and fro, flings herself down again, and rocks and moans. The horror that is upon her, is unutterable. If she really were the murderess, it could hardly be, for the moment, more intense.

For now she sees that when he used to be on the watch before her, and she used to think, "if some mortal stroke would but fall on this old man and take him from my way!" it was but wishing that all he held against her in his hand might be flung to the winds, and chance-sown in many places. So, too, with the wicked relief she has felt in his death. What was his death but the key-stone of a gloomy arch removed, and now the arch begins to fall in a thousand fragments, each crushing and mangling piecemeal!

Thus, a terrible impression steals upon and overshadows her, that from this pursuer, living or dead – obdurate and imperturbable before her in his well-remembered shape, or obdurate and imperturbable in his coffin-bed – there is no escape but in death. Hunted, she flies. The complication of her shame, her dread, remorse, and misery, overwhelms her at its height; and even her strength of self-reliance is overturned and whirled away, like a leaf before a mighty wind.

She hurriedly addresses these lines to her husband, seals, and leaves them on her table.

"If I am sought for, or accused of, his murder, believe that I am wholly innocent. Believe no other good of me; for I am innocent of nothing else that you have heard, or will hear, laid to my charge. He prepared me, on that fatal night, for his disclosure of my guilt to you. After he had left me, I went out, on pretence of walking in the garden where I sometimes walk, but really to follow him, and make one last petition that he would not protract the dreadful suspense on which I had been racked by him, you do not know how long, but would mercifully strike next morning.

I found his house dark and silent. I rang twice at his door, but there was no reply, and I came home.

"I have no home left. I will encumber you no more. May you, in your just resentment, be able to forget the unworthy woman on whom you have wasted a most generous devotion – who avoids you, only with a deeper shame than that with which she hurries from herself – and who writes this last adieu."

She veils and dresses quickly, leaves all her jewels and her money, listens, goes downstairs at a moment when the hall is empty, opens and shuts the great door; flutters away, in the shrill frosty wind.

CHAPTER 34

Pursuit

The Dedlock town-house changes not externally, and hours pass before its exalted dullness is disturbed within. But a little scream acquires a considerable augmentation and the house is quickly in commotion. Servants tear up and downstairs, bells are violently rung, doctors are sent for, and Lady Dedlock is sought in all directions, but not found. Nobody has seen or heard her since she last rang her bell. Her letter to Sir Leicester is discovered on her table, unopened.

They lay him down upon his bed, and chafe, and rub, and fan, and put ice to his head, and try every means of restoration. But the day has ebbed away, and it is night in his room, before his stertorous breathing lulls or his fixed eyes show any consciousness of the candle that is occasionally passed before them. But when this change begins, it goes on; and by and by he nods, or moves his eyes, or even his hand, in token that he hears and comprehends.

He fell down, this morning, a handsome stately gentleman; somewhat infirm, but of a fine presence, and with a well-filled face. He lies upon his bed, an aged man with sunken cheeks, the decrepit shadow of himself. His voice was rich and mellow; and he had so long been thoroughly persuaded of the weight and import to man-kind of any word he said, that his words really had come to sound as if there were something in them. But now he can only whisper; and what he whispers sounds like what it is – mere jumble and jargon.

His favourite and faithful housekeeper stands at his bedside. It is the first act he notices, and he clearly derives pleasure from it. After vainly trying to make himself understood in speech, he makes signs for a pencil.

So inexpressively, that they cannot at first understand him; it is his old housekeeper who makes out what he wants, and brings in a slate.

After pausing for some time, he slowly scrawls upon it, in a hand that is not his, "Chesney Wold?"

No, she tells him; he is in London. He was taken ill in the library, this morning. Right thankful she is that she happened to come to London, and is able to attend upon him.

"It is not an illness of any serious consequence, Sir Leicester. You will be much better to-morrow, Sir Leicester. All the gentlemen say so." This, with the tears coursing down her fair old face.

After making a survey of the room, and looking with particular attention all round the bed where the doctors stand, he writes, "My Lady."

"My Lady went out, Sir Leicester, before you were taken ill, and don't know of your illness yet."

He points again, in great agitation, at the two words. They all try to quiet him, but he points again with increased agitation. On their looking at one another, not knowing what to say, he takes the slate once more and writes "My Lady. For God's sake, where?" And makes an imploring moan.

It is thought better that his old housekeeper should give him Lady Dedlock's letter, the contents of which no one knows or can surmise. She opens it for him, and puts it out for his perusal. Having read it twice by a great effort, he turns it down so that it shall not be seen, and lies moaning. He passes into a kind of relapse, or into a swoon; and it is an hour before he opens his eyes, reclining on his faithful and attached old servant's arm. The doctors know that he is best with her; and when not actively engaged about him, stand aloof.

The slate comes into requisition again; but the word he wants to write he cannot remember. His anxiety, his eagerness, and affliction, at this pass, are pitiable to behold. It seems as if he must go mad, in the necessity he feels for haste, and the inability under which he labours of expressing to do what, or to fetch whom. He has written the letter B, and there stopped. Of a sudden, in the height of his misery, he puts Mr before it. The old housekeeper suggests Bucket. Thank Heaven! That's his meaning.

Mr Bucket is found to be downstairs, by appointment. Shall he come up?

There is no possibility of misconstruing Sir Leicester's burning wish to see him, or the desire he signifies to have the room cleared of every one but the housekeeper. It is speedily done; and Mr Bucket appears. Of all men upon earth, Sir Leicester seems fallen from his high estate to place his sole trust and reliance upon this man.

"Sir Leicester Dedlock, Baronet, I'm sorry to see you like this. I hope you'll cheer up. I'm sure you will, on account of the family credit."

Leicester puts her letter in his hands, and looks intently in his face while he reads it. A new intelligence comes into Mr Bucket's eye, as he reads on; with one hook of his finger, while that eye is still glancing over the words, he indicates, "Sir Leicester Dedlock, Baronet, I understand you."

Sir Leicester writes upon the slate. "Full forgiveness. Find – " Mr Bucket stops his hand.

"Sir Leicester Dedlock, Baronet, I'll find her. But my search after her must be begun out of hand. Not a minute must be lost."

With the quickness of thought, he follows Sir Leicester Dedlock's look towards a little box upon a table.

"Bring it here, Sir Leicester Dedlock, Baronet? Certainly. Open it with one of these here keys? Certainly. The littlest key? To be sure. Take the notes out? So I will. Count 'em? That's soon done. Twenty and thirty's fifty, and twenty's seventy, and fifty's one twenty, and forty's one sixty. Take 'em for expenses? That I'll do, and render an account of course. Don't spare money? No I won't."

The velocity and certainty of Mr Bucket's interpretation on all these heads is little short of miraculous. Mrs Rouncewell, who holds the light, is giddy with the swiftness of his eyes and hands, as he starts up, furnished for his journey.

"You're George's mother, old lady; that's about what you are, I believe?" says Mr Bucket, aside, with his hat already on, and buttoning his coat.

"Yes, sir, I am his distressed mother."

"So I thought, according to what he mentioned to me just now. Well, then, I'll tell you something. You needn't be distressed no more. Your son's all right. Now, don't you begin a crying; because what you've got to do is to take care of Sir Leicester Dedlock, Baronet, and you won't do that by crying. As to your son, he's all right, I tell you; and he sends his loving duty, and hoping you're the same. He's discharged honourable;

that's about what he is; with no more imputation on his character than there is on yours, and yours is a tidy one, I'll bet a pound. You may trust me, for I took your son. He conducted himself in a game way, too, on that occasion; and he's a fine-made man, and you're a fine-made old lady. Sir Leicester Dedlock, Baronet, what you've trusted to me I'll go through with. Don't you be afraid of my turning out of my way, right or left; or taking a sleep, or a wash, or a shave, 'till I have found what I go in search of. Say everything as is kind and forgiving on your part? Sir Leicester Dedlock, Baronet, I will. And I wish you better, and these family affairs smoothed over – as, Lord, many other family affairs equally has been, and equally will be, to the end of time."

With this peroration, Mr Bucket; buttoned up, goes quietly out, looking steadily before him as if he were already piercing the night, in quest of the fugitive.

His first step is to take himself to Lady Dedlock's rooms, and look all over them for any trifling indication that may help him. "Spicy boudoir, this," says Mr Bucket. "Must have cost a sight of money. Rum articles to cut away from, these; she must have been hard put to it!"

Ever looking about, he has opened a dainty little chest in an inner drawer. His great hand, turning over some gloves which it can scarcely feel, they are so light and soft within it, comes upon a white handkerchief.

"Hum! Let's have a look at you," says Mr Bucket, putting down the light. "What should you be kept by yourself for? What's your motive? Are you her ladyship's property, or somebody else's? You've got a mark upon you somewheres or another, I suppose?"

He finds it as he speaks, "Esther Summerson."

"O!" says Mr Bucket, pausing, with his finger at his ear. "Come, I'll take you."

He completes his observations as quietly and carefully as he has carried them on, leaves everything else precisely as he found it, glides away after some five minutes in all, and passes into the street. With a glance upward at the dimly lighted windows of Sir Leicester's room, he sets off, full-swing, to the nearest coach-stand, picks out the horse for his money, and directs to be driven to the Shooting Gallery.

He dashes to his destination at such a speed, that when he stops, the horse half smothers him in a cloud of steam.

"Unbear him half a moment to freshen him up, and I'll be back."

140

He runs up the long wooden entry, and finds the trooper smoking his pipe.

"I thought I should, George, after what you have gone through, my lad. I haven't a word to spare. Now, honour! All to save a woman. Miss Summerson that was here when Jo died – that was the name, I know – all right – where does she live?"

The trooper has just come from there, and gives him the address, near Oxford Street.

"You won't repent it, George. Good night!"

He is off again, with an impression of having seen Phil sitting by the frosty fire, staring at him open-mouthed; and gallops away again, and gets out in a cloud of steam again.

Mr Jarndyce, the only person up in the house, is just going to bed; rises from his book, on hearing the rapid ringing at the bell; and comes down to the door in his dressing-gown.

"Don't be alarmed, sir." In a moment his visitor is confidential with him in the hall, has shut the door, and stands with his hand upon the lock. "I've had the pleasure of seeing you before. Inspector Bucket. Look at that handkerchief, sir, Miss Esther Summerson's. Found it myself put away in a drawer of Lady Dedlock's, quarter of an hour ago. Not a moment to lose. Matter of life or death. You know Lady Dedlock?"

"Yes."

"There has been a discovery there, to-day. Family affairs have come out. Sir Leicester Dedlock, Baronet, has had a fit – apoplexy or paralysis – and couldn't be brought to, and precious time has been lost. Lady Dedlock disappeared this afternoon, and left a letter for him that looks bad. Run your eye over it. Here it is!"

Mr Jarndyce, having read it, asks him what he thinks.

"I don't know. It looks like suicide. Anyways, there's more and more danger, every minute, of its drawing to that. I'd give a hundred pound an hour to have got the start of the present time. Now, Mr Jarndyce, I am employed by Sir Leicester Dedlock, Baronet, to follow her and find her, to save her, and take her his forgiveness. I have money and full power, but I want something else: I want Miss Summerson."

Mr Jarndyce, in a troubled voice, repeats, "Miss Summerson?"

"Now, Mr Jarndyce;" – Mr Bucket has read his face with the greatest attention all along; "I speak to you as a gentleman of a humane heart, and

141

under such pressing circumstances as don't often happen. If ever delay was dangerous, it's dangerous now; and if ever you couldn't afterwards forgive yourself for causing it, this is the time. Eight or ten hours, worth, as I tell you, a hundred pound a-piece at least, have been lost since Lady Dedlock disappeared. I am charged to find her. Besides all the rest that's heavy on her, she has upon her, as she believes, suspicion of murder. If I follow her alone, she, being in ignorance of what Sir Leicester Dedlock, Baronet, has communicated to me, may be driven to desperation. But if I follow her in company with a young lady, answering to the description of a young lady that she has a tenderness for – I ask no question, and I say no more than that – she will give me credit for being friendly. Let me come up with her, and be able to have the hold upon her of putting that young lady for'ard, and I'll save her and prevail with her if she is alive. Let me come up with her alone – a hard matter – and I'll do my best; but I don't answer for what the best may be. Time flies; it's getting on for one o'clock. When one strikes, there's another hour gone, and it's worth a thousand pound now, instead of a hundred."

This is all true, and the pressing nature of the case cannot be questioned. Mr Jarndyce begs him to remain there, while he speaks to Miss Summerson. Mr Bucket says he will; but, acting on his usual principle, does no such thing – following upstairs instead, and keeping his man in sight. So he remains, dodging and lurking about in the gloom of the staircase, while they confer. In a very little time Mr Jarndyce comes down, and tells him that Miss Summerson will join him directly, and place herself under his protection, to accompany him where he pleases. Mr Bucket, satisfied, expresses high approval; and awaits her coming, at the door.

There, he mounts a high tower in his mind, and looks out, far and wide. Many solitary figures he perceives, creeping through the streets; many solitary figures out on heaths, and roads, and lying under haystacks. But the figure that he seeks, is not among them.

Where is she? Living or dead, where is she? If, as he folds the handkerchief and carefully puts it up, it were able, with an enchanted power, to bring before him the place where she found it, and the night-landscape near the cottage where it covered the little child, would he see her there? On the waste, where the brick-kilns are burning with a pale blue flare; where the straw-roofs of the wretched huts in which the bricks are made, are being scattered by the wind; where the clay and water are hard frozen, traversing this deserted, blighted spot, there is a lonely figure with the sad world to itself, pelted by the snow and driven by the wind, and cast out, it would seem, from all companionship. It is the figure of a woman, too; but it is miserably dressed, and no such clothes ever came through the hall, and out at the great door, of the Dedlock mansion.

CHAPTER 35

Esther's Narrative

I had gone to bed and fallen asleep, when my guardian knocked at the door of my room and begged me to get up directly. On my hurrying to speak to him and learn what had happened, he told me, after a word or two of preparation, that there had been a discovery at Sir Leicester Dedlock's. That my mother had fled; that a person was now at our door who was empowered to convey to her the fullest assurances of affectionate protection and forgiveness, if he could possibly find her; and that I was sought for to accompany him, in the hope that my entreaties might prevail upon her, if his failed. I was thrown into such a tumult of alarm, and hurry and distress, that in spite of every effort I could make to subdue my agitation, I did not seem, to myself, fully to recover my right mind until hours had passed.

But, I dressed and wrapped up expeditiously and went down to Mr Bucket, who was the person entrusted with the secret. In taking me to him my guardian told me this, and also explained how it was that he had come to think of me. Mr Bucket, in a low voice, by the light of my guardian's candle, read to me, in the hall, a letter that my mother had left upon her table; and, I suppose within ten minutes of my having been aroused, I was sitting beside him, rolling swiftly through the streets.

His manner was very keen, and yet considerate when he explained to me that a great deal might depend on my being able to answer, without confusion, a few questions that he wished to ask me. These were, chiefly, whether I had had much communication with my mother (to whom he only referred as Lady Dedlock); when and where I had spoken with her last; and how she had become possessed of my handkerchief.

143

We had not driven very far from our lodgings, when we stopped in a bye-street, at a public-looking place lighted up with gas. Mr Bucket took me in and sat me in an arm-chair, by a bright fire. It was now past one, as I saw by the clock against the wall. Two police officers, looking in their perfectly neat uniform not at all like people who were up all night, were quietly writing at a desk; and the place seemed very quiet altogether, except for some beating and calling out at distant doors underground, to which nobody paid any attention.

A third man in uniform, whom Mr Bucket called and to whom he whispered his instructions, went out; and then the two others advised together, while one wrote from Mr Bucket's subdued dictation. It was a description of my mother that they were busy with; for Mr Bucket brought it to me when it was done, and read it in a whisper. It was very accurate indeed.

The second officer, who had attended to it closely, then copied it out, and called in another man in uniform (there were several in an outer room) who took it up and went away with it. All this was done with the greatest dispatch, and without the waste of a moment; yet nobody was at all hurried. As soon as the paper was sent out upon its travels, the two officers resumed their former quiet work of writing with neatness and care. Mr Bucket thoughtfully came and warmed the soles of his boots, first one and then the other, at the fire.

"Are you well wrapped up, Miss Summerson?" he asked me, as his eyes met mine. "It's a desperate sharp night for a young lady to be out in."

I told him I cared for no weather, and was warmly clothed.

"It may be a long job," he observed; "but so that it ends well, never mind, miss."

"I pray to Heaven it may end well!" said I.

He nodded comfortingly. "You see, whatever you do, don't you go and fret yourself. You keep yourself cool, and equal for anything that may happen; and it'll be the better for you, the better for me, the better for Lady Dedlock, and the better for Sir Leicester Dedlock, Baronet."

He gave me his arm, and the two officers courteously bowed me out, and we found at the door a phaeton or barouche, with a postillion and post horses. Mr Bucket handed me in, and took his own seat on the box. The man in uniform whom he had sent to fetch this equipage, then handed him up a dark lantern at his request; and when he had given a few directions to the driver, we rattled away.

I was far from sure that I was not in a dream. We rattled with great rapidity through such a labyrinth of streets, that I soon lost all idea where we were. At length we stopped at the corner of a little slimy turning, which the wind from the river, rushing up it, did not purify; and I saw my companion, by the light of his lantern, in conference with several men, who looked like a mixture of police and sailors. Against the mouldering wall by which they stood, there was a bill, on which I could discern the words, "*Found drowned*;" and this, and an inscription about Drags, possessed me with the awful suspicion shadowed forth in our visit to that place.

I remained quiet; but what I suffered in that dreadful spot, I never can forget. And still it was like the horror of a dream. A man yet dark and muddy, in long swollen sodden boots and a hat like them, was called out of a boat, and whispered with Mr Bucket, who went away with him down some slippery steps – as if to look at something secret that he had to show. They came back, wiping their hands upon their coats, after turning over something wet; but thank God it was not what I feared!

After some further conference, Mr Bucket (whom everybody seemed to know and defer to) went in with the others at a door, and left me in the carriage; while the driver walked up and down by his horses, to warm himself. The tide was coming in, as I judged from the sound it made; and I could hear it break at the end of the alley, with a little rush towards me. It never did so – and I thought it did so, hundreds of times, in what can have been at the most a quarter of an hour, and probably was less – but the thought shuddered through me that it would cast my mother at the horses' feet.

Mr Bucket came out again, exhorting the others to be vigilant, darkened his lantern, and once more took his seat. "Don't you be alarmed, Miss Summerson, on account of our coming down here," he said, turning to me. "I only want to have everything in train, and to know that it is in train by looking after it myself. Get on, my lad!"

We appeared to retrace the way we had come. Not that I had taken note of any particular objects in my perturbed state of mind, but judging from the general character of the streets. We called at another office or station for a minute, and crossed the river again. During the whole of this time, and during the whole search, my companion, wrapped up on the box, never relaxed in his vigilance a single moment; but, when we crossed the bridge he seemed, if possible, to be more on the alert than before. He stood up to look over the parapet; he alighted, and went back after a shadowy female figure that flitted past us; and he gazed into the profound black pit of water, with a face that made my heart die within me.

Clattering and clattering through the empty streets, we came at length from the pavement on to dark smooth roads, and began to leave the houses behind us. After a while, I recognised the familiar way to Saint Albans. At Barnet, fresh horses were ready for us, and we changed and went on. It was very cold indeed; and the open country was white with snow, though none was falling then.

"An old acquaintance of yours, this road, Miss Summerson," said Mr Bucket cheerfully.

"Yes," I returned. "Have you gathered any intelligence?"

"None that can be quite depended on as yet," he answered; "but it's early times as yet."

He had gone into every late or early public-house where there was a light (they were not a few at that time, the road being then much frequented by drovers), and had got down to talk to the turnpike-keepers. I had heard him ordering drink, and chinking money, and making himself agreeable and merry everywhere; but whenever he took his seat upon the box again, his face resumed its watchful steady look, and he always said to the driver in the same business tone, "Get on, my lad!"

With all these stoppages, it was between five and six o'clock and we were yet a few miles short of Saint Albans, when he came out of one of these houses and handed me in a cup of tea.

"Drink it, Miss Summerson, it'll do you good. You're beginning to get more yourself now, ain't you?"

I thanked him, and said I hoped so.

"You was what you may call stunned at first," he returned; "and Lord, no wonder! Don't speak loud, my dear. It's all right. She's on a-head."

I don't know what joyful exclamation I made, or was going to make, but he put up his finger, and I stopped myself.

"Passed through here on foot, this evening, about eight or nine. I heard of her first at the archway toll, over at Highgate, but couldn't make quite sure. Traced her all along, on and off. Picked her up at one place, and dropped her at another; but she's before us now, safe. Take hold of this cup and saucer, Ostler. Now, my lad, try a gallop!"

We were soon in Saint Albans, and alighted a little before day, when I was just beginning to arrange and comprehend the occurrences of the night, and really to believe that they were not a dream. Leaving the carriage at the posting-house, and ordering fresh horses to be ready, my companion gave me his arm, and we went towards home.

"As this is your regular abode, Miss Summerson, you see," he observed, "I should like to know whether you've been asked for by any stranger answering the description, or whether Mr Jarndyce has. I don't much expect it, but it might be."

As we ascended the hill, he looked about him with a sharp eye – the day was now breaking – and reminded me that I had come down it one night, as I had reason for remembering, with my little servant and poor Jo: whom he called Toughey.

I wondered how he knew that.

"When you passed a man upon the road, just yonder, you know," said Mr Bucket.

Yes, I remembered that too, very well.

"That was me," said Mr Bucket.

Seeing my surprise, he went on:

"I drove down in a gig that afternoon, to look after that boy. You might have heard my wheels when you came out to look after him yourself, for I was aware of you and your little maid going up, when I was walking the horse down. Making an inquiry or two about him in the town, I soon heard what company he was in; and was coming among the brick-fields to look for him, when I observed you bringing him home here."

"Had he committed any crime?" I asked.

"None was charged against him," said Mr Bucket, coolly lifting off his hat; "but I suppose he wasn't over-particular. No. What I wanted him for, was in connexion with keeping this very matter of Lady Dedlock quiet. He had been making his tongue more free than welcome, as to a small accidental service he had been paid for by the deceased Mr Tulkinghorn; and it wouldn't do, at any sort of price, to have him playing those games. So having warned him out of London, I made an afternoon of it to warn him to keep out of it now he was away, and go farther from it, and maintain a bright look out that I didn't catch him coming back again."

"Poor creature!" said I.

"Poor enough," assented Mr Bucket, "and trouble enough, and well enough away from London, or anywhere else. I was regularly turned on my back when I found him taken up by your establishment, I do assure you.

I asked him why. "Why, my dear?" said Mr Bucket. "Naturally there was no end to his tongue then. He might as well have been born with a yard and a half of it, and a remnant over."

He often spoke to me of indifferent things, while his face was busy with the one object that we had in view. He still pursued this subject, as we turned in at the garden gate.

We were now in front of the house; he looked attentively and closely at the gravel for footprints, before he raised his eyes to the windows.

"Do you generally put that elderly young gentleman in the same room, when he's on a visit here, Miss Summerson?" he inquired, glancing at Mr Skimpole's usual chamber.

"You know Mr Skimpole!" said I.

"What do you call him again?" returned Mr Bucket, bending down his ear. "Skimpole, is it? I've often wondered what his name might be. Skimpole. Not John, I should say, nor yet Jacob?"

"Harold," I told him.

"Harold. Yes. He's a queer bird is Harold," said Mr Bucket, eyeing me with great expression.

"He is a singular character," said I.

"No idea of money," observed Mr Bucket. – "He takes it though!"

I involuntarily returned for answer, that I perceived Mr Bucket knew him.

"Why, now I'll tell you, Miss Summerson," he replied. "Your mind will be all the better for not running on one point too continually, and I'll tell you for a change. It was him as pointed out to me where Toughey was. I made up my mind, that night, to come to the door and ask for Toughey, if that was all; but, willing to try a move or so first, if any such was on the board, I just pitched up a morsel of gravel at that window where I saw a shadow. As soon as Harold opens it and I have had a look at him, thinks I, you're the man for me. So I smoothed him down a bit, about not wanting to disturb the family after they was gone to bed, and about its being a thing to be regretted that charitable young ladies should harbour vagrants; and then, when I pretty well understood his ways, I said, I should consider a five pun note well bestowed if I could relieve the premises of Toughey without causing any noise or trouble. Then says he, lifting up his eyebrows in the gayest way, 'It's no use mentioning a five pun note to me, my friend, because I'm a mere child in such matters, and have no idea of money.' Of course I understood what his taking it so easy meant; and being now quite sure he was the man for me, I wrapped the note round a little stone and threw it up to him. Well of course he told me where to find Toughey, and I found him."

I regarded this as very treacherous on the part of Mr Skimpole towards my guardian, and as passing the usual bounds of his childish innocence.

"Bounds, my dear?" returned Mr Bucket. "Bounds? Now, Miss Summerson, I'll give you a piece of advice. Whenever a person says to you that they are as innocent as can be in all concerning money, look well after your own money, for they are dead certain to collar it, if they can. Whenever a person proclaims to you 'In worldly matters I'm a child,' you consider that that person is only a crying off from being held accountable, and that you have got that person's number, and it's Number One. With which caution to the unwary, my dear, I take the liberty of pulling this here bell, and so go back to our business."

I believe it had not been for a moment out of his mind, any more than it had been out of my mind, or out of my face. The whole household were amazed to see me, without any notice, at that time in the morning, and so accompanied; and their surprise was not diminished by my inquiries. No one, however, had been there. It could not be doubted that this was the truth.

"Then, Miss Summerson," said my companion, "we can't be too soon at the cottage where those brickmakers are to be found. Most inquiries there I leave to you, if you'll be so good as to make 'em. The naturalest way is the best way, and the naturalest way is your own way."

We set off again immediately. On arriving at the cottage, we found it shut up, and apparently deserted; but one of the neighbours who knew me, and who came out when I was trying to make some one hear, informed me that the two women and their husbands now lived together in another house, made of loose rough bricks, which stood on the margin of the piece of ground where the kilns were, and where the long rows of bricks were drying. We lost no time in repairing to this place, which was within a few hundred yards; and as the door stood ajar, I pushed it open.

There were only three of them sitting at breakfast; the child lying asleep on a bed in the corner. Jenny, the befriender of Jo, was absent. The other woman rose on seeing me; and the men, though they were, as usual, sulky and silent, each gave me a morose nod of recognition. A look passed between them when Mr Bucket followed me in, and I was surprised to see that the woman evidently knew him.

I had asked leave to enter, of course. Liz (the only name by which I knew her) rose to give me her own chair, but I sat down on a stool near the fire, and Mr Bucket took a corner of the bedstead. Now that I had to speak, and was among people with whom I was not familiar, I became conscious of being hurried and giddy. It was very difficult to begin, and I could not help bursting into tears.

"Liz," said I, "I have come a long way in the night and through the snow, to inquire after a lady – ."

"Who has been here, you know," Mr Bucket struck in, addressing the whole group, with a composed propitiatory face; "that's the lady the young lady means. The lady that was here last night, you know."

"And who told you as there was anybody here?" inquired Jenny's husband, who had made a surly stop in his eating, to listen, and now measured him with his eye.

"He's out of employment, I believe," said Mr Bucket, apologetically for his informant, "and so gets talking."

The woman had not resumed her chair, but stood faltering with her hand upon its broken back, looking at me. I thought she would have spoken to me privately, if she had dared. She was still in this attitude of uncertainty, when her husband, who was eating with a lump of bread and fat in one hand, and his clasp-knife in the other, struck the handle of his knife violently on the table, and told her with an oath to mind her own business at any rate, and sit down.

"I should like to have seen Jenny very much," said I, "for I am sure she would have told me all she could about this lady, whom I am very anxious indeed – you cannot think how anxious – to overtake. Will Jenny be here soon? Where is she?"

The woman had a great desire to answer, but the man, with another oath, openly kicked at her foot with his heavy boot. He left it to Jenny's husband to say what he chose, and after a dogged silence the latter turned his shaggy head towards me.

"I'm not partial to gentlefolks coming into my place, as you've heerd me say afore now, I think, miss. Howsoever, I don't so much complain of you as of some others; and I'm agreeable to make you a civil answer. Will Jenny be here soon? No she won't. Where is she? She's gone up to Lunnun."

"Did she go last night?" I asked.

"Did she go last night? Ah! She went last night," he answered with a sulky jerk of his head.

"But was she here when the lady came? And what did the lady say to her? And where is the lady gone? I beg and pray you to be so kind as to tell me," said I, "for I am in great distress to know."

"If my master would let me speak, and not say a word of harm – " the woman timidly began.

"Your master," said her husband, muttering an imprecation with slow emphasis, "will break your neck if you meddle with wot don't concern you."

After another silence, the husband of the absent woman, turning to me again, answered me with his usual grumbling unwillingness.

"Wos Jenny here when the lady from off the London road come? Yes, she wos here when the lady come. Wot did the lady say to her? Well, I'll tell you wot the lady said to her. She said, 'You remember me as come one time to talk to you about the young lady as had been a-wisiting of you? You remember me as give you somethink handsome for a handkercher wot the young lady from Bleak House had lost?' Ah, she remembered. So we all did. Well, then, wos that young lady up at the house now? No, she warn't up at the house now. Well, then, lookee here. The lady was upon a journey all alone, strange as we might think it, and could she rest herself where you're a setten, for a hour or so. Yes she could, and so she did. Then she went – it might be at twenty minutes past eleven, and it might be at twenty minutes past twelve; we ain't got no watches here to know the time by, nor yet clocks. Where did she go? I don't know where she go'd. She went one way, and Jenny went another; one went right to Lunnun, and t'other went right from it. That's all about it. Ask this man. He heerd it all, and see it all. He knows."

The other man repeated, "That's all about it."

"Was the lady crying?" I inquired.

"Devil a bit," returned the first man. "Her shoes was the worse, and her clothes was the worse, but she warn't – not as I see."

The woman sat with her arms crossed, and her eyes upon the ground. Her husband had turned his seat a little, so as to face her; and kept his hammer-like hand upon the table, as if it were in readiness to execute his threat if she disobeyed him.

"I hope you will not object to my asking your wife," said I, "how the lady looked."

"Come, then!" he gruffly cried to her. "You hear wot she says. Cut it short, and tell her."

"Bad," replied the woman. "Pale and exhausted. Very bad."

"Did she speak much?"

"Not much, but her voice was hoarse."

She answered, looking all the while at her husband for leave.

"Was she faint?" said I. "Did she eat or drink here?"

"Go on!" said the husband, in answer to her look. "Tell her, and cut it short."

"She had a little water, miss, and Jenny fetched her some bread and tea. But she hardly touched it."

"And when she went from here," – I was proceeding, when Jenny's husband impatiently took me up.

"When she went from here, she went right away Nor'ard by the high road. Ask on the road if you doubt me, and see if it warn't so. Now, there's the end. That's all about it."

I glanced at my companion; and finding that he had already risen and was ready to depart, thanked them for what they had told me, and took my leave. The woman looked full at Mr Bucket as he went out, and he looked full at her.

"Now, Miss Summerson," he said to me, as we walked quickly away. "They've got her ladyship's watch among 'em. That's a positive fact."

"You saw it?" I exclaimed.

"Just as good as saw it," he returned. "Else why should he talk about his 'twenty minutes past,' and about his having no watch to tell the time by? Now, you see, either her ladyship gave him that watch, or he took it. I think she gave it him. Now, what should she give it him for? What should she give it him for?"

152

He repeated this question to himself several times, as we hurried on; appearing to balance between a variety of answers that arose in his mind.

"If time could be spared," said Mr Bucket "I might get it out of that woman; but it's too doubtful a chance to trust to, under present circumstances. They are up to keeping a close eye upon her, and any fool knows that a poor creetur like her, beaten and kicked and scarred and bruised from head to foot, will stand by the husband that ill uses her, through thick and thin. There's something kept back. It's a pity but what we had seen the other woman."

I regretted it exceedingly; for she was very grateful, and I felt sure would have resisted no entreaty of mine.

"It's possible, Miss Summerson," said Mr Bucket, pondering on it, "that her ladyship sent her up to London with some word for you, and it's possible that her husband got the watch to let her go. It don't come out altogether so plain as to please me, but it's on the cards. So far, our road is for'ard – straight ahead – and keeping everything quiet!"

We called at home once more, that I might send a hasty note to my guardian, and then we hurried back to where we had left the carriage. The horses were brought out as soon as we were seen coming, and we were on the road again in a few minutes.

It had set in snowing at daybreak, and it now snowed hard. The air was so thick with the darkness of the day and the density of the fall, that we could see but a very little way in any direction. One horse fell three times in this first stage, and trembled so, and was so shaken, that the driver had to dismount from his saddle and lead him at last.

I could eat nothing, and could not sleep; and I grew so nervous under those delays, and the slow pace at which we travelled, that I had an unreasonable desire upon me to get out and walk. Yielding to my companion's better sense, however, I remained where I was. All this time, kept fresh by a certain enjoyment of the work in which he was engaged, he was up and down at every house we came to; addressing people whom he had never beheld before, as old acquaintances; running in to warm himself at every fire he saw; talking and drinking and shaking hands, at every bar and tap; friendly with every wagoner, wheelwright, blacksmith, and toll-taker; yet never seeming to lose time, and always mounting to the box again with his watchful, steady face, and his business-like "Get on, my lad!"

When we were changing horses the next time, he came from the stable-yard, with the wet snow encrusted upon him, and dropping off him – crashing through it to his wet knees, as he had been doing frequently since we left Saint Albans – and spoke to me at the carriage side.

"Keep up your spirits. It's certainly true that she came on here, Miss Summerson. There's not a doubt of the dress by this time, and the dress has been seen here."

"Still on foot?" said I.

"Still on foot. But whatever you do, don't you fall a crying, my dear; and don't you worry yourself no more than you can help. Get on my lad!"

The sleet fell all that day unceasingly, a thick mist came on early, and it never rose or lightened for a moment. Such roads I had never seen. I sometimes feared we had missed the way, and got into the ploughed grounds, or the marshes.

As we advanced, I began to feel misgivings that my companion lost confidence. He was the same as before with all the roadside people, but he looked graver when he sat by himself on the box. I saw his finger uneasily going across and across his mouth, during the whole of one long weary stage. I overheard that he began to ask the drivers of coaches and other vehicles coming towards us, what passengers they had seen in other coaches and vehicles that were in advance. Their replies did not encourage him. He always gave me a re-assuring beck of his finger, and lift of his eyelid as he got upon the box again; but he seemed perplexed now, when he said, "Get on, my lad!"

At last he told me that he had lost the track of the dress so long that he began to be surprised. It was nothing, he said, to lose such a track for one while, and to take it up for another while, and so on; but it had disappeared here in an unaccountable manner, and we had not come upon it since. But, I was not to be down-hearted, he told me, for it was as likely as not that the next stage might set us right again.

The next stage, however, ended as that one ended; we had no new clue. There was a spacious inn here, solitary, but a comfortable substantial building, and as we drove in under a large gateway, before I knew it, where a landlady and her pretty daughters came to the carriage door, entreating me to alight and refresh myself while the horses were making ready, I thought it would be uncharitable to refuse. They took me upstairs to a warm room, and left me there.

Night was setting in, and its bleakness was enhanced by the contrast of the pictured fire glowing and gleaming in the window-pane. As I looked among the stems of the trees, and followed the discoloured marks in the snow where the thaw was sinking into it and undermining it, I thought of the motherly face brightly set off by daughters that had just now welcomed me, and of my mother lying down in such a wood to die.

I was frightened when I found them all about me, but I remembered that before I fainted I tried very hard not to do it; and that was some little comfort. They cushioned me up, on a large sofa by the fire; and then the comely landlady told me that I must travel no further to-night, but must go to bed. But this put me into such a tremble lest they should detain me there, that she soon recalled her words, and compromised for a rest of half-an-hour.

A good endearing creature she was. She, and her three fair girls, all so busy about me. I was to take hot soup and broiled fowl, while Mr Bucket dried himself and dined elsewhere; but I could not do it when a snug round table was presently spread by the fireside, though I was very unwilling to disappoint them. However, I could take some toast and some hot negus; and as I really enjoyed that refreshment, it made some recompense.

Punctual to the time, at the half-hour's end the carriage came rumbling under the gateway, and they took me down, warmed, refreshed, comforted by kindness, and safe (I assured them) not to faint any more. After I had got in and had taken a grateful leave of them all, the youngest daughter – a blooming girl of nineteen, got upon the carriage step, reached in, and kissed me. I have never seen her, from that hour, but I think of her to this hour as my friend.

We went on with toil enough but the dismal roads were not much worse than they had been, and the stage was only nine miles. My companion smoking on the box – I had thought at the last inn of begging him to do so, when I saw him standing at a great fire in a comfortable cloud of tobacco – was as vigilant as ever; and as quickly down and up again, when we came to any human abode or any human creature. He had lighted his little dark lantern, which seemed to be a favourite with him, for we had lamps to the carriage; and every now and then he turned it upon me, to see that I was doing well. There was a folding-window to the carriage-head, but I never closed it, for it seemed like shutting out hope.

We came to the end of the stage, and still the lost trace was not recovered. I looked at him anxiously when we stopped to change horses; but I knew by his yet graver face, as he stood watching the ostlers, that he had heard nothing. Almost in an instant afterwards, as I leaned back in my seat, he looked in, with his lighted lantern in his hand, an excited and quite different man.

"What is it?" said I, starting. "Is she here?"

"No, no. Don't deceive yourself, my dear. Nobody's here. But I've got it!"

The crystallised snow was in his eyelashes, in his hair, lying in ridges on his dress. He had to shake it from his face, and get his breath, before he spoke to me.

"Now, Miss Summerson," said he, beating his finger on the apron, "don't you be disappointed at what I'm a going to do. You know me. I'm Inspector Bucket, and you can trust me. We've come a long way; never mind. Four horses out there for the next stage up! Quick!"

There was a commotion in the yard, and a man came running out of the stables to know "if he meant up or down?"

"Up, I tell you! Up! Ain't it English? Up!"

"Up?" said I, astonished. "To London! Are we going back?"

"Miss Summerson," he answered, "back. Straight back as a die. You know me. Don't be afraid. I'll follow the other, by G – ."

"The other?" I repeated. "Who?"

"You called her Jenny, didn't you? I'll follow her. Bring those two pair out here, for a crown a man. Wake up, some of you!"

"You will not desert this lady we are in search of; you will not abandon her on such a night, and in such a state of mind as I know her to be in!" said I, in an agony, and grasping his hand.

"You are right, my dear, I won't. But I'll follow the other. Look alive here with them horses. My darling, don't you be afraid!"

These orders, and the way in which he ran about the yard, urging them, caused a general excitement that was scarcely less bewildering to me than the sudden change. But, in the height of the confusion, a mounted man galloped away to order the relays, and our horses were put to with great speed.

"My dear," said Mr Bucket, jumping to his seat, and looking in again, – "you'll excuse me if I'm too familiar – don't you fret and worry

156

yourself no more than you can help. I say nothing else at present; but you know me, my dear; now, don't you?"

I endeavoured to say that I knew he was far more capable than I of deciding what we ought to do; but was he sure that this was right? Could I not go forward by myself in search of – I grasped his hand again in my distress, and whispered it to him – of my own mother.

"My dear," he answered, "I know, I know, and would I put you wrong do you think? Inspector Bucket. Now you know me, don't you?"

What could I say but yes!

"Then you keep up as good a heart as you can, and you rely upon me for standing by you, no less than by Sir Leicester Dedlock, Baronet. Now, are you right there?"

"All right, sir!"

"Off she goes, then. And get on, my lads!"

We were again upon the melancholy road by which we had come; tearing up the miry sleet and thawing snow, as if they were torn up by a waterwheel.

CHAPTER 36

A Wintry Day and Night

It is given out that my Lady has gone down into Lincolnshire, but is expected to return presently.

Rumour, busy overmuch, however, will not go down into Lincolnshire. It persists in flitting and chattering about town. It knows that that poor unfortunate man, Sir Leicester, has been sadly used. It hears, my dear child, all sorts of shocking things. It makes the world of five miles round, quite merry. One of the peachy-cheeked charmers with the skeleton throats, is already apprised of all the principal circumstances that will come out before the Lords, on Sir Leicester's application for a bill of divorce.

Thus rumour thrives in the capital, and will not go down into Lincolnshire. By half-past five, post meridian, Horse Guards' time, it has even elicited a new remark from the Honourable Mr Stables, to the effect that although he always knew she was the best-groomed woman in the stud, he had no idea she was a bolter. It is immensely received in turf-circles.

At feasts and festivals also: in firmaments she has often graced, and among constellations she outshone but yesterday, she is still the prevalent subject. What is it? Who is it? When was it? Where was it? How was it? She is discussed by her dear friends with all the genteelest slang in vogue, with the last new word, the last new manner, the last new drawl, and the perfection of polite indifference. And not the least amazing circumstance connected with her being vaguely the town talk, is, that people who know nothing and ever did know nothing about her, think it essential to their reputation to pretend that she is their topic too; and to retail her at second-hand with the last new word and the last new manner, and the last new drawl, and the last new polite indifference, and all the rest of it, all at second-hand but considered equal to new.

So goes the wintry day outside the Dedlock mansion. How within it?

Sir Leicester lying in his bed can speak a little, though with difficulty and indistinctness. He is enjoined to silence and to rest, and they have given him some opiate to lull his pain; for his old enemy is very hard with him. He is never asleep, though sometimes he seems to fall into a dull waking doze. He caused his bedstead to be moved out nearer to the window, when he heard it was such inclement weather; and his head to be so adjusted, that he could see the driving snow and sleet. He watches it as it falls, throughout the whole wintry day.

Upon the least noise in the house, which is kept hushed, his hand is at the pencil. The old housekeeper, sitting by him, knows what he would write and whispers, "No, he has not come back yet, Sir Leicester. It was late last night when he went. He has been but a little time gone yet."

He withdraws his hand, and falls to looking at the sleet and snow again, until they seem, by being long looked at, to fall so thick and fast, that he is obliged to close his eyes for a minute on the giddy whirl of white flakes and icy blots.

He began to look at them as soon as it was light. The day is not yet far spent, when he conceives it to be necessary that her rooms should be prepared for her. It is very cold and wet. Let there be good fires. Let them know that she is expected. Please see to it yourself. He writes to this purpose on his slate, and Mrs Rouncewell with a heavy heart obeys.

"For I dread, George," the old lady says to her son, who waits below to keep her company when she has a little leisure; "I dread, my dear, that my Lady will never more set foot within these walls."

"That's a bad presentiment, mother."

"Nor yet within the walls of Chesney Wold, my dear."

"That's worse. But why, mother!"

"It's going on for sixty year that I have been in this family, and I never had any fears for it before. But it's breaking up, my dear; the great old Dedlock family is breaking up."

"I hope not, mother."

"I am thankful I have lived long enough to be with Sir Leicester in this illness and trouble, for I know I am not too old, nor too useless, to be a welcomer sight to him than anybody else in my place would be. But the step on the Ghost's Walk will walk my Lady down, George; it has been many a day behind her, and now it will pass her, and go on."

"Well, mother dear, I say again, I hope not."

"Ah, so do I, George," the old lady returns, shaking her head, and parting her folded hands. "But if my fears come true, and he has to know it, who will tell him!"

"Are these her rooms?"

"These are my Lady's rooms, just as she left them."

"Why, now," says the trooper, glancing round him, and speaking in a lower voice, "I begin to understand how you come to think as you do think, mother. Rooms get an awful look about them when they are fitted up, like these, for one person you are used to see in them, and that person is away under any shadow: let alone being God knows where."

He is not far out. My Lady's state has a hollow look, thus gloomy and abandoned; and in the inner apartment, where Mr Bucket last night made his secret perquisition, the traces of her dresses and her ornaments, even the mirrors accustomed to reflect them when they were a portion of herself, have a desolate and vacant air. Dark and cold as the wintry day is, it is darker and colder in these deserted chambers; and though the servants heap fires in the grates, and set the couches and the chairs within the warm glass screens, there is a heavy cloud upon the rooms which no light will dispel.

The old housekeeper and her son remain until the preparations are complete, and then she returns upstairs. Sir Leicester watches the sleet and snow, and listens for the returning steps that he expects. In the ears of his old servant, looking as if she had stepped out of an old picture-frame to attend a summoned Dedlock to another world, the silence is fraught with echoes of her own words, "Who will tell him!"

He has been under his valet's hands this morning, to be made presentable; and is as well got up as the circumstances will allow. He is propped with pillows, his grey hair is brushed in its usual manner, his linen is arranged to a nicety, and he is wrapped in a responsible dressing-gown. His eye-glass and his watch are ready to his hand. It is necessary – less to his own dignity now perhaps, than for her sake – that he should be seen as little disturbed, and as much himself, as may be. He is very ill; but he makes his present stand against distress of mind and body, most courageously.

Sir Leicester breaks silence with a harsh cry. "George? Your son George come home, Mrs Rouncewell?"

The old housekeeper wipes her eyes. "Thank God. Yes, Sir Leicester."

Does this discovery of some one lost, this return of some one so long gone, come upon him as a strong confirmation of his hopes? Does he think, "Shall I not, with the aid I have, recall her safely after this?"

It is of no use entreating him; he is determined to speak now, and he does. In a thick crowd of sounds, but still intelligibly enough to be understood.

"Why did you not tell me, Mrs Rouncewell?"

"It happened only yesterday, Sir Leicester, and I doubted your being well enough to be talked to of such things."

"Where is your son George, Mrs Rouncewell?" asks Sir Leicester.

Mrs Rouncewell, not a little alarmed by his disregard of the doctor's injunctions, replies, in London.

"Where in London?"

Mrs Rouncewell is constrained to admit that he is in the house.

"Bring him here to my room. Bring him directly."

The old lady can do nothing but go in search of him. Sir Leicester, with such power of movement as he has, arranges himself a little, to receive him. When he has done so, he looks out again at the falling sleet and snow, and listens again for the returning steps. A quantity of straw has been tumbled down in the street to deaden the noises there, and she might be driven to the door perhaps without his hearing wheels.

He is lying thus, apparently forgetful of his newer and minor surprise, when the housekeeper returns, accompanied by her trooper son. Mr George approaches softly to the bedside, makes his bow, squares his chest, and stands, with his face flushed, very heartily ashamed of himself.

"Good heaven, and it is really George Rouncewell!" exclaims Sir Leicester. "Do you remember me, George?"

The trooper needs to look at him, and to separate this sound from that sound, before he knows what he has said; but doing this, and being a little helped by his mother, he replies:

"I must have a very bad memory, indeed, Sir Leicester, if I failed to remember you."

"When I look at you, George Rouncewell," Sir Leicester observes with difficulty, "I see something of a boy at Chesney Wold – I remember well – very well."

He looks at the trooper until tears come into his eyes, and then he looks at the sleet and snow again.

"I ask your pardon, Sir Leicester," says the trooper, "but would you accept of my arms to raise you up? You would lie easier, Sir Leicester, if you would allow me to move you."

"If you please, George Rouncewell; if you will be so good."

The trooper takes him in his arms like a child, lightly raises him, and turns him with his face more towards the window. "Thank you. You have your mother's gentleness," returns Sir Leicester, "and your own strength. Thank you."

He signs to him with his hand not to go away. George quietly remains at the bedside, waiting to be spoken to.

"You find me," says Sir Leicester, whose eyes are much attracted towards him, "far from well, George Rouncewell."

"I am very sorry both to hear it and to see it, Sir Leicester."

"I am sure you are. No. In addition to my older malady, I have had a sudden and bad attack. Something that deadens " making an endeavour to pass one hand down one side, "and confuses," touching his lips.

George, with a look of assent and sympathy, makes another bow.

Sir Leicester, evidently with a great determination to say, in his own manner, something that is on his mind before relapsing into silence, tries to raise himself among his pillows a little more. George, observant of the action, takes him in his arms again and places him as he desires to be.

161

"Thank you, George. You are another self to me. You have often carried my spare gun at Chesney Wold, George. You are familiar to me in these strange circumstances, very familiar." He has put Sir Leicester's sounder arm over his shoulder in lifting him up, and Sir Leicester is slow in drawing it away again as he says these words.

"I was about to add," he presently goes on, "I was about to add, respecting this attack, that it was unfortunately simultaneous with a slight misunderstanding between my Lady and myself. I do not mean that there was any difference between us (for there has been none), but that there was a misunderstanding of certain circumstances important only to ourselves, which deprives me, for a little while, of my Lady's society. She has found it necessary to make a journey – I trust will shortly return. Mrs Rouncewell do I make myself intelligible? The words are not quite under my command, in the manner of pronouncing them."

The housekeeper understands him perfectly; and in truth he delivers himself with far greater plainness than could have been supposed possible a minute ago. The effort by which he does so, is written in the anxious and labouring expression of his face. Nothing but the strength of his purpose enables him to make it.

"Therefore, I desire to say in the presence of my old retainer and friend, Mrs Rouncewell, whose truth and fidelity no one can question, and in the presence of her son George, who comes back like a familiar recollection of my youth in the home of my ancestors at Chesney Wold – in case I should relapse, in case I should not recover, in case I should lose both my speech and the power of writing, though I hope for better things – therefore I desire to say, and to call you all to witness most solemnly – that I am on unaltered terms with Lady Dedlock. That I assert no cause whatever of complaint against her. That I have ever had the strongest affection for her, and that I retain it undiminished. Say this to herself, and to every one. If you ever say less than this, you will be guilty of deliberate falsehood to me."

Overpowered by his exertions, he lays his head back on his pillows, and closes his eyes; for not more than a minute; when he again resumes his watching of the weather and his attention to the muffled sounds. In the rendering of those little services, and in the manner of their acceptance, the trooper has become installed as necessary to him. Nothing has been said, but it is quite understood. He falls a step or two backward to be out of sight, and mounts guard a little behind his mother's chair.

The day is now beginning to decline. The mist, and the sleet into which the snow has all resolved itself, are darker, and the blaze begins to tell more vividly upon the room walls and furniture.

Now, does Sir Leicester become worse; restless, uneasy, and in great pain.

"Mrs Rouncewell, I am weak – and he has been so long gone."

"Not so very long, Sir Leicester. Not twenty-four hours yet."

"But that is a long time. O, it is a long time!"

He says it with a groan that wrings her heart.

But they find that, however dejected and ill he is, he brightens when a quiet pretence is made of looking at the fires in her rooms, and being sure that everything is ready to receive her. Poor pretence as it is, these allusions to her being expected keep up hope within him.

Midnight comes, and with it the same blank. Upon this wintry night it is so still, that listening to the intense silence is like looking at intense darkness. If any distant sound be audible in this case, it departs through the gloom like a feeble light in that, and all is heavier than before.

The corporation of servants are dismissed to bed (not unwilling to go, for they were up all last night), and only Mrs Rouncewell and George keep watch in Sir Leicester's room. As the night lags tardily on – or rather when it seems to stop altogether, at between two and three o'clock – they find a restless craving on him to know more about the weather, now he cannot see it. Hence George, patrolling regularly every half-hour to the rooms so carefully looked after, extends his march to the hall-door, looks about him, and brings back the best report he can make of the worst of nights; the sleet still falling and even the stone footways lying ankle-deep in icy sludge.

"All is still in readiness, George Rouncewell?"

"Quite orderly and right, Sir Leicester."

"No word of any kind?"

The trooper shakes his head.

"No letter that can possibly have been overlooked?"

But he knows there is no such hope as that, and lays his head down without looking for an answer.

Very familiar to him, as he said himself some hours ago, George

Rouncewell lifts him into easier positions through the long remainder of the blank wintry night, and equally familiar with his unexpressed wish, extinguishes the light and undraws the curtains at the first late break of day. The day comes like a phantom. Cold, colourless, and vague, it sends a warning streak before it of a deathlike hue, as if it cried out, "Look what I am bringing you, who watch there! Who will tell him!"

CHAPTER 37

Esther's Narrative

It was three o'clock in the morning when the houses outside London did at last begin to exclude the country, and to close us in with streets. We had made our way along roads in a far worse condition than when we had traversed them by daylight, both the fall and the thaw having lasted ever since; but the energy of my companion never slackened. I had never heard any variation in his cool, "Get on, my lads!"

The steadiness and confidence with which he had directed our journey back, I could not account for. Never wavering, he never even stopped to make an inquiry until we were within a few miles of London. A very few words, here and there, were then enough for him; and thus we came, at between three and four o'clock in the morning, into Islington.

We stopped in a high-street where there was a coach-stand. My companion paid our two drivers, who were as completely covered with splashes as if they had been dragged along the roads like the carriage itself; and giving them some brief direction where to take it, lifted me out of it, and into a hackney-coach he had chosen from the rest.

"Why, my dear!" he said as he did this. "How wet you are!"

I had not been conscious of it. But the melted snow had found its way into the carriage; and I had got out two or three times when a fallen horse was plunging and had to be got up; and the wet had penetrated my dress. I assured him it was no matter; but the driver, who knew him, would not be dissuaded by me from running down the street to his stable, whence he brought an armful of clean dry straw. They shook it out and strewed it well about me, and I found it warm and comfortable.

"Now, my dear," said Mr Bucket, with his head in at the window after I was shut up. "We're a-going to mark this person down. It may take a little time, but you don't mind that. You're pretty sure that I've got a motive. Ain't you?"

I little thought what it was – little thought in how short a time I should understand it better; but I assured him that I had confidence in him.

"So you may have, my dear," he returned. "And I tell you what! If you only repose half as much confidence in me as I repose in you, that'll do. Lord! You're no trouble at all." said Mr Bucket warmly.

I told him I was very glad, as indeed I was, to have been no hindrance to him; and that I hoped I should be none now.

"My dear," he returned, "when a young lady is as mild as she's game, and as game as she's mild, that's all I ask, and more than I expect. She then becomes a Queen, and that's about what you are yourself."

With these encouraging words – they really were encouraging to me under those lonely and anxious circumstances – he got upon the box, and we once more drove away. Where we drove, I neither knew then, nor have ever known since; but we appeared to seek out the narrowest and worst streets in London.

Sometimes we emerged upon a wider thoroughfare, or came to a larger building than the generality, well lighted. Then we stopped at offices like those we had visited when we began our journey, and I saw him in consultation with others. Sometimes he would get down by an archway, or at a street corner, and mysteriously show the light of his little lantern. This would attract similar lights from various dark quarters, like so many insects, and a fresh consultation would be held. By degrees we appeared to contract our search within narrower and easier limits. Single police-officers on duty could now tell Mr Bucket what he wanted to know, and point to him where to go. At last we stopped for a rather long conversation between him and one of these men, which I supposed to be satisfactory from his manner of nodding from time to time. When it was finished he came to me, looking very busy and very attentive.

"Now, Miss Summerson," he said to me, "We have marked this person down, and you may be of use to me before I know it myself. I don't like to ask such a thing, my dear, but would you walk a little way?"

Of course I got out directly, and took his arm.

"It ain't so easy to keep your feet," said Mr Bucket; "but take time."

Although I looked about me confusedly and hurriedly, as we crossed the street, I thought I knew the place. "Are we in Holborn?" I asked him.

"Yes," said Mr Bucket. "Do you know this turning?"

"It looks like Chancery Lane."

"And was christened so, my dear," said Mr Bucket.

We turned down it; and as we went, shuffling through the sleet, I heard the clocks strike half-past five. We passed on in silence, and as quickly as we could with such a foothold; when some one coming towards us on the narrow pavement, wrapped in a cloak, stopped and stood aside to give me room. In the same moment I heard an exclamation of wonder, and my own name, from Mr Woodcourt. I knew his voice very well.

It was so unexpected, and so – I don't know what to call it, whether pleasant or painful – to come upon it after my feverish wandering journey, and in the midst of the night, that I could not keep back the tears from my eyes. It was like hearing his voice in a strange country.

"My dear Miss Summerson, that you should be out at this hour, and in such weather!"

He had heard from my guardian of my having been called away on some uncommon business, and said so to dispense with any explanation. I told him that we had but just left a coach, and were going – but then I was obliged to look at my companion.

"Why, you see, Mr Woodcourt;" he had caught the name from me; "we are a-going at present into the next street. – Inspector Bucket."

Mr Woodcourt, disregarding my remonstrances, had hurriedly taken off his cloak, and was putting it about me. "That's a good move, too," said Mr Bucket, assisting, "a very good move."

"May I go with you?" said Mr Woodcourt. I don't know whether to me or to my companion.

"Why, Lord!" exclaimed Mr Bucket, taking the answer on himself. "Of course you may."

It was all said in a moment, and they took me between them, wrapped in the cloak.

"I have just left Richard," said Mr Woodcourt. "I have been sitting with him since ten o'clock last night."

"O, dear me, he is ill!"

"No, no, believe me; not ill, but not quite well. He was depressed and faint and Ada sent to me of course. Richard revived so much after a little while, and Ada was so happy that I remained with him until he had been fast asleep some hours. As fast asleep as she is now, I hope!"

We now turned into another narrow street. "Mr Woodcourt," said Mr Bucket, who had eyed him closely as we came along, "our business takes us to a law-stationer's here; a certain Mr Snagsby's. What, you know him, do you?" He was so quick that he saw it in an instant.

"Yes, I know a little of him, and have called upon him at this place."

"Indeed, sir?" said Mr Bucket. "Then you will be so good as to let me leave Miss Summerson with you for a moment, while I go and have half a word with him?"

The last police-officer with whom he had conferred was standing silently behind us. I was not aware of it until he struck in, on my saying I heard some one crying.

"Don't be alarmed, miss," he returned. "It's Snagsby's servant."

"Why, you see," said Mr Bucket, "the girl's subject to fits, and has 'em bad upon her to-night. A most contrary circumstance it is, for I want certain information out of that girl, and she must be brought to reason somehow."

"At all events, they wouldn't be up yet, if it wasn't for her, Mr Bucket," said the other man. "She's been at it pretty well all night, sir."

"Well, that's true," he returned. "My light's burnt out. Show yours a moment."

In the little round of light produced for the purpose, Mr Bucket went up to the door and knocked. The door was opened, after he had knocked twice; and he went in, leaving us standing in the street.

"Miss Summerson," said Mr Woodcourt, "if without obtruding myself on your confidence, I may remain near you, pray let me do so."

"You are truly kind," I answered. "I need wish to keep no secret of my own from you; if I keep any, it is another's."

"I quite understand. Trust me, I will remain near you only so long as I can fully respect it."

"I trust implicitly to you," I said.

After a short time the little round of light shone out again, and Mr Bucket advanced towards us in it with his earnest face. "Please to come in, Miss Summerson," he said, "and sit down by the fire. Mr Woodcourt, from information I have received I understand you are a medical man. Would you look to this girl and see if anything can be done to bring her round. She has a letter somewhere that I particularly want. It's not in her box, and I think it must be about her; but she is so twisted and clenched up, that she is difficult to handle without hurting."

We all three went into the house together; although it was cold and raw, it smelt close too from being up all night. In the passage behind the door, stood a scared, sorrowful-looking little man in a grey coat, who seemed to have a naturally polite manner and spoke meekly.

"Downstairs, if you please, Mr Bucket," said he. "The back is Guster's bedroom, and in it she's a carrying on, poor thing, to a frightful extent!"

We went downstairs, followed by Mr Snagsby, as I soon found the little man to be. He appeared so miserable, sitting with his head upon his hand, and I appeared so unwelcome, that I was going to offer an apology, when Mr Bucket took the matter on himself.

"Now, Mr Snagsby," said he, "the best thing you can do, is to go along with Mr Woodcourt to look after your Guster and to hold the candle, or hold her, or make yourself useful in any way you're asked. Mr Woodcourt, would you be so good as see to her, and if you can get that letter from her, to let me have it as soon as ever you can?"

As they went out, Mr Bucket made me sit down in a corner by the fire, and take off my wet shoes, which he turned up to dry upon the fender. I involuntarily clasped my hands, and felt the room turning away from me. But it stopped as Mr Woodcourt came in, put a paper into his hand, and went away again.

"Now my dear, you're steady, and quite sure of yourself?"

"Quite," said I.

"Whose writing is that?"

It was my mother's. A pencil-writing, on a crushed and torn piece of paper, blotted with wet. Folded roughly like a letter, and directed to me, at my guardian's.

"You know the hand," he said, "and if you are firm enough to read it to me, do! But be particular to a word."

It had been written in portions, at different times. I read what follows:

"I came to the cottage with two objects. First, to see the dear one, if I could, once more – but only to see her – not to speak to her, or let her know that I was near. The other object, to elude pursuit, and to be lost. Do not blame the mother for her share. The assistance that she rendered me, she rendered on my strongest assurance that it was for the dear one's good. You remember her dead child. The men's consent I bought, but her help was freely given."

"That was written," said my companion, "when she rested there. It bears out what I made of it. I was right."

The next was written at another time:

"I have wandered a long distance, and for many hours, and I know that I must soon die. These streets! I have no purpose but to die. Cold, wet, and fatigue are sufficient causes for my being found dead; but I shall die of others, though I suffer from these. It was right that all that had sustained me should give way at once and that I should die of terror and my conscience."

"Take courage," said Mr Bucket. "There's only a few words more."

Those, too, were written at another time. To all appearance, almost in the dark:

"I have done all I could do to be lost. I shall be soon forgotten so, and shall disgrace him least. I have nothing about me by which I can be recognised. This paper I part with now. The place where I shall lie down, if I can get so far, has been often in my mind. Farewell. Forgive."

Mr Bucket, supporting me with his arm, lowered me gently into my chair. "Cheer up! Don't think me hard with you, my dear, but, as soon as ever you feel equal to it, get your shoes on and be ready."

I did as he required; but I was left there a long time, praying for my unhappy mother. They were all occupied with the poor girl, and I heard Mr Woodcourt directing them, and speaking to her often. At length he came in with Mr Bucket; and said that as it was important to address her gently, he thought it best that I should ask her for whatever information we desired to obtain. There was no doubt that she could now reply to questions, if she were soothed, and not alarmed. The questions, Mr Bucket said, were, how she came by the letter, what passed between her and the person who gave her the letter, and where the person went. Holding my mind as steadily as I could to these points, I went into the next room with them. Mr Woodcourt would have remained outside, but at my solicitation went in with us.

The poor girl was sitting on the floor where they had laid her down.

They stood around her, though at a little distance, that she might have air. She was not pretty, and looked weak and poor; but she had a plaintive and a good face, though it was still a little wild. I kneeled on the ground beside her, and put her poor head upon my shoulder; whereupon she drew her arm round my neck, and burst into tears.

"My poor girl," said I, laying my face against her forehead; for indeed I was crying too, and trembling; "it seems cruel to trouble you now, but more depends on our knowing something about this letter, than I could tell you in an hour."

She began piteously declaring that she didn't mean any harm, she didn't mean any harm.

"We are all sure of that," said I. "But pray tell me how you got it."

"Yes, dear lady, I will, and tell you true."

"I am sure of that," said I. "And how was it?"

"I had been out on an errand, dear lady – long after it was dark – quite late; and when I came home, I found a common-looking person, all wet and muddy, looking up at our house. When she saw me coming in at the door, she called me back, and said did I live here? and I said yes, and she said she knew only one or two places about here, but had lost her way, and couldn't find them. O, what shall I do, what shall I do! They won't believe me! She didn't say any harm to me, and I didn't say any harm to her."

It was necessary to comfort her before she could be got beyond this.

"She could not find those places," said I.

"No!" cried the girl, shaking her head. "No! Couldn't find them. And she was so faint, and lame, and miserable, O so wretched, that if you had seen her, Mr Snagsby, you'd have given her half-a-crown, I know!"

"Well, Guster, my girl," said he, at first not knowing what to say. "I hope I should."

"And yet she was so well spoken," said the girl, looking at me with wide-open eyes, "that it made a person's heart bleed. And so she said to me, did I know the way to the burying ground? And I asked her which burying-ground. And she said, the poor burying-ground not very far from here, where there was an archway, and a step, and an iron gate."

As I watched her face, and soothed her to go on, I saw that Mr Bucket received this with a look of alarm.

"O, dear, dear!" cried the girl, pressing her hair back with her hands. "What shall I do, what shall I do! She meant the burying-ground where the man was buried that took the sleeping-stuff – that you came home and told us of, Mr Snagsby – that frightened me so. O, I am frightened again. Hold me!"

"You are so much better now," said I. "Pray, pray tell me more."

"Yes I will, yes I will! But don't be angry with me, that's a dear lady, because I have been so ill."

Angry with her, poor soul!

"There! Now I will, now I will. So she said, could I tell her how to find it, and I said yes, and I told her; and she looked at me with eyes like almost as if she was blind, and herself all waving back. And so she took out the letter, and showed it me, and said would I take it from her, and send it, and the messenger would be paid at the house? And so I said yes, if it was no harm, and she said no – no harm. And so I took it from her, and she said she had nothing to give me, and I said I was poor myself and consequently wanted nothing. And so she said God bless you, and went."

"And did she go – "

"Yes," cried the girl, anticipating the inquiry. "Yes! She went the way I had shown her."

Mr Woodcourt took her kindly from me. Mr Bucket wrapped me up, and immediately we were in the street. Mr Woodcourt hesitated, but I said, "Don't leave me now!" and Mr Bucket added, "You'll be better with us, we may want you; don't lose time!"

I have the most confused impressions of that walk. I recollect that it was neither night nor day; that morning was dawning, but the street-lamps were not yet put out; that the sleet was still falling, and that all the ways were deep with it. I recollect a few chilled people passing in the streets. I recollect the wet housetops, the clogged and bursting gutters and water-spouts, the mounds of blackened ice and snow over which we passed, the narrowness of the courts by which we went. At the same time I remember, that the poor girl seemed to be yet telling her story audibly and plainly in my hearing; that I could feel her resting on my arm.

At last we stood under a dark and miserable covered way, where one lamp was burning over an iron gate, and where the morning faintly struggled in. The gate was closed. Beyond it, was a burial-ground – a dreadful spot in which the night was very slowly stirring; but where I could dimly see heaps of dishonoured graves and stones, hemmed in by filthy houses with a few dull lights in their windows, and on whose walls

171

a thick humidity broke out like a disease. On the step at the gate, drenched in the fearful wet of such a place, which oozed and splashed down everywhere, I saw, with a cry of pity and horror, a woman lying – Jenny, Jo's old friend from the brickworks.

I ran forward, but they stopped me, and Mr Woodcourt entreated me, with the greatest earnestness, even with tears, before I went up to the figure to listen for an instant to what Mr Bucket said.

"Miss Summerson, you'll understand me, if you think a moment. They changed clothes at the cottage."

They changed clothes at the cottage. I could repeat the words in my mind, and I knew what they meant of themselves; but I attached no meaning to them in any other connexion.

"And one returned," said Mr Bucket, "and one went on. And the one that went on, only went on a certain way agreed upon to deceive, and then turned across country, and went home. Think a moment!"

I could repeat this in my mind too, but I had not the least idea what it meant. I saw before me, lying on the step, the mother of the dead child. She lay there, with one arm creeping round a bar of the iron gate, and seeming to embrace it. She lay there, who had so lately spoken to my mother. She lay there, a distressed, unsheltered, senseless creature. She who had brought my mother's letter, who could give me the only clue to where my mother was; she, who was to guide us to rescue and save her whom we had sought so far, who had come to this condition by some means connected with my mother that I could not follow, and might be passing beyond our reach and help at that moment; she lay there, and they stopped me! I saw, but did not comprehend, the solemn and compassionate look in Mr Woodcourt's face. I saw, but did not comprehend, his touching the other on the breast to keep him back. I saw him stand uncovered in the bitter air, with a reverence for something. But my understanding for all this was gone.

I even heard it said between them:

"Shall she go?"

"She had better go. Her hands should be the first to touch her. They have a higher right than ours."

I passed on to the gate, and stooped down. I lifted the heavy head, put the long dank hair aside, and turned the face. And it was my mother, cold and dead.

CHAPTER 38

Perspective

I had an illness, but it was not a long one; and I would avoid even this mention of it, if I could quite keep down the recollection of their sympathy.

I proceed to other passages of my narrative.

During the time of my illness, we were still in London, where Mrs Woodcourt had come, on my guardian's invitation, to stay with us. When my guardian thought me well and cheerful enough to talk with him in our old way I resumed my work, and my chair beside his. He had appointed the time himself, and we were alone.

"Dame Trot," said he, receiving me with a kiss, "welcome to the Growlery again, my dear. I have a scheme to develop, little woman. I propose to remain here, perhaps for six months, perhaps for a longer time – as it may be. Quite to settle here for a while, in short."

"And in the meanwhile leave Bleak House?" said I.

"Bleak House," he repeated, "must learn to take care of itself. It is a long way from Ada, my dear, and Ada stands much in need of you."

"It is like you, guardian," said I, "to have been taking that into consideration, for a happy surprise to both of us."

"I wish to hear as much and as often of Ada as I can, in this condition of estrangement from poor Rick. Not of her alone, but of him too, poor fellow."

"Have you seen Mr Woodcourt, this morning, guardian?"

"I see Mr Woodcourt every morning, Dame Durden."

"Does he still say the same of Richard?"

"Just the same. He knows of no direct bodily illness that he has; on the contrary, he believes that he has none. Yet he is not easy about him; who can be?"

"Dear, unfortunate, mistaken Richard," said I. "When will he awake from his delusion!"

"He is not in the way to do so now, my dear," replied my guardian. "The more he suffers, the more averse he will be to me: having made me the principal representative of the great occasion of his suffering."

I could not help adding, "So unreasonably!"

"Ah, Dame Trot, Dame Trot," returned my guardian, "what shall we find reasonable in Jarndyce and Jarndyce! Unreason and injustice at the top, unreason and injustice at the heart and at the bottom, unreason and injustice from beginning to end – if it ever has an end – how should poor Rick, always hovering near it, pluck reason out of it?"

His gentleness and consideration for Richard, whenever we spoke of him, touched me so, that I was always silent on this subject very soon.

"Well, well, little woman! To go on, my dear. This rock we must leave to time, chance, and hopeful circumstance. We must not shipwreck Ada upon it. She cannot afford, and he cannot afford, the remotest chance of another separation from a friend. Therefore, I have particularly begged of Woodcourt, and I now particularly beg of you, my dear, not to move this subject with Rick. Let it rest. Next week, next month, next year, sooner or later, he will see me with clearer eyes. I can wait."

But I had already discussed it with him, I confessed; and so, I thought, had Mr Woodcourt.

"So he tells me," returned my guardian. "Very good. He has made his protest, and Dame Durden has made hers, and there is nothing more to be said about it."

"Good," said my guardian. "Carried unanimously."

"Carried unanimously," I repeated, going on with my work.

It was a cover for his book-table that I happened to be ornamenting. It had been laid by on the night preceding my sad journey, and never resumed. I showed it to him now, and he admired it highly.

"You said, dear guardian, when we spoke of Mr Woodcourt before Ada left us, that you thought he would give a long trial to another country. Have you been advising him since?"

"Yes, little woman; pretty often."

"Has he decided to do so?"

"I rather think not."

"Some other prospect has opened to him, perhaps?" said I.

"Why – yes – perhaps," returned my guardian, beginning his answer in a very deliberate manner. "About half a year hence or so, there is a medical attendant for the poor to be appointed at a certain place in Yorkshire. It is a thriving place, pleasantly situated; streams and streets, town and country, mill and moor; and seems to present an opening for such a man. It is Woodcourt's kind."

"And will he get this appointment?" I asked.

"Why, little woman," returned my guardian, smiling, "not being an oracle, I cannot confidently say; but I think so. His reputation stands very high; strange to say, I believe the best man has the best chance. You must not suppose it to be a fine endowment. It is a very, very commonplace affair, my dear; an appointment to a great amount of work and a small amount of pay; but better things will gather about it, it may be fairly hoped."

"The poor of that place will have reason to bless the choice, if it falls on Mr Woodcourt, guardian."

"You are right, little woman; that I am sure they will."

We said no more about it, nor did he say a word about the future of Bleak House. But it was the first time I had taken my seat at his side in my mourning dress, and that accounted for it I considered.

I now began to visit my dear girl every day, in the dull dark corner where she lived. The morning was my usual time; but whenever I found I had an hour or so to spare, I put on my bonnet and bustled off to Chancery Lane. They were both so glad to see me at all hours, and used to brighten up so when they heard me opening the door and coming in (being quite at home, I never knocked), that I had no fear of becoming troublesome just yet.

On these occasions I frequently found Richard absent. At other times he would be writing, or reading papers in the Cause, at that table of his, so covered with papers, which was never disturbed. Sometimes I would meet him in the neighbourhood, lounging about, and biting his nails. I often met him wandering in Lincoln's Inn, near the place where I had first seen him, O how different, how different!

That the money Ada brought him was melting away with the candles I used to see burning after dark, I knew very well. My dear made the best of housekeepers, and tried hard to save; but I knew that they were getting poorer and poorer every day.

She shone in the miserable corner like a beautiful star. She adorned and graced it so, that it became another place. Paler than she had been at home, and a little quieter than I had thought natural when she was yet so cheerful and hopeful, her face was so unshadowed, that I half believed she was blinded by her love for Richard to his ruinous career.

I went one day to dine with them, while I was under this impression.

We sat down to dinner, and I had an opportunity of observing Richard, anxiously. I found Richard thin and languid, slovenly in his dress, abstracted in his manner, forcing his spirits now and then, and at other intervals relapsing into a dull thoughtfulness. About his large bright eyes that used to be so merry, there was a wanness and a restlessness that changed them altogether. I cannot use the expression that he looked old. There is a ruin of youth which is not like age; and into such a ruin, Richard's youth and youthful beauty had all fallen away.

He ate little, and seemed indifferent what it was; showed himself to be much more impatient than he used to be; and was quick, even with Ada. I thought, at first, that his old light-hearted manner was all gone; but it shone out of him sometimes, as I had occasionally known little momentary glimpses of my own old face to look out upon me from the glass. His laugh had not quite left him either; but it was like the echo of a joyful sound, and that is always sorrowful.

Yet he was as glad as ever, in his old affectionate way, to have me there; and we talked of the old times pleasantly.

Then he threw himself on the sofa, tired out; and Ada and I put things to rights, for they had no other servant than the woman who attended to the chambers. My dear girl had a cottage piano there, and quietly sat down to sing some of Richard's favourites; the lamp being first removed into the next room, as he complained of its hurting his eyes.

I sat between them, at my dear girl's side, and felt very melancholy listening to her sweet voice. I think Richard did too; I think he darkened the room for that reason. She had been singing some time, rising between whiles to bend over him and speak to him; when Mr Woodcourt came in. Then he sat down by Richard; and half playfully, half earnestly, quite naturally and easily, found out how he felt, and where he had been all day. Presently he proposed to accompany him in a short walk on one of the bridges, as it was a moonlight airy night; and Richard readily consenting, they went out together.

They left my dear girl still sitting at the piano, and me still sitting beside her. When they were gone out, I drew my arm round her waist. She put her left hand in mine (I was sitting on that side), but kept her right upon the keys – going over and over them, without striking any note.

"Esther, my dearest," she said, breaking silence, "Richard is never so well, and I am never so easy about him, as when he is with Allan Woodcourt. We have to thank you for that."

I pointed out to my darling how this could scarcely be, because Mr Woodcourt had come to her cousin John's house, and had known us all there; and because he had always liked Richard, and Richard had always liked him, and – and so forth.

"All true," said Ada; "but that he is such a devoted friend to us, we owe to you."

I thought it best to let my dear girl have her way, and to say no more about it. So I said as much. I said it lightly, because I felt her trembling.

"When I married Richard, I was not insensible to what was before him. I had been perfectly happy for a long time with you, and I had never known any trouble or anxiety, so loved and cared for; but I understood the danger he was in, dear Esther."

"I know, I know, my darling."

"When we were married, I had some little hope that I might be able to convince him of his mistake; that he might come to regard it in a new way as my husband, and not pursue it all the more desperately for my sake – as he does. But if I had not had that hope, I would have married him just the same, Esther. Just the same!"

In the momentary firmness of the hand that was never still – a firmness inspired by the utterance of these last words, and dying away with them – I saw the confirmation of her earnest tones.

"You are not to think, my dearest Esther, that I fail to see what you see, and fear what you fear. No one can understand him better than I do. The greatest wisdom that ever lived in the world could scarcely know Richard better than my love does."

She spoke so modestly and softly, and her trembling hand expressed such agitation, as it moved to and fro upon the silent notes!

"I see him at his worst, every day. I watch him in his sleep. I know every change of his face. But when I married Richard I was quite determined, Esther, if Heaven would help me, never to show him that I grieved for what he did, and so to make him more unhappy. I want him, when he comes home, to find no trouble in my face. I want him, when he looks at me, to see what he loved in me. I married him to do this, and this supports me."

I felt her trembling more. I waited for what was yet to come, and I now thought I began to know what it was.

"And something else supports me, Esther."

She stopped a minute. Stopped speaking only; her hand was still in motion.

"I look forward a little while, and there may be something lying on my breast with greater power than mine to show him his true course, and win him back."

Her hand stopped now. She clasped me in her arms, and I clasped her in mine. O, my sweet girl, what a heart was that which beat so fast against me!

"These hopes uphold me, my dear Esther, and I know they will. Though sometimes even they depart from me, before a dread that arises when I look at Richard."

I tried to cheer my darling, and asked her what it was. Sobbing and weeping, she replied:

"That he may not live to see his child."

CHAPTER 39

A Discovery

Not a day passed, without my going there, of course. At first I found Mr Skimpole there, on two or three occasions, idly playing the piano, and talking in his usual vivacious strain. Now, besides my mistrusting his being there without making Richard poorer, I felt as if there were something in his careless gaiety, too inconsistent with what I knew of the depths of Ada's life. I clearly perceived, too, that Ada shared my feelings. I therefore resolved, after much thinking of it, to make a private visit to Mr Skimpole and try delicately to explain myself.

I set off one morning, accompanied by Charley, for Somers Town. I knocked with a trembling hand at Mr Skimpole's door – literally with a hand, for the knocker was gone – and after a long parley gained admission.

Mr Skimpole, lying on the sofa in his room, playing the flute a little, declared he was enchanted to see me.

I replied, half defeated already, that I wished to speak to himself only, if he would give me leave.

"My dear Miss Summerson, most joyfully! Of course," he said, bringing his chair nearer mine, and breaking into his fascinating smile, "of course it's not business. Then it's pleasure!"

I said it certainly was not business that I came upon, but it was not quite a pleasant matter.

"Then, my dear Miss Summerson," said he, with the frankest gaiety, "don't allude to it. Why should you allude to anything that is not a pleasant matter? I never do. So that's disposed of, and we will talk of something else."

"Mr Skimpole," said I, raising my eyes to his, "I have so often heard you say that you are unacquainted with the common affairs of life that perhaps you will excuse my boldness on that account. I think you ought most seriously to know that Richard is poorer than he was."

"Dear me!" said Mr Skimpole. "So am I, they tell me."

"And in very embarrassed circumstances."

"Parallel case, exactly!" said Mr Skimpole with a delighted countenance.

"This at present naturally causes Ada much secret anxiety; and as I think she is less anxious when no claims are made upon her by visitors, and as Richard has one uneasiness always heavy on his mind, it has occurred to me to take the liberty of saying that – if you would – not – ."

I was coming to the point with great difficulty, when he took me by both hands, and, with a radiant face and in the liveliest way, anticipated it.

"Not go there? Certainly not, my dear Miss Summerson, most assuredly not. Why should I go there? When I go anywhere, I go for pleasure. I don't go anywhere for pain, because I was made for pleasure. Pain comes to me when it wants me. Now I have had very little pleasure at our dear Richard's, lately. Why should I go to see them therefore? Absurd!"

Through the beaming smile with which he regarded me, as he reasoned thus, there now broke forth a look of disinterested benevolence quite astonishing. He finished by genially kissing my hand and thanking me. Nothing but Miss Summerson's fine tact, he said, would have found this out for him.

179

I was much disconcerted; but I had determined to mention something else, however, and I thought I was not to be put off in that.

"Mr Skimpole," said I, "I must take the liberty of saying, before I conclude my visit, that I was much surprised to learn, on the best authority, some little time ago, that you knew with whom that poor boy left Bleak House, and that you accepted a present on that occasion. I have not mentioned it to my guardian, for I fear it would hurt him unnecessarily; but I may say to you that I was much surprised."

He thought about it for a little while, with a highly agreeable and whimsical expression of face; then quite gave it up, and said, in his most engaging manner.

"You know what a child I am. Why surprised?"

I gave him to understand, in the gentlest words I could use, that his conduct seemed to involve a disregard of several moral obligations. He was much amused and interested when he heard this, and said, "No, really?" with ingenuous simplicity.

"You know I don't intend to be responsible. I never could do it. Responsibility is a thing that has always been above me – or below me," said Mr Skimpole.

I suggested, as I rose to go, that it was not right to betray my guardian's confidence for a bribe.

"My dear Miss Summerson," he returned with a candid hilarity that was all his own, "I can't be bribed."

"Not by Mr Bucket?" said I.

"No," said he. "Not by anybody. I don't attach any value to money. I don't care about it, I don't know about it, I don't want it, I don't keep it – it goes away from me directly. How can I be bribed?"

Anything to equal the lightness of his manner, and the playful impartiality with which he seemed to convince himself, as he tossed the matter about like a ball of feathers, was surely never seen in anybody else!

I had nothing to offer in reply to this exposition, and therefore took my leave.

As it so happened that I never saw Mr Skimpole again, I may at once finish what I know of his history. A coolness arose between him and my guardian, based principally on the foregoing grounds, and on his having heartlessly disregarded my guardian's entreaties in reference to

Richard. His being heavily in my guardian's debt, had nothing to do with their separation.

And now I come to a part of my story, touching myself very nearly indeed, and for which I was quite unprepared when the circumstance occurred.

The months were gliding away; and my dear girl, sustained by the hopes she had confided to me, was the same beautiful star in the miserable corner. Richard, more worn and haggard, haunted the Court day after day; listlessly sat there the whole day long, when he knew there was no remote chance of the suit being mentioned; and became one of the stock sights of the place.

It was only Mr Woodcourt who could occasionally divert his attention, for a few hours at a time; and rouse him, even when he sunk into a lethargy of mind and body that alarmed us greatly, and the returns of which became more frequent as the months went on. My dear girl was right in saying that he only pursued his errors the more desperately for her sake. I have no doubt that his desire to retrieve what he had lost, was rendered the more intense by his grief for his young wife, and became like the madness of a gamester.

I was there, as I have mentioned, at all hours. When I was there at night, I generally went home with Charley in a coach; sometimes my guardian would meet me in the neighbourhood, and we would walk home together. One evening, he had arranged to meet me at eight o'clock and it was within a few minutes of the hour, when I gave my darling my last kiss for the night, and hurried downstairs. Mr Woodcourt went with me, as it was dusk.

When we came to the usual place of meeting, my guardian was not there. We agreed that he was either prevented from coming or that he had come, and gone away; and Mr Woodcourt proposed to walk home with me.

Arriving at home and going upstairs, we found that my guardian was out. We were standing by the opened window looking down into the street, when Mr Woodcourt spoke to me. I learned in a moment that he loved me. I learned in a moment that my scarred face was all unchanged to him. I learned in a moment that what I had thought was pity and compassion, was devoted, generous, faithful love. O, too late to know it now, too late. That was the first ungrateful thought I had. Too late.

"Heaven knows, beloved of my life," said he, "that my praise is not a lover's praise, but the truth. You do not know what all around you see in Esther Summerson, how many hearts she touches and awakens, what sacred admiration and what love she wins."

"O, Mr Woodcourt," cried I, "it is a great thing to win love! I am proud of it, and honoured by it; and the hearing of it causes me to shed these tears of mingled joy and sorrow, but I am not free to think of yours."

He broke the silence.

"I should poorly show the trust that I have in the dear one who will evermore be as dear to me as now," and the deep earnestness with which he said it, at once strengthened me and made me weep, "if, after her assurance that she is not free to think of my love, I urged it. Dear Esther, I have always feared that I should tell it you in vain. I distress you. I have said enough."

I wished to help him in his trouble, as I had wished to do when he showed that first commiseration for me.

"Dear Mr Woodcourt," said I, "before we part to-night, something is left for me to say. I never could say it as I wish – I never shall – but – ."

I had to think again of being more deserving of his love, and his affliction, before I could go on.

"I am deeply sensible of your generosity, and I shall treasure its remembrance to my dying hour. I know full well how changed I am, I know you are not unacquainted with my history, and I know what a noble love that is which is so faithful. It shall not be lost. It shall make me better."

He covered his eyes with his hand, and turned away his head. How could I ever be worthy of those tears?

"And never believe, dear dear Mr Woodcourt, never believe, that I forget this night; or that while my heart beats it can be insensible to the pride and joy of having been beloved by you."

He took my hand, and kissed it. He was like himself again, and I felt still more encouraged.

"I am induced, by what you said just now," said I, "to hope that you have succeeded in your endeavour."

"I have," he answered. "With such help from Mr Jarndyce, as you who know him so well can imagine him to have rendered me, I have succeeded."

"Heaven bless him for it," said I, giving him my hand; "and Heaven bless you in all you do!"

"I shall do it better for the wish," he answered; "it will make me enter on these new duties, as on another sacred trust from you."

"Ah! Richard!" I exclaimed involuntarily, "What will he do when you are gone!"

"I am not required to go yet; I would not desert him, dear Miss Summerson, even if I were."

One other thing I felt it needful to touch upon, before he left me. I knew that I should not be worthier of the love I could not take, if I reserved it.

"Mr Woodcourt," said I, "From my childhood I have been the object of the untiring goodness of the best of human beings; to whom I am so bound by every tie of attachment, gratitude, and love, that nothing I could do in the compass of a life could express the feelings of a single day."

"I share those feelings," he returned; "You speak of Mr Jarndyce."

"You know his virtues well," said I, "but few can know the greatness of his character as I know it. All its highest and best qualities have been revealed to me in nothing more brightly, than in the shaping out of that future in which I am so happy."

I gave him my hand again. "Good-night," I said, "good-bye."

"The first, until we meet to-morrow; the second, as a farewell to this theme between us for ever."

"Yes."

"Good-night; good-bye."

He left me, and I stood at the dark window watching the street. His love, in all its constancy and generosity, had come so suddenly upon me, that he had not left me a minute when my fortitude gave way again, and the street was blotted out by my rushing tears.

CHAPTER 40

Another Discovery

I had not the courage to see any one that night. I had not even the courage to see myself, for I was afraid that my tears might a little reproach me. I went up to my room in the dark, and prayed in the dark, and lay down in the dark to sleep. I had no need of any light to read my guardian's letter by, for I knew it by heart. I took it from the place where I kept it, and repeated its contents by its own clear light of integrity and love, and went to sleep with it on my pillow.

After breakfast, I waited my opportunity, and peeped about a little, until I saw my guardian in his own room – the room of last night – by himself. Then I made an excuse to go in with my housekeeping keys, shutting the door after me.

"Well, Dame Durden?" said my guardian; the post had brought him several letters, and he was writing. "You want money?"

"No, indeed, I have plenty in hand."

"There never was such a Dame Durden," said my guardian, "for making money last."

He had laid down his pen, and leaned back in his chair looking at me. I have often spoken of his bright face, but I thought I had never seen it look so bright and good. There was a high happiness upon it, which made me think, "he has been doing some great kindness this morning."

"There never was," said my guardian, musing as he smiled upon me, "such a Dame Durden for making money last."

He had never yet altered his old manner. I loved it, and him, so much, that when I now went up to him and took my usual chair, which was always put at his side.

"Dear guardian," said I, "I want to speak to you. Have I been remiss in anything?"

"Remiss in anything, my dear!"

"Have I not been what I have meant to be, since – I brought the answer to your letter, guardian?"

"You have been everything I could desire, my love."

"I am very glad indeed to hear that," I returned. "You know, you said to me, was this the mistress of Bleak House. And I said, yes."

"Yes," said my guardian, nodding his head. He had put his arm about me, as if there were something to protect me from; and looked in my face, smiling.

"Since then," said I, "we have never spoken on the subject except once."

"And then I said, Bleak House was thinning fast; and so it was, my dear."

"And I said," I timidly reminded him, "but its mistress remained."

184

He still held me, in the same protecting manner, and with the same bright goodness in his face.

"Dear guardian," said I, "I know how you have felt all that has happened, and how considerate you have been. As so much time has passed, and as you spoke only this morning of my being so well again, perhaps you expect me to renew the subject. Perhaps I ought to do so. I will be the mistress of Bleak House when you please."

"See," he returned gaily, "what a sympathy there must be between us! I have had nothing else, poor Rick excepted, in my mind. When you came in, I was full of it. When shall we give Bleak House its mistress, little woman?"

"When you please."

"Next month?"

"Next month, dear guardian."

"The day on which I take the happiest and best step of my life – the day on which I shall be a man more exulting and more enviable than any other man in the world – the day on which I give Bleak House its little mistress – shall be next month, then," said my guardian.

I put my arms round his neck and kissed him, just as I had done on the day when I brought my answer.

A servant came to the door to announce Mr Bucket, which was quite unnecessary, for Mr Bucket was already looking in over the servant's shoulder. "Mr Jarndyce and Miss Summerson," said he, rather out of breath, "with all apologies for intruding, will you allow me to order up a person that's on the stairs, and that objects to being left there in case of becoming the subject of observations in his absence? Thank you. Be so good as chair that there Member in this direction, will you?" said Mr Bucket, beckoning over the banisters.

This singular request produced an old man in a black skull-cap, unable to walk, who was carried up by a couple of bearers, and deposited in the room near the door. Mr Bucket immediately got rid of the bearers, mysteriously shut the door, and bolted it.

"Now you see, Mr Jarndyce," he then began, putting down his hat, and opening his subject with a flourish of his well-remembered finger, "you know me, and Miss Summerson knows me. This gentleman likewise knows me, and his name is Smallweed and he's what you may call a dealer in bills. Now, Mr Jarndyce, I address myself to you. I've been negotiating with this gentleman on behalf of Sir Leicester Dedlock, Baronet; and one way and another I've been in and out and about his premises a deal. His premises are the premises formerly occupied by Krook, Marine Store Dealer – a relation of this gentleman's that you saw in his life-time if I don't mistake?"

My guardian replied, "Yes."

"Well! You are to understand," said Mr Bucket, "that this gentleman he come into Krook's property. Vast lots of waste paper among the rest. Among them odd heaps of old papers, this gentleman naturally begins to rummage, don't you see?" said Mr Bucket.

"To which? Say that again," cried Mr Smallweed, in a shrill, sharp voice.

"To rummage," repeated Mr Bucket. "Being a prudent man, and accustomed to take care of your own affairs, you begin to rummage among the papers as you have come into; don't you?"

"Of course I do," cried Mr Smallweed.

"Of course you do," said Mr Bucket, conversationally, "and much to blame you would be if you didn't. And so you chance to find, you know," Mr Bucket went on, stooping over him with an air of cheerful raillery which Mr Smallweed by no means reciprocated, "and so you chance to find, you know, a paper with the signature of Jarndyce to it. Don't you?"

Mr Smallweed glanced with a troubled eye at us, and grudgingly nodded assent.

"And coming to look at that paper, at your full leisure and convenience, what do you find it to be but a Will, you see. That's the drollery of it," said Mr Bucket, with the same lively air of recalling a joke for the enjoyment of Mr Smallweed, who had the same crest-fallen appearance of not enjoying it at all; "what do you find it to be, but a Will?"

"I don't know that it's good as a Will, or as anything else," snarled Mr Smallweed.

Mr Bucket eyed the old man for a moment – he had slipped and shrunk down in his chair into a mere bundle – as if he were much disposed to pounce upon him; nevertheless, he continued to bend over him with the same agreeable air, keeping the corner of one of his eyes upon us.

"And as you've heard a good deal mentioned regarding a celebrated Chancery Will case, of the same name, you begin to think – and you never was more correct in your born days – 'Ecod, if I don't look about me, I may get into trouble regarding this Will.'"

"Now, mind how you put it, Bucket," cried the old man anxiously, with his hand at his ear. However, as soon as he could be heard through Mr Smallweed's coughing, and his vicious ejaculations of "O, my bones! O, dear! I've no breath in my body! I'm worse than the chattering, clattering, brimstone pig at home!" Mr Bucket proceeded, in the same convivial manner as before.

"So, as I happen to be in the habit of coming about your premises, you take me into your confidence, don't you?"

I think it would be impossible to make an admission with more ill-will, and a worse grace, than Mr Smallweed displayed when he admitted this; rendering it perfectly evident that Mr Bucket was the very last person he would have thought of taking into his confidence, if he could by any possibility have kept him out of it.

"And I go into the business with you, – very pleasant we are over it; and I confirm you in your well-founded fears, that you will-get-yourself-in-to-a-most precious line if you don't come out with that there Will," said Mr Bucket, emphatically; "and accordingly you arrange with me that it shall be delivered up to this present Mr Jarndyce, on no conditions. If it should prove to be valuable, you trusting yourself to him for your reward; that's about where it is, ain't it?"

"That's what was agreed," Mr Smallweed assented, with the same bad grace.

"In consequence of which," said Mr Bucket, dismissing his agreeable manner all at once, and becoming strictly business-like, "you've got that Will upon your person at the present time; and the only thing that remains for you to do is, just to out with it!"

Having given us one glance out of the watching corner of his eye, and having given his nose one triumphant rub with his fore-finger, Mr Bucket stood with his eyes fastened on his confidential friend, and his hand stretched forth ready to take the paper and present it to my guardian. Little by little, Mr Smallweed very slowly took from a breast-pocket a stained discoloured paper, which was much singed upon the outside, and a little burnt at the edges, as if it had long ago been thrown upon a fire; and hastily snatched off again. Mr Bucket lost no time in transferring this paper, with the dexterity of a conjuror, from Mr Smallweed to Mr Jarndyce. As he gave it to my guardian, he whispered behind his fingers:

"Hadn't settled how to make their market of it. Quarrelled and hinted about it. I laid out twenty pound upon it. First, the avaricious grandchildren split upon him, on account of their objections to his living so unreasonably long, and then they split on one another. Lord!"

"Mr Bucket," said my guardian aloud, "whatever the worth of this paper may be to any one, my obligations are great to you; and if it be of any worth, I hold myself bound to see Mr Smallweed remunerated accordingly."

"Not according to your merits, you know," said Mr Bucket, in friendly explanation to Mr Smallweed. "Don't you be afraid of that. According to its value."

"That is what I mean," said my guardian. "You may observe, Mr Bucket, that I abstain from examining this paper myself. The plain truth is, I have forsworn and abjured the whole business these many years, and my soul is sick of it. But Miss Summerson and I will immediately place the paper in the hands of my solicitor in the cause, and its existence shall be made known without delay to all other parties interested."

"Mr Jarndyce can't say fairer than that, you understand," observed Mr Bucket, to his fellow visitor. "And it being now made clear to you that nobody's a-going to be wronged – which must be a great relief to your mind – we may proceed with the ceremony of chairing you home again."

He unbolted the door, called in the bearers, wished us good morning, and with a look full of meaning, and a crook of his finger at parting, went his way.

We went our way too, which was to Lincoln's Inn, as quickly as possible. Mr Kenge was disengaged; and we found him at his table in his dusty room, with the inexpressive-looking books, and the piles of papers. Chairs having been placed for us by Mr Guppy, Mr Kenge expressed the surprise and gratification he felt at the unusual sight of Mr Jarndyce in his office.

"I hope," said Mr Kenge, "that the genial influence of Miss Summerson," he bowed to me, "may have induced Mr Jarndyce," he bowed to him, "to forego some little of his animosity towards a Cause and towards a Court which are – shall I say, which take their place in the stately vista of the pillars of our profession?"

"I am inclined to think," returned my guardian, "that Miss Summerson has seen too much of the effects of the Court and the Cause to exert any influence in their favour. Nevertheless, they are a part of the occasion of my being here. Mr Kenge, before I lay this paper on your desk and have done with it, let me tell you how it has come into my hands."

He did so shortly and distinctly.

"It could not, sir," said Mr Kenge, "have been stated more plainly and to the purpose, if it had been a case at law."

"Did you ever know English law, or equity either, plain and to the purpose?" said my guardian.

"O, fie!" said Mr Kenge.

At first he had not seemed to attach much importance to the paper, but when he saw it he appeared more interested, and when he had opened and read a little of it through his eye-glass, he became amazed. "Mr Jarndyce," he said, looking off it, "you have perused this?"

"Not I!" returned my guardian.

"But, my dear sir," said Mr Kenge, "it is a Will of later date than any in the suit. It appears to be all in the Testator's handwriting. It is duly executed and attested. And even if intended to be cancelled, as might possibly be supposed to be denoted by these marks of fire, it is not cancelled. Here it is, a perfect instrument!"

"Well!" said my guardian. "What is that to me?"

You ask me what is this to you, Mr Jarndyce. If you had perused this document, you would have seen that it reduces your interest considerably, though still leaving it a very handsome one, still leaving it a very handsome one," said Mr Kenge, waving his hand persuasively and blandly. "You would further have seen that the interests of Mr Richard Carstone, and of Miss Ada Clare, now Mrs Richard Carstone, are very materially advanced by it."

"Kenge," said my guardian, "if all the flourishing wealth that the suit brought into this vile court of Chancery could fall to my two young cousins, I should be well contented. But do you ask me to believe that any good is to come of Jarndyce and Jarndyce?"

"O, really, Mr Jarndyce! Prejudice, prejudice. My dear sir, this is a very great country, a very great country. Its system of equity is a very great system, a very great system. And when the Cause is in the paper next Term, this document will be an unexpected and interesting feature in it," said Mr Kenge, looking loftily at my guardian.

"And when," asked my guardian, rising after a pause, "is next Term?"

"Next Term, Mr Jarndyce, will be next month," said Mr Kenge. "Of course we shall at once proceed to do what is necessary with this document, and to collect the necessary evidence concerning it; and of course you will receive our usual notification of the Cause being in the paper."

"To which I shall pay, of course, my usual attention."

"Still bent, my dear sir," said Mr Kenge, shewing us through the outer office to the door, "still bent, even with your enlarged mind, on echoing a popular prejudice? This is a great system, Mr Jarndyce, and would you wish a great country to have a little system? Now, really, really!"

He said this at the stair-head, gently moving his right hand as if it were a silver trowel, with which to spread the cement of his words on the structure of the system, and consolidate it for a thousand ages.

CHAPTER 41

Esther's Narrative

Soon after I had that conversation with my guardian, he put a sealed paper in my hand one morning, and said, "This is for next month, my dear." I found in it two hundred pounds.

I now began very quietly to make such preparations as I thought were necessary. Regulating my purchases by my guardian's taste, which I knew very well of course, I arranged my wardrobe to please him, and hoped I should be highly successful. I did it all so quietly, because I was not quite free from my old apprehension that Ada would be rather sorry, and because my guardian was so quiet himself. I had no doubt that under all the circumstances we should be married in the most private and simple manner. Perhaps I should only have to say to Ada, "Would you like to come and see me married to-morrow, my pet?" Perhaps our wedding might even be as unpretending as her own, and I might not find it necessary to say anything about it until it was over. I thought that if I were to choose, I would like this best.

Meanwhile, I must say, I could not agree with my guardian on the subject of the Will, and I had some sanguine hopes of Jarndyce and Jarndyce. Which of us was right will soon appear, but I certainly did encourage expectations. In Richard, the discovery gave occasion for a burst of business and agitation that buoyed him up for a little time; but he had lost the elasticity even of hope now, and seemed to me to retain only its feverish anxieties. From something my guardian said one day, when we were talking about this, I understood that my marriage would not take place until after the Term-time we had been told to look forward to; and I thought the more, for that, how rejoiced I should be if I could be married when Richard and Ada were a little more prosperous.

The Term was very near indeed, when my guardian was called out of town, and went down into Yorkshire on Mr Woodcourt's business. He had told me beforehand that his presence there would be necessary. I had just come in one night from my dear girl's, and was sitting in the midst of all my new clothes, looking at them all around me and thinking, when a letter from my guardian was brought to me. It asked me to join him in the country; and mentioned by what stage-coach my place was taken, and at what time in the morning I should have to leave town. It added in a postscript that I would not be many hours from Ada.

I expected few things less than a journey at that time, but I was ready for it in half-an-hour, and set off as appointed early next morning. I travelled all day, wondering all day what I could be wanted for at such a distance; now I thought it might be for this purpose, and now I thought it might be for that purpose; but I was never, never, never near the truth.

It was night when I came to my journey's end, and found my guardian waiting for me. This was a great relief, for towards evening I had begun to fear (the more so as his letter was a very short one) that he might be ill. However, there he was, as well as it was possible to be; and when I saw his genial face again at its brightest and best, I said to myself he has been doing some other great kindness. Not that it required much penetration to say that, because I knew that his being there at all was an act of kindness.

Supper was ready at the hotel, and when we were alone at table he said:

"Full of curiosity, no doubt, little woman, to know why I have brought you here?"

"Well, guardian," said I, "I am a little curious about it."

"Then to ensure your night's rest, my love," he returned, gaily, "I won't wait until to-morrow to tell you. I have very much wished to express to Woodcourt, somehow, my sense of his humanity to poor unfortunate Jo, his inestimable services to my young cousins, and his value to us all.

When it was decided that he should settle here, it came into my head that I might ask his acceptance of some unpretending and suitable little place, to lay his own head in. I therefore caused such a place to be looked out for, and such a place was found on very easy terms, and I have been touching it up for him and making it habitable. However, when I walked over it the day before yesterday, and it was reported ready, I found that I was not housekeeper enough to know whether things were all as they ought to be. So I sent off for the best little housekeeper that could possibly be got, to come and give me her advice and opinion. And here she is," said my guardian, "laughing and crying both together!"

Because he was so dear, so good, so admirable. I tried to tell him what I thought of him, but I could not articulate a word.

"Tut, tut!" said my guardian. "You make too much of it, little woman. Why, how you sob, Dame Durden, how you sob!"

"It is with exquisite pleasure, guardian – with a heart full of thanks."

"Well, well," said he. "I am delighted that you approve. I thought you would. I meant it as a pleasant surprise for the little mistress of Bleak House."

I kissed him, and dried my eyes. "I know now!" said I. "I have seen this in your face a long while."

"No; have you really, my dear?" said he. "What a Dame Durden it is to read a face!"

A most beautiful summer morning succeeded; and after breakfast we went out arm in arm, to see the house of which I was to give my mighty housekeeping opinion. We entered a flower-garden by a gate in a side wall, of which he had the key; and the first thing I saw, was, that the beds and flowers were all laid out according to the manner of my beds and flowers at home.

"You see, my dear," observed my guardian, standing still, with a delighted face, to watch my looks; "knowing there could be no better plan, I borrowed yours."

We went on by a pretty little orchard, where the cherries were nestling among the green leaves, and the shadows of the apple-trees were sporting on the grass, to the house itself, – a cottage, quite a rustic cottage of doll's rooms; but such a lovely place, so tranquil and so beautiful. And still, as we went through the pretty rooms, out at the little rustic verandah doors, and underneath the tiny wooden colonnades, garlanded with woodbine, jasmine, and honey-suckle, I saw, in the papering on the walls, in the colours of the furniture, in the arrangement of all the pretty objects, my little tastes and fancies, my little methods and inventions which they used to laugh at while they praised them, my odd ways everywhere.

I could not say enough in admiration of what was all so beautiful, but one secret doubt arose in my mind, when I saw this. I thought, O would he be the happier for it! Would it not have been better for his peace that I should not have been so brought before him? Because, although I was not what he thought me, still he loved me very dearly, and it might remind him mournfully of what be believed he had lost.

"And now, little woman," said my guardian, whom I had never seen so proud and joyful as in showing me these things, and watching my appreciation of them, "now, last of all, for the name of this house."

"What is it called, dear guardian?"

"My child," said he, "come and see."

He took me to the porch, which he had hitherto avoided, and said, pausing before we went out:

"My dear child, don't you guess the name?"

"No!" said I.

We went out of the porch; and he showed me written over it, *Bleak House*.

He led me to a seat among the leaves close by, and sitting down beside me, and taking my hand in his, spoke to me thus:

"My darling girl, in what there has been between us, I have, I hope, been really solicitous for your happiness. When I wrote you the letter to which you brought the answer," smiling as he referred to it, "I had my own too much in view; but I had yours too. Whether, under different circumstances, I might ever have renewed the old dream I sometimes dreamed when you were very young, of making you my wife one day, I need not ask myself. I did renew it, and I wrote my letter, and you brought your answer. You are following what I say, my child?"

I was cold, and I trembled violently; but not a word he uttered was lost.

"Hear me, my love, but do not speak. It is for me to speak now. When it was that I began to doubt whether what I had done would really make you happy, is no matter. Woodcourt came and I soon had no doubt at all."

I clasped him round the neck, and hung my head upon his breast, and wept. "Lie lightly, confidently, here, my child," said he, pressing me gently to him. "I am your guardian and your father now. Rest confidently here."

Soothingly, like the gentle rustling of the leaves; and genially, like the ripening weather; and radiantly and beneficently, like the sunshine; he went on.

"Understand me, my dear girl. I had no doubt of your being contented and happy with me, being so dutiful and so devoted; but I saw with whom you would be happier. Well! I have long been in Allan Woodcourt's confidence, although he was not, until yesterday, a few hours before you came here, in mine. But I would not have my Esther's bright example lost; I would not have a jot of my dear girl's virtues unobserved and unhonoured."

He stopped to kiss me on the forehead, and I sobbed and wept afresh. For I felt as if I could not bear the painful delight of his praise.

"Hush, little woman! Don't cry; this is to be a day of joy. I have looked forward to it," he said, exultingly, "for months on months!"

He tenderly raised my head, and as I clung to him, kissed me in his old fatherly way again and again. What a light, now, on the protecting manner I had thought about!

"One more last word. When Allan Woodcourt spoke to you, my dear, he spoke with my knowledge and consent – but I gave him no encouragement, not I, for these surprises were my great reward, and I was too miserly to part with a scrap of it. He was to come, and tell me all that passed; and he did. I have no more to say. My dearest, Allan Woodcourt stood beside your father when he lay dead – stood beside your mother. This is Bleak House. This day I give this house its little mistress; and before God, it is the brightest day in all my life!"

He rose, and raised me with him. We were no longer alone. My husband – I have called him by that name full seven happy years now – stood at my side.

"Allan," said my guardian, "take from me, a willing gift, the best wife that ever man had. What more can I say for you, than that I know you deserve her! Take with her the little home she brings you. You know what she will make it; you know what she has made its namesake. Let me share its felicity sometimes, and what do I sacrifice? Nothing, nothing."

He kissed me once again; and now the tears were in his eyes, as he said more softly:

"Esther, my dearest, after so many years, there is a kind of parting in this too. I know that my mistake has caused you some distress. Forgive your old guardian, in restoring him to his old place in your affections; and blot it out of your memory. Allan, take my dear."

He moved away from under the green roof of leaves, and stopping in the sunlight outside, and turning cheerfully towards us, said:

"I shall be found about here somewhere. Let no one thank me any more; for I am going to revert to my bachelor habits, and if anybody disregards this warning, I'll run away, and never come back!"

What happiness was ours that day, what joy, what rest, what hope, what gratitude, what bliss! We were to be married before the month was out; but when we were to come and take possession of our own house, was to depend on Richard and Ada.

We all three went home together next day. As soon as we arrived in town, Allan went straight to see Richard, and to carry our joyful news to him and my darling.

CHAPTER 42

Beginning the World

The Term had commenced, and my guardian found an intimation from Mr Kenge that the Cause would come on in two days. As I had sufficient hopes of the Will to be in a flutter about it, Allan and I agreed to go down to the Court that morning. Richard was extremely agitated, and was so weak and low, though his illness was still of the mind, that my dear girl indeed had sore occasion to be supported. But she looked forward to the help that was to come to her, and never drooped.

We left home directly after breakfast, to be at Westminster Hall in good time; and walked down there through the lively streets – so happily and strangely it seemed! – together.

When we came to Westminster Hall we found that the day's business was begun. Worse than that, we found such an unusual crowd in the Court of Chancery that it was full to the door, and we could neither see nor hear what was passing within. It appeared to be something droll, for occasionally there was a laugh, and a cry of "Silence!" It appeared to be something interesting, for every one was pushing and striving to get nearer. It appeared to be something that made the professional gentlemen very merry, for there were several young counsellors in wigs and whiskers on the outside of the crowd, and when one of them told the others about it, they put their hands in their pockets, and quite doubled themselves up with laughter, and went stamping about the pavement of the hall.

We asked a gentleman by us, if he knew what cause was on? He told us Jarndyce and Jarndyce. We asked him if he knew what was doing in it. He said, really no he did not, nobody ever did; but as well as he could make out, it was over. Over for the day? we asked him. No, he said; over for good. Over for good!

When we heard this unaccountable answer, we looked at one another quite lost in amazement. Could it be possible that the Will had set things right at last, and that Richard and Ada were going to be rich? It seemed too good to be true. Alas it was!

Our suspense was short; for a break-up soon took place in the crowd, and the people came streaming out looking flushed and hot, and bringing a quantity of bad air with them. Still they were all exceedingly amused, and were more like people coming out from a Farce or a Juggler than from a court of Justice. We stood aside, watching for any countenance we knew; and presently great bundles of paper began to be carried out – bundles in bags, bundles too large to be got into any bags, immense masses of papers of all shapes and no shapes, which the bearers staggered under, and threw down for the time being, anyhow, on the Hall pavement, while they went back to bring out more. Even these clerks were laughing. We glanced at the papers, and seeing Jarndyce and Jarndyce everywhere, asked an official-looking person who was standing in the midst of them, whether the cause was over.

"Yes," he said; "it was all up with it at last!" and burst out laughing too.

At this juncture, we perceived Mr Kenge coming out of court with an affable dignity upon him.

"How do you do? " said Mr Kenge, raising his hat to me with polished politeness. "Glad to see you. Mr Jarndyce is not here?"

No. He never came there, I reminded him.

"Really," returned Mr Kenge, "it is as well that he is not here to-day, for his indomitable singularity of opinion might have been strengthened, perhaps; not reasonably, but might have been strengthened."

"Pray what has been done to-day?" asked Allan.

"I beg your pardon?" said Mr Kenge, with excessive urbanity.

"What has been done to-day?"

"What has been done," repeated Mr Kenge. "Quite so. Yes. Why, not much has been done; not much. We have been checked – brought up suddenly, I would say – upon the – shall I term it threshold?"

"Is this Will considered a genuine document, sir?" said Allan; "Will you tell us that?"

"You are to reflect, Mr Woodcourt," observed Mr Kenge, using his silver trowel, persuasively and smoothingly, "that this has been a great cause, that this has been a protracted cause, that this has been a complex cause. Jarndyce and Jarndyce has been termed, not inaptly, a Monument of Chancery practice."

"And Patience has sat upon it a long time," said Allan.

"Very well indeed, sir," returned Mr Kenge, with a certain condescending laugh he had. "Very well! You are further to reflect, Mr Woodcourt," becoming dignified almost to severity, "that on the numerous difficulties, contingencies, masterly fictions, and forms of procedure in this great cause, there has been expended study, intellect, Mr Woodcourt, high intellect. For many years, the flower of the Bar has been lavished upon Jarndyce and Jarndyce and it must be paid for, in money or money's worth, sir."

"Mr Kenge," said Allan, appearing enlightened all in a moment. "Excuse me, our time presses. Do I understand that the whole estate is found to have been absorbed in costs?"

"Hem! I believe so," returned Mr Kenge.

"And that thus the suit lapses and melts away?"

"Probably," returned Mr Kenge.

"My dearest life," whispered Allan, "this will break Richard's heart!"

There was such a shock of apprehension in his face, and he knew Richard so perfectly, and I too had seen so much of his gradual decay, that what my dear girl had said to me in the fullness of her foreboding love, sounded like a knell in my ears.

"My dear love," said Allan, "leave to me, for a little while, the charge you gave me. Go home with this intelligence, and come to Ada's by-and-by!"

I would not let him take me to a coach, but entreated him to go to Richard without a moment's delay, and leave me to do as he wished. Hurrying home, I found my guardian, and told him gradually with what news I had returned.

"Little woman," said he, quite unmoved for himself, "to have done with the suit on any terms, is a greater blessing than I had looked for. But my poor young cousins!"

We talked about them all the morning, and discussed what it was possible to do. In the afternoon, my guardian walked with me to Symond's Inn, and left me at the door. I went upstairs. When my darling heard my footsteps, she came out into the small passage and threw her arms round my neck; but she composed herself directly, and said that Richard had asked for me several times. Allan had found him sitting in the corner of the court, she told me, like a stone figure. On being roused, he had broken away, and made as if he would have spoken in a fierce voice to the judge. He was stopped by his mouth being full of blood, and Allan had brought him home.

He was lying on a sofa with his eyes closed, when I went in. There were restoratives on the table; the room was made as airy as possible, and was darkened, and was very orderly and quiet. Allan stood behind him, watching him gravely. His face appeared to me to be quite destitute of colour, and now that I saw him without his seeing me, I fully saw, for the first time, how worn away he was. But he looked handsomer than I had seen him look for many a day.

I sat down by his side in silence. Opening his eyes by-and-by, he said, in a weak voice but with his old smile, "Dame Durden, kiss me, my dear!"

It was a great comfort and surprise to me, to find him in his low state cheerful and looking forward. He was happier, he said, in our intended marriage, than he could find words to tell me. My husband had been a guardian angel to him and Ada, and he blessed us both, and wished us all the joy that life could yield us.

We spoke of the future as much as possible, and he said several times that he must be present at our marriage if he could stand upon his feet. Ada would contrive to take him, somehow, he said. "Yes, surely, dearest Richard!" But as my darling answered him thus hopefully, so serene and beautiful, with the help that was to come to her so near, – I knew – I knew!

198

It was not good for him to talk too much; and when he was silent, we were silent too. Sitting beside him, I made a pretence of working for my dear, as he had always been used to joke about my being busy. Ada leaned upon his pillow, holding his head upon her arm. He dozed often; and whenever he awoke without seeing him, said first of all, "Where is Woodcourt?"

Evening had come on, when I lifted up my eyes, and saw my guardian standing in the little hall.

"Who is that, Dame Durden?" Richard asked me. The door was behind him, but he had observed in my face that some one was there.

I looked to Allan for advice, and as he nodded "Yes," bent over Richard and told him. My guardian saw what passed, came softly by me in a moment, and laid his hand on Richard's. "O sir," said Richard, "you are a good man, you are a good man!" and burst into tears for the first time.

My guardian, the picture of a good man, sat down in my place, keeping his hand on Richard's.

"My dear Rick," said he, "the clouds have cleared away, and it is bright now. We can see now. We were all bewildered, Rick, more or less. And how are you, my dear boy?"

"I am very weak, sir, but I hope I shall be stronger. I have to begin the world."

"Aye, truly; well said!" cried my guardian.

"I will not begin it in the old way now," said Richard with a sad smile. "I have learned a lesson now, sir. It was a hard one; but you shall be assured, indeed, that I have learned it."

"Well, well," said my guardian, comforting him; "well, well, well, dear boy!"

"I was thinking, sir," resumed Richard, "that there is nothing on earth I should so much like to see as their house – Dame Durden's and Woodcourt's house. If I could be removed there when I begin to recover my strength, I feel as if I should get well there, sooner than anywhere."

"Why, so have I been thinking, too, Rick," said my guardian, "and our little woman likewise; she and I have been talking of it, this very day. I dare say her husband won't object. What do you think?"

Richard smiled; and lifted up his arm to touch him, as he stood behind the head of his couch.

"I say nothing of Ada," said Richard, "but I think of her, and have thought of her very much. Look at her! See her here, sir, bending over this pillow when she has so much need to rest upon it herself, my dear love, my poor girl!"

He clasped her in his arms, and none of us spoke. He gradually released her; and she looked upon us, and looked up to Heaven, and moved her lips.

"When I get down to Bleak House," said Richard, "I shall have much to tell you, sir, and you will have much to show me. You will go, won't you?"

"Undoubtedly, dear Rick."

"Thank you; like you, like you," said Richard. "But it's all like you. They have been telling me how you planned it, and how you remembered all Esther's familiar tastes and ways. It will be like coming to the old Bleak House again."

"And you will come there too, I hope, Rick. I am a solitary man now, you know, and it will be a charity to come to me. A charity to come to me, my love!" he repeated to Ada.

"It was a troubled dream?" said Richard, clasping both my guardian's hands eagerly.

"Nothing more, Rick; nothing more."

"And you, being a good man, can pass it as such, and forgive and pity the dreamer, and be lenient and encouraging when he wakes?"

"Indeed I can. What am I but another dreamer, Rick?"

"I will begin the world!" said Richard, with a light in his eyes.

My husband drew a little nearer towards Ada, and I saw him solemnly lift up his hand to warn my guardian.

"When shall I go from this place, to that pleasant country where the old times are, where I shall have strength to tell what Ada has been to me, where I shall be able to recall my many faults and blindnesses, where I shall prepare myself to be a guide to my unborn child?" said Richard. "When shall I go?"

"Dear Rick, when you are strong enough," returned my guardian.

"Ada, my darling!"

He sought to raise himself a little. Allan raised him so that she could hold him on her bosom; which was what he wanted.

"I have done you many wrongs, my own. I have fallen like a poor stray shadow on your way, I have married you to poverty and trouble, I have scattered your means to the winds. You will forgive me all this, my Ada, before I begin the world?"

A smile irradiated his face, as she bent to kiss him. He slowly laid his face down upon her bosom, drew his arms closer round her neck, and with one parting sob began the world. Not this world, O not this! The world that sets this right.

CHAPTER 43

Down in Lincolnshire

There is a hush upon Chesney Wold in these altered days, as there is upon a portion of the family history. The story goes, that Sir Leicester paid some who could have spoken out, to hold their peace; but it is a lame story, feebly whispering and creeping about, and any brighter spark of life it shows soon dies away. It is known for certain that the handsome Lady Dedlock lies in the mausoleum in the park, where the trees arch darkly overhead, and the owl is heard at night making the woods ring; but whence she was brought home, to be laid among the echoes of that solitary place, or how she died, is all mystery.

Up from among the fern in the hollow, and winding by the bridle-road among the trees, comes sometimes to this lonely spot the sound of horses' hoofs. Then may be seen Sir Leicester – invalided, bent, and almost blind, but of worthy presence yet – riding with a stalwart man beside him, constant to his bridle-rein. When they come to a certain spot before the mausoleum door, Sir Leicester's accustomed horse stops of his own accord, and Sir Leicester, pulling off his hat, is still for a few moments before they ride away.

In one of the lodges of the Park the stalwart man, the trooper formerly, is housed. Some relics of his old calling hang upon the walls, and these it is the chosen recreation of a little lame man about the stable-yard to keep gleaming bright. A busy little man he always is, in the polishing at harness-house doors, of stirrup-irons, bits, curb-chains, harness-bosses, anything in the way of a stable-yard that will take a polish: leading a life of friction. A shaggy little damaged man, withal, not unlike an old dog of some mongrel breed, who has been considerably knocked about. He answers to the name of Phil.

A goodly sight it is to see the grand old housekeeper (harder of hearing now) going to church on the arm of her son, and to observe the relations of both towards Sir Leicester, and his towards them.

The greater part of the house is shut up, and it is a show-house no longer; yet Sir Leicester holds his shrunken state in the long drawing-room for all that, and reposes in his old place before my Lady's picture. Closed in by night with broad screens, and illumined only in that part, the light of the drawing-room seems gradually contracting and dwindling until it shall be no more. A little more, in truth, and it will be all extinguished for Sir Leicester; and the damp door in the mausoleum which shuts so tight, and looks so obdurate, will have opened and received him.

Thus Chesney Wold. With so much of itself abandoned to darkness and vacancy; with so little change under the summer shining or the wintry lowering; so sombre and motionless always – no flag flying now by day, no rows of lights sparkling by night; with no family to come and go, no visitors to be the souls of pale cold shapes of rooms, no stir of life about it; – passion and pride, even to the stranger's eye, have died away from the place in Lincolnshire, and yielded it to dull repose.

CHAPTER 44

The Close of Esther's Narrative

Full seven happy years I have been the mistress of Bleak House. They gave my darling into my arms, and through many weeks I never left her. The little child who was to have done so much was born before the turf was planted on its father's grave. It was a boy; and I, my husband, and my guardian gave him his father's name.

The help that my dear counted on did come to her; to bless and restore his mother, not his father, was the errand of this baby and its power was mighty to do it. When I saw the strength of the weak little hand and how its touch could heal my darling's heart and raised hope within her, I felt a new sense of the goodness and the tenderness of God.

They throve; and by degrees I saw my dear girl pass into my country garden and walk there with her infant in her arms. I was married then. I was the happiest of the happy.

It was at this time that my guardian joined us and asked Ada when she would come home?

"Both houses are your home, my dear," said he, "but the older Bleak House claims priority. When you and my boy are strong enough to do it, come and take possession of your home."

Ada called him "her dearest cousin, John." But he said, No, it must be guardian now. He was her guardian henceforth, and the boy's; and he had an old association with the name. So she called him guardian, and has called him guardian ever since. The children know him by no other name. – I say the children; I have two little daughters.

With the first money we saved at home, we added to our pretty house by throwing out a little Growlery expressly for my guardian; which we inaugurated with great splendour the next time he came down to see us. I try to write all this lightly, because my heart is full in drawing to an end; but when I write of him, my tears will have their way.

I never look at him, but I hear our poor dear Richard calling him a good man. To Ada and her pretty boy, he is the fondest father; to me, he is what he has ever been, and what name can I give to that! He is my husband's best and dearest friend, he is our children's darling, he is the object of our deepest love and veneration. Yet while I feel towards him as if he were a superior being, I am so familiar with him, and so easy with him, that I almost wonder at myself. I have never lost my old names, nor has he lost his; nor do I ever, when he is with us, sit in any other place than in my old chair at his side, Dame Trot, Dame Durden, Little Woman! – all just the same as ever; and I answer, Yes, dear guardian! – just the same.

I think my darling girl is more beautiful than ever. Sometimes, when I raise my eyes and see her, in the black dress that she still wears, teaching my Richard, I feel – it is difficult to express – as if it were so good to know that she remembers her dear Esther in her prayers.

I call him my Richard! But he says that he has two mamas, and I am one.

We are not rich in the bank, but we have always prospered, and we have quite enough. I never walk out with my husband, but I hear the people bless him. I never go into a house of any degree, but I hear his praises, or see them in grateful eyes. I never lie down at night, but I know that in the course of that day he has alleviated pain, and soothed some fellow-creature in the time of need. I know that from the beds of those who were past recovery, thanks have often, often gone up, in the last hour, for his patient ministration. Is not this to be rich?

The people even praise me as the doctor's wife. The people even like me as I go about, and make so much of me that I am quite abashed. I owe it all to him, my love, my pride! They like me for his sake, as I do everything I do in life for his sake.

A night or two ago, after bustling about preparing for my darling and my guardian and little Richard, who are coming tomorrow, I was sitting out in the porch of all places, that dearly memorable porch, when Allan came home.

So he said, "My precious little woman, what are you doing here?" And I said, "The moon is shining so brightly, Allan, and the night is so delicious, that I have been sitting here, thinking."

"What have you been thinking about, my dear?" said Allan then.

"How curious you are!" said I. "I am almost ashamed to tell you, but I will. I have been thinking about my old looks – such as they were."

"And what have you been thinking about them, my busy bee?" said Allan.

"I have been thinking, that I thought it was impossible that you could have loved me any better, even if I had retained them."

"Such as they were?" said Allan, laughing.

"Such as they were, of course."

"My dear Dame Durden," said Allan, drawing my arm through his, "do you ever look in the glass?"

"You know I do; you see me do it."

"And don't you know that you are prettier than you ever were?"

"I did not know that; I am not certain that I know it now. But I know that my dearest little pets are very pretty, and that my darling is very beautiful, and that my husband is very handsome, and that my guardian has the brightest and most benevolent face that ever was seen; and that they can very well do without much beauty in me – even supposing ...